The AMERICAN Wives Club

Praise for Anna Durand's Books

"*Brit vs. Scot* was a whole lot of fun to read! [Anna Durand] did an excellent job of keeping me guessing about what was going to happen next [and] developing her characters. As a man, I sympathized with Grey Dixon. Sometimes he messes up royally, and that's part of what makes him an appealing character. [...] Another charming aspect of Brit vs. Scot is its British and Scottish terminology. [...] I recommend *Brit vs. Scot* to rom-com fans."
Joe Wisinski, Readers' Favorite

"Wow! I'm so happy I picked up [*Natural Passion*]. [...] Refreshing, funny, and sexy, with a unique twist on a vacation spot. [...] Another author to add to my favorites list, and I can't wait for Ollie and Mara's story in *Natural Impulse*."
Sharon Clayton, The Eclectic Review

"Durand's Hot Scots series has been loads of fun to read, and this newest installment in the series is no exception. [...] The author's action-packed and suspenseful plot keeps the reader on their toes, and the grown-up sizzle never disappoints."
Jack Magnus, Readers' Favorite

" I loved the slow-burn, should we-shouldn't we, what's right, dilemma and desire that built and built until the steam had to escape. [*One Hot Chance*] is equal parts fun, steam, and moral quandary. [...] I am in love with Chance and his brothers already."
MaryLou Hoffman, Page Princess blog

"[*Lethal in a Kilt* is] full of hot sex, adventure, and so much laughter. I found myself laughing-out-loud at the antics of the Witches of Ballachulish (Logan's sisters) and the hilarious flirting and sexy banter between Serena and Logan. [...] Recommend highly! "
Sharon Clayton, The Eclectic Review

"I loved the Scottish in Ian and the strength of Rae, but the love of one little girl makes [*Notorious in a Kilt*] something to behold."
Coffee Time Romance

"I have enjoyed this whole series, but Emery and Rory [from *Scandalous in a Kilt*] have stolen my heart and are now my favorites!"
The Romance Reviews

Other Books by Anna Durand

Brit vs. Scot (A Hot Brits/Hot Scots/Au Naturel Crossover Book)
Lachlan in a Kilt (The Ballachulish Trilogy, Book One)
Aidan in a Kilt (The Ballachulish Trilogy, Book Two)
Rory in a Kilt (The Ballachulish Trilogy, Book Three)
Dangerous in a Kilt (Hot Scots, Book One)
Wicked in a Kilt (Hot Scots, Book Two)
Scandalous in a Kilt (Hot Scots, Book Three)
The MacTaggart Brothers Trilogy (Hot Scots, Books 1-3)
Gift-Wrapped in a Kilt (Hot Scots, Book Four)
Notorious in a Kilt (Hot Scots, Book Five)
Insatiable in a Kilt (Hot Scots, Book Six)
Lethal in a Kilt (Hot Scots, Book Seven)
Irresistible in a Kilt (Hot Scots, Book Eight)
Devastating in a Kilt (Hot Scots, Book Nine)
Spellbound in a Kilt (Hot Scots, Book Ten)
Relentless in a Kilt (Hot Scots, Book Eleven)
One Hot Chance (Hot Brits, Book One)
One Hot Roomie (Hot Brits, Book Two)
One Hot Crush (Hot Brits, Book Three)
The Dixon Brothers Trilogy (Hot Brits, Books 1-3)
One Hot Escape (Hot Brits, Book Four)
One Hot Rumor (Hot Brits, Book Five)
One Hot Christmas (Hot Brits, Book Six)
Natural Passion (Au Naturel Trilogy, Book One)
Natural Impulse (Au Naturel Trilogy, Book Two)
Natural Satisfaction (Au Naturel Trilogy, Book Three)
Fired Up (a standalone romance)
Echo Dominion (Echo Power Trilogy, Book Two)
Echo Unbound (Echo Power Trilogy, Book Three)
The Mortal Falls (Undercover Elementals, Book One)
The Mortal Fires (Undercover Elementals, Book Two)
The Mortal Tempest (Undercover Elementals, Book Three)
The Janusite Trilogy (Undercover Elementals, Books 1-3)
Obsidian Hunger (Undercover Elementals, Book Four)
Unbidden Hunger (Undercover Elementals, Book Five)
The Thirteenth Fae (Undercover Elementals, Book Six)
Willpower (Psychic Crossroads, Book One)
Intuition (Psychic Crossroads, Book Two)
Kinetic (Psychic Crossroads, Book Three)
Passion Never Dies: The Complete Reborn Series

A Hot Brits / Hot Scots / Au Naturel
Crossover Book

ANNA DURAND

JACOBSVILLE BOOKS · MARIETTA, OHIO

ISBN: 978-1-949406-91-7 (paperback)
ISBN: 978-1-949406-92-4 (ebook)
ISBN: 978-1-949406-93-1 (audiobook)

Manufactured in the United States.

Jacobsville Books
www.JacobsvilleBooks.com

Publisher's Cataloging-in-Publication Data
provided by Five Rainbows Cataloging Services

Names: Durand, Anna, author.
Title: The American wives club : a Hot Brits/Hot Scots/Au Naturel crossover book / Anna Durand.
Description: Marietta, OH : Jacobsville Books, 2022.
Identifiers: ISBN 978-1-949406-91-7 (paperback) | ISBN 978-1-949406-92-4 (ebook) | ISBN 978-1-949406-93-1 (audiobook)
Subjects: LCSH: Man-woman relationships--Fiction. | Friendship--Fiction. | Scots--Fiction. | Americans--Fiction. | Highlands (Scotland)--Fiction. | Romance fiction. | BISAC: FICTION / Romance / Contemporary. | FICTION / Romance / Romantic Comedy. | GSAFD: Love stories.
Classification: LCC PS3604.U724 A44 2022 (print) | LCC PS3604.U724 (ebook) | DDC 813/.6--dc23.

Chapter One

Callum

THE GRUMBLE OF MY HARLEY'S ENGINE SPUTTERS OUT AS I remove my helmet and gaze at the nondescript brick building in front of me, where I have volunteered to be tortured for three days every week. Well, "volunteered" might be a slight exaggeration. My brother gave me no choice. Jack tried to convince me this is physical therapy for my knee, which I injured a few weeks ago, but I know he has ulterior motives. No idea what they are, not yet, but I have no doubts I'll find out soon.

With my helmet tucked under one arm, I stride across the pavement to the front doors of the therapy clinic. All right, maybe I limp over to the doors. And it might've taken me twice as long as it should have, and I probably growled and groaned the whole time. My bloody knee bloody hurts.

Aye, I shouldn't have come on my Harley. Jack will have my hide if he finds out I did that.

I take a deep breath, straighten my posture, and march—all right, limp—into the building. A receptionist greets me, and I sign in for my appointment, then sit down in a chair that feels like a torture device. I'd known physical therapy would be painful, but I hadn't expected the torment to start in the waiting room. I sit here squirming and grimacing as the seconds tick by. Since the clinic doesn't have a clock on the wall, I keep glancing at the one on my mobile.

Two minutes. Five minutes. Seven minutes.

Why do medical people always make their patients wait?

"Callum?" a female voice calls out.

I stuff my mobile into my pocket and struggle to get up out of my chair.

A bonnie lass with golden red hair glances my way. "Do you need some help?"

"No." I can't stop myself from sounding grumpy. Accepting help, especially from a woman, is not something I like to do. As I reach the lass, though, my mood brightens. She's not only bonnie, but she has beautiful green eyes, sensuous lips, and a toned body. I smile and offer her my hand. "Callum MacTaggart. Are you my physical therapist?"

"Yes." The lass shakes my hand. "Kate Wagner. Come with me, please."

I'll follow her anywhere.

She sweeps her gaze over my entire body, but it doesn't seem like sexual interest. No, I get the feeling she's analyzing me. As she takes in my clothes, her brows wrinkle. I'm wearing jeans, a black T-shirt, leather boots, and a black leather jacket, along with a black helmet tucked under my arm. Why should she seem confused by that?

The lass twists her mouth into what seems like a disapproving expression. "Did you come here on a motorcycle?"

"Aye."

"Why would you do that? It's bad for your knee." She lifts her gaze to my face. "Your brother said you were coming from Loch Fairbairn. Did you ride your bike all the way here? It's got to be three hours away."

"I towed my Harley to Inverness on a trailer, then rode it here."

"You still shouldn't be doing that."

I struggle to stay calm despite her mother-knows-best tone and the way she's squinting at me. "It's my life. If I want to ride a Harley, I'll do it. When I'm here in this clinic, I'll do what you say. But the rest of my life is none of your business."

"All of your life is my business, Callum." She leans in to stare into my eyes, though she has to stand on her tiptoes to do that. "I'm not just your physical therapist. I'm your counselor too."

"Counselor?"

"Your brother hired me to rehabilitate your knee and your mind."

Cannae help it. I clench my jaw and hiss a breath out through my nostrils. Counseling? Jack is going to pay for this.

I take a deep breath to calm myself, which doesn't work, and look at Kate Wagner. "Thank you for the offer, but I donnae need a mental counselor."

She shakes her head. "Sorry. I'm under strict orders to refurbish you, inside and out."

Refurbish? Ahmno a piece of furniture.

"Your brother paid for four weeks in advance," Kate says. "The clinic doesn't offer refunds. So if you walk out the door—"

"Aye, ahmno a bairn. I understand the situation."

My brother has tricked me into psychotherapy, that's the situation. And he paid in advance to make sure I'd have no choice but to stay. At least I can go home to my cousin Evan's luxury apartment after my thrice weekly torture sessions. Having a billionaire for a cousin has its benefits.

"Come with me," Kate says, turning toward the doorway she'd come through a moment ago. "We'll start with your body, then move on to your mind."

I might like that if I didn't know she means to rummage around in my head after tormenting every muscle in my body.

Kate leads me through the door and down a hallway that has more doors on both sides. Most of them are closed. The therapists here wouldn't want anyone to see them strapping their patients on the rack while asking how it makes them feel.

At the end of the hall, we stop beside the only open door.

She waves for me to go inside the room. "Welcome to your home away from home for the next four weeks."

I limp into the small room, which has a padded bench in the middle of it and a wheeled stool nearby. Cabinets line the wall at floor level and up higher too. She must store her torture devices in there.

Kate shuts the door.

When I stop halfway into the room, she walks past me to pat the bench. "Have a seat, and we'll get started. You can hang your jacket on the hook over there."

She points toward the coat rack in the corner.

I dutifully remove my jacket and hang it on the hook. Then I rest my erse on the bench, wincing a wee bit when I bend my knee.

Kate settles her bonnie erse on the stool and rolls it closer to me. She's sitting an arm's length away, and thanks to the fact her stool is shorter than my bench, I can see down the front of her T-shirt, giving me a glimpse of her breasts. But the shirt isn't low-cut enough to reveal much.

"Let's get started," Kate says. "Tell me how you injured your knee."

"I was building a cabinet when I dropped my hammer and had to bend down to get it. My foot slipped, and my knee got wrenched."

"Start at the beginning, Callum. How many times have you injured your knee?"

"Three. The first time was nine months ago."

"I see." She folds her arms over her chest and tips her head to the side while she studies me. "You were a firefighter, right? Before you became a carpenter."

"Aye."

"Why did you quit?"

I huff. "Because I injured my bloody knee. A firefighter needs to be agile."

"Can't be just your knee. There's something else going on under the surface, and together, we're going to dig down to the root cause."

"Sounds like fun." Aye, my tone implies the opposite. I donnae want therapy of any kind, but Jack has ensured I have to go through with this.

"Therapy isn't supposed to be a party. This will hurt, and you'll probably want to swear at me often. But if you do what I say, I guarantee you'll feel better when we're done."

"Never heard of a therapist guaranteeing results. Are you sure you're licensed for this?"

She shakes her head. "That won't work. I've dealt with men who are much more pigheaded than you."

"I am not pigheaded. Donnae want to spill my ruddy guts to a stranger, that's all."

Kate is still eying me with her head tipped to the side, but now she's squinting too. "Jack led me to believe you're a cheerful, laid-back guy. But you're grumpy and uncooperative."

"Ye met me two minutes ago. Isn't it unprofessional to make snap judgments?"

Her sexy mouth curls into a smug smile. "You just proved my point. Grumpy, uncooperative, *and* argumentative."

I groan and rub my eyes. "Can we get on with the physical therapy?"

"Sure. Just tell me how you injured your knee the first time."

Kate won't give up, will she? The woman is much more bloody-minded than I am.

I blow out a sigh. "Have it your way. I was injured on the job. It was a house fire."

"There's more to the story, for sure. But we'll set that aside for now." She pats my knee—the good one. "Let's get started on the physical side of your therapy. I need to evaluate you."

"All right."

"Lie down."

I stretch out on the padded bench, linking my hands over my belly.

Kate pulls a lever on the underside of her stool to lift it to the height of the bench. "First, I'm going to gently explore your knee. Let me know if anything hurts."

She lays her hands on my calf, just below my knee, and works her way up while cautiously palpating my flesh. I wince when she presses on my knee, but she keeps going, her fingers exploring every side of my leg.

"That one spot hurt, right?" she asks. "But was there any other discomfort?"

"No. Only that spot."

She inches her fingers up my thigh, gently poking and prodding as she goes. When her fingers come within a few inches of my groin, my entire body flinches.

"What's wrong?" she asks. "Is it really painful there?"

"No, it's—Just donnae touch me there." Because her fingers are inching too close to my cock, and the last thing I want is to get an erection while my physical therapist examines me.

"Are you sure it doesn't hurt there? Could be a more widespread problem if—"

"There's no pain. Just stick to my knee, all right?"

"Sure. I don't want to cause you too much discomfort."

Kate stands up and kicks the stool out of her way. Then she takes hold of my calf with both hands. "Try to relax and just let me move your muscles for you. Okay?"

"I'll try." Not much chance I'll relax, but I can give it a go.

With her hands around my calf, she exerts light pressure to bend my knee, then slides her hand up. "Still okay?"

"Aye."

She sets my foot down on the bench, leaving my knee bent. Then she runs her hands down my thigh and back up to my knee. When she starts massaging my flesh while she moves her hands up my thigh, I fight the urge to clench my jaw. My gaze stays riveted to her fingers while they crawl closer to my groin and she kneads my thigh. I grip the sides of the bench, but she keeps going until her fingers graze my cock. I grimace, but she doesn't seem to notice what part of me she's touching.

Any second, I'll get an erection. In front of Kate.

"Stop," I growl.

"Does it hurt?" She stays focused on my thigh, still massaging me.

"No, it bloody doesn't hurt. Just stop. *Now.*"

She freezes, but doesn't remove her wee hands from my leg. "What's wrong?"

And that's when it happens. I get an erection.

"*Mhac na galla,*" I snarl. "Didn't I tell you to stop doing that? Donnae ye ever listen?"

"What is your problem?"

I cover my face with one hand and mutter, "My *slat.*"

"Your what?"

"My cock, ye daft woman." I spread both palms over my face, then drop them. But I still can't look at her. "I have—*Bod an Donais.* I told ye not to touch me there."

Finally, she glances at the offending body part. Her eyes go wide, though only for a second. "Oh. Sorry."

She pulls her hands away.

But it's too late.

Chapter Two

Kate

CALLUM IS EMBARRASSED. I GET THAT, AND I FEEL BAD FOR putting him in this situation. But honestly, I've seen men with erections before. It doesn't bother me, though it clearly bothers him, and I need to figure out how to soothe his wounded pride. Men can be so sensitive about their dicks. But I never would've expected Callum to react that way, not after his grumpy behavior leading up to this little incident.

Not that his dick is little. Oh no, even before the erection issue, I could tell he has the kind of equipment every woman dreams of experiencing. I won't do that, though. No sex with clients. I don't like grumpy guys anyway, and I absolutely do not like bikers. At least Callum wears a helmet, but I will never get anywhere near his "equipment" or his motorcycle.

"I'm sorry," I tell Callum. "Didn't mean to make you uncomfortable. But I've seen this reaction before when I start evaluating a man, so you have no reason to feel weird about it."

"No reason?" He scowls at me. "It's your fault. *Coinbheineadh* my *slat* is not professional."

He told me *slat* means penis, but the other thing has me flummoxed. "What did you just say? Is that Gaelic?"

"Aye. And I said feeling up my cock is not professional."

"There was no feeling up of any part of you. I was doing my job."

He still looks annoyed, but at least he's not scowling anymore. "Fine. I'll let it go. But donnae be putting your fingers anywhere near—" He scrunches up his face. "You know where I mean."

I guess he can't even bring himself to say the word *slat* anymore, much less erection or penis. But I have to ask, "You said a couple of other Gaelic things. What did they mean?"

He scratches the back of his neck, his head bowed. "*Mhac na galla* means son of a bitch. And *bod an Donais* means, ah...the devil's penis."

"I see."

"They're curse words."

"Uh-huh." I step back. "The physical evaluation is over. Let's move on to phase two."

"How many phases are there?"

"Three. We did the exam. Later, we'll start your physical therapy, but now it's time for the mental portion."

Callum groans and shakes his head. "Ahmno talking about my feelings with you."

"Who would you talk about that with?"

"No one." He pushes up into a sitting position. "Psychotherapy is rubbish."

"Do you tell your brother that? He's a psychologist, after all."

Callum rolls his eyes. "Jack is different."

"Because he's your brother." I want to point out the hypocrisy in that, but it would be unprofessional. Instead, I drop onto my stool and wheel it backward to give Callum some space. "Tell me about your relationship with your brother."

"It's fine."

"Be more specific, please."

"Jack and I get on well enough. No problems there, so I have nothing to tell you about that."

Uncooperative doesn't even begin to describe Callum MacTaggart. While Jack had told me his brother is easygoing and happy, he'd left out the details about Callum's current attitude problem. To be fair, though, Jack did mention his brother had changed lately, ever since he reinjured his knee. My job is to find out why.

This might take more than four weeks.

"So, there isn't anyone you would talk to," I say. "Not even a friend? Or one of your cousins? Jack said you have lots of those."

"Aye, I do." Callum swings his legs off the bench. "But I donnae share my innermost feelings with them either. It's private."

"But you do have things you need to discuss with someone. Right?"

"I can work it out on my own."

Oh yeah, more than four weeks. This might take years.

Since it's my job to be nosy, I press on. "You must have one friend."

He flattens his lips, then blows out a breath. "Ye willnae give up, will ye?"

"Nope. Might as well share one little thing with me. If you answer this question honestly, with no evasion, then we can go into the exercise room to start your recovery routine."

The pigheaded Scot growls under his breath. "I have a friend. Hugh Parrish has been my best mate for years."

"But you won't talk to him either."

Callum shrugs. "Hugh lives in England, and he's busy with family matters. We haven't seen each other in person since last summer and haven't spoken for almost two months."

"You've never heard of the telephone?"

He flashes me another scowl. "Of course I have. But we both have too much going on in our lives to be havering every night the way lasses do. We email, though."

"You should do more than that." I hop off my stool. "If you agree to call Hugh tonight, I won't ask any more nosy questions today."

"But you'll harass me again on Wednesday."

"Yes." I lean in to stare straight into his gorgeous blue eyes. "It's my job to harass, harangue, and generally hound you. That's therapy."

"I will ring Hugh tonight. Satisfied?"

"This is for your benefit, not mine. But yes, I'm glad you're going to talk to your best friend. Now, let's head into the exercise room to start your physical therapy."

"Ahmno leaving this room until—Well, just not yet."

Oh, I get it. He's still freaked about the hard-on incident. I glance at his groin, and I see why. He's still semi-hard.

"If you need a minute," I say, "I can wait in the hall until you're ready."

"In the hall? How am I meant to, ah...recover when I know you're standing just outside the door?"

Wow, he's bent out of shape about this. "Okay. I'll go into the exercise room to get things set up. As soon as you're ready, just turn right when you leave this room and go all the way to the end of the hall. You'll see the sign for the exercise room."

"All right."

I leave, shutting the door behind me, and head for the exercise room. For the next ten minutes, I putter around getting things set up for Callum's session. It doesn't take me that long, but I do things very slowly to waste time until the grumpy Scot recovers his male pride. Cheerful and laid-back? Oh yeah, Jack MacTaggart has some explaining to do. Either that, or I bring out the snarling jerk hidden inside Callum. I know I can be a bit tough, but I do it for my clients' own good.

Just as I'm wondering what to do now that I've set everything up, Callum pushes through the swinging doors and limps into the room. He stops a couple of feet inside the doorway, glancing around the space like he's never seen an exercise facility before.

I wave to him. "Over here, Callum."

He swerves his attention to me, nods once, and scuffles this way. His gaze narrows when he sees the equipment beside me. "Is that a stationary bicycle?"

"Yes. It's for warming up before we get into the real therapy."

"But you scolded me for riding a motorcycle. That's a kind of bike."

"This is different. It doesn't have an engine that rattles your bones with its vibrations, and you won't sit on it without moving your legs."

He gives the bike a dirty look. "Donnae need warming up."

"Yes, you do. Unless you want to get leg cramps later." I pick up a stack of folded clothing. "You can borrow these sweats for today, but you'll need to get your own before your next appointment."

"I donnae wear sweats."

"As long as you're my client, you will. Jeans aren't flexible enough." I thrust the clothes at him. "Get changed, Callum. Now. The bathroom is over there."

I stab a finger in the air to indicate where he should go.

He squints at me while a muscle jumps in his jaw. Then he snatches the clothes away from me and hobbles off to the bathroom faster than he should, considering his injury. Oh, that stubborn, rude man. I don't care how attractive he is. Callum MacTaggart is a jackass.

My reluctant client hobbles back to me a few minutes later, now wearing gray sweatpants and a gray T-shirt. I'd borrowed the clothes from a coworker who's not as, um, well-built as Callum. The T-shirt clings to every muscle on his torso, and the pants mold to his groin and thighs. He might be a jerk, but damn, he's got a killer body.

"Are the clothes too tight?" I ask.

"No, they're fine."

"Good. Now, get on the bike."

Though I can tell he wants to gripe about it, he sighs and climbs onto the bicycle. "How long am I meant to do this?"

"Five minutes. There's a timer on the dashboard." I point at the box attached to the middle of the handlebars and the four zeros displayed on its screen. "Right there."

He starts pedaling, though he refuses to touch the handlebars, and instead locks his arms over his chest while he glares at the wall on the other side of the room.

Yeah, Jack is definitely getting an earful from me. Callum might turn out to be the most difficult client I've ever had.

I stand beside the bike while Callum pedals away, strictly to keep an eye on him and get an idea of how his knee is doing. He doesn't pedal too fast, so I don't need to "scold" him about that. I bet he drives his motorcycle faster than the speed limit. He seems like that kind of guy. My mind decides now is a good time to make me imagine Callum astride his motorcycle, those powerful thighs hugging the machine while it rumbles and vibrates, roaring down the road. And naturally, that fantasy spurs my gaze to gravitate toward the man himself and slide down to his thighs before my focus lifts to his arms and the thick muscles of his biceps.

What would it feel like to go for a ride on his motorcycle, with my body strapped to his, the engine vibrations shivering through my flesh and exciting my body? Is it possible to have sex on a motorcycle? Not while we're driving down the road, obviously. But we could pull over and—

No. I do not get down and dirty with my clients. Especially not rude ones.

But maybe I could have sex with him once, strictly to get this inappropriate lust out of my system.

Ugh, woman, what is wrong with you?

I shift my gaze to the timer on the handlebars. He's been pedaling for four minutes and twenty seconds. Thank goodness. I won't have time to fantasize about the jerk's body once we get started on his physical therapy.

The timer hits five minutes.

"All done," I say. "Now I need to evaluate you a little more."

"More?" He hops off the bike. "We did that already."

"When you were lying down. Now I need to see you in motion." Since he's just standing there, I lay a palm on his back and give him a little shove. It barely disturbs him. "Walk across the room and back so I can watch how you move."

"Is this really necessary?"

"Yes, it is." I give him another shove. "Get moving."

He warps his mouth into an irritable slant but starts striding across the room.

Though I should be watching how he walks, I can't stop staring at his toned ass. Oh yeah, sex with him could be amazing. I mean, with all those muscles... But no, I can't get naked with him.

So I focus on watching his knee, the way he moves it and how much he limps. His warm-up on the stationary bike seems to have limbered him up, and the longer he walks, the less he hobbles. When he turns around and ambles back to me, I pat his shoulder. "Good job. I don't think your knee is as bad as you think. Maybe it's partly psychosomatic."

"Are you claiming I imagined injuring myself?"

"No. I'm saying there might be a psychological component to your physical problem."

"That's bollocks."

"We'll see." I grasp his upper arm to urge him to come with me to the area where I've set things up for his physical therapy session. We end up standing beside a foam mat that I had spread out on the floor earlier. "Lie down. It's time for straight leg raises."

For once, he doesn't grouse. Callum lies down on the mat and follows my instructions for this exercise, doing two repetitions of ten stretches each. I turn sideways to him so I can watch how he moves his leg and count the reps for him. He makes a face when I do that, but he doesn't say anything.

I swear he's ogling my ass, though. His lips kink up the tiniest bit at the corners.

No sex with Callum. No way.

Chapter Three

Callum

KATE WAGNER TORTURED ME TODAY. THAT WOMAN IS A MEN-ace, and she shouldn't be allowed to give any kind of therapy to anyone. Psychosomatic? What a load of bollocks. I didn't imagine I sprained my knee, and if that's what she thinks, then I need a different therapist. There's no way in hell I'm letting that she-demon root around in my brain. She'll probably try to convince me I have a serious mental defect just so she can make more money off my brother's misguided generosity.

But I know Kate will harass me even more on Wednesday if I don't try at least one wee thing she demanded I do. I decide to call Hugh Parrish, my best mate. But before I can do that, my mobile rings. I barely get to say hello before the caller starts talking, but I would've recognized Alex Thorne's British voice even if he weren't married to my cousin Catriona.

"Good afternoon, Callum," he says. "I've rung to warn you. The American Wives Club is mobilizing."

"To do what?"

"Help you, of course. Once those lovely lasses have set their sights on a goal, there's no stopping them."

"I donnae need help." Especially not from the American wives of my brother and our cousins. I love those women, but they need to have more bairns to keep them busy, so they'll stop harassing the single men in the family. "Tell Cat to call off the dogs, Alex. My life doesn't need fixing."

Maybe it does, but that's none of anyone's business. Besides, the American Wives Club specializes in engineering romance, and I do not need that sort of meddling.

"I wouldn't order Catriona to stop meddling even if I could," Alex says. "Maybe I appreciated it slightly when those luscious ladies interfered in my life. At any rate, the train has already left the station."

"Enough rubbish metaphors, Alex."

Underneath the snarky attitude, Alex is a good bloke. And he's warning me about the latest meddling scheme, so I can't get too annoyed with him. A wee bit will do.

"All right," he says. "No more metaphors. But you know you can't stop the American Wives Club. And I hear the British Branch is mobilizing too."

"To do what? They're in England. Are they planning to send me emails ordering me to find a girlfriend?"

"No," Alex says with a chuckle. "They're plotting an invasion."

Maybe I'm thickheaded today because I still don't understand. "Invasion of what?"

"Scotland." Alex lowers his voice to almost a whisper. "They're coming for you, mate."

Coming? To Scotland? No, they can't do that. Their husbands won't let them. Aye, because men have such cracking luck talking women out of interfering in...anything.

"Well, I've warned you," Alex says. "Cheers, Callum."

"Aye, cheers."

My chat with Alex has convinced me I do need to talk to Hugh. He lives down there in England where the British Branch of the American Wives Club is "mobilizing." *Iasg is feòil.* No, I won't growl that to those women when and if they turn up in Scotland. They wouldn't understand it, especially if I told them the phrase means "fish and flesh." Curses aren't meant to be literal. But I might swear at Jack when I see him again because this must be his fault somehow.

"Greetings from Sommerleigh House," Hugh says when I ring him. "How is bonnie Scotland?"

"Cloudy. You're at home today? Thought you swore you'd only go back there for Christmas, Boxing Day, and New Year's. 'I love London and hate the country,' that's what you said."

"Yes, but it's more convenient to stay here for a day or two. Ben and Sam are having a do at their house tomorrow, and his wife is dying to meet me."

I snort. "Aye, I'm sure Sam will fall at your feet and beg you to shag her. She's married, ye erse."

"You're in a mood today. When you can't handle my humor, I know there's trouble brewing."

"Aye, there is." I drop onto an armchair, one of four arrayed around the living room in this bloody enormous apartment. "Jack sent me to physical therapy in Inverness, but he didn't warn me I'd be getting psychotherapy too. It's a package deal—physical and mental torture simultaneously."

"A therapist who does the body and the mind? Can't picture you submitting to either one."

"I have no choice. Jack paid for it—in advance. No refunds."

"Blimey. You must be in hell."

Aye, I can always count on Hugh to be on my side. "I'm meant to suffer through a month of thrice-weekly torture sessions."

"Must take a very brawny chap to keep you in line."

I squirm in my seat, wincing though Hugh can't see that. "My therapist is a bossy lass who scolded me for riding my Harley."

"Bossy *lass*?" He chuckles. "She must be one sexy bird to get you tied up in knots."

"Kate is a she-demon."

Hugh laughs louder this time. "Poor Callum. A luscious lass is laying her hands on you three times a week. Most men would love that, but you make it sound like a life sentence in hell."

"Ye havenae met Kate, so ye donnae know what you're on about."

"That's true. Maybe I should come for a visit and meet the she-demon. Can't let my best mate suffer alone."

I groan. "You want to come here so you can have a poke with her."

"Well, if you don't like her..."

"She might be married, you know. Maybe that's why she acts like such a shrew."

"Oh, I must meet his woman immediately."

My conversation with Alex resurfaces in my mind, and I decide telling Hugh about the invasion is the best way to change the subject. "It gets worse. The American Wives Club is mobilizing to interfere in my life, and the British Branch wants to invade Scotland."

"Do they? This sounds more intriguing by the second." He switches to an overly dramatic voice. "I definitely need to rush up there to save my best mate from a meddling campaign. Lord Sommerleigh to the rescue, eh?"

"I donnae need rescuing. But maybe I wouldn't mind having one person on my side."

"Brilliant. I'll be there the day after tomorrow. Can't miss Ben and Sam's party."

"No rush. It'll take time for those lasses to get mobilized."

"You don't understand women at all, do you?"

He could be right about that.

We say goodbye, and I wander over to the windows to gaze out at the grey sky. I have nothing to do tomorrow, no one to see, nowhere to go. I could take a ride on my Harley, but Kate will scowl at me if she finds out I've done that. And she will know. I'm sure the she-demon can see me wherever I go.

Luckily, my cousin Evan left food in the refrigerator. After a few hours of staring at the television, I make myself dinner and eat it while...watching TV. I need a life, don't I? *Bod an Donais.* I know exactly what Hugh would say. *You need to get laid, mate.* And he'd be right.

I manage to sleep that night, despite hearing in my head the voices of everyone I know telling me to stop acting like a numpty. When I do fall asleep, I have dreams that ensure I wake up not at all rested.

Because I dream of Kate Wagner.

She's naked, of course, and not behaving like a professional therapist. In my fantasies, she does things that would make an adult film star blush, and I wake up with the stiffest morning hard-on I've ever had. Aye, the lass is bonnie and sexy, but I can't get past her rigid attitude about...everything. Maybe I drive her to act that way. Donnae know. I haven't seen her with other people, so maybe she treats all her patients like naughty children.

Though I wouldn't mind if she spanked me...

Bloody hell. I do not want Kate. She's the most annoying woman I've ever met.

Since I have an entire day to do anything I want, before I return to the torture chamber tomorrow, I decide to go sightseeing. When Jack suggested this therapeutic getaway in Inverness, I'd told him I would go back to my carpentry work on the days when I didn't have physical therapy sessions. He threatened to take away my car keys and my Harley if I tried to do any sort of work.

"You need to recuperate," Jack had said. "Your knee will never fully heal if you don't give it a chance."

Then he offered to pay all my living expenses for the month that I'm in Inverness. I wanted to tell him "away and chew a brush," but I knew Jack wouldn't give up that easily. So I took the coward's route and agreed to his plan.

Sightseeing by myself isn't any fun at all. I stare at Loch Ness for a while, then I shop for souvenirs to give to my family. Since they are all Scottish, except for the American women so many of them have married, souvenirs seem like a moronic idea. I do it anyway. Aye, I'm an eejit. I spend the rest of the day watching football on TV.

And then it's doomsday, otherwise known as my second appointment with Kate.

Seconds after I sit down in the waiting room, Hugh rings me. "Has the she-demon gnawed all the flesh off your bones yet?"

"No, ye *cacan*. I haven't seen her yet."

"Are you sure you're Callum MacTaggart? An alien parasite must've taken over your body, because my best mate would never call me a wee shit."

"Of course I would."

"But only in a cheeky tone."

I rub my eyes and groan. "Sorry, Hugh. When will you get here?"

"Should be there to meet you after your appointment. I'm in the air as we speak, flying across Scotland."

"All right. See you in a while."

"Cheers, Callum."

I grumble and end the call. Aye, I'm glad Hugh is coming for a visit, but I do not look forward to my next therapy session.

"Callum."

Kate's voice snaps me out of my thoughts. She's standing on the other side of the waiting room, holding the door to the torture chamber open while looking at me. I heave myself off my chair, and every part of me feels stiff from just sitting in the hard, uncomfortable seat. Why do medical places always have chairs that a robot wouldn't want to sit on?

I hobble toward Kate and follow her down the hall and into the exercise room. "Walk around the room briskly for five minutes."

"Havenae ye heard of the word please?" I ask. "Ahmno a dog."

"But I already know how difficult you are, so I'm taking a no-nonsense approach."

"You have a nonsense-only approach too? Or half-nonsense?"

She ignores my comments and waves her hand in a circular gesture. "Walk around the room for five minutes. It's your warm-up for today." She lays a hand on my arm, opening her mouth like she wants to speak, but she hesitates, eying my biceps. "You must work out when you're at home."

"Aye."

The lass gives my arm a gentle squeeze. Then she blinks rapidly, focusing on my face. "That's good. It'll make physical therapy much easier. Now, get moving."

I salute her.

She shakes her head and crosses her arms over her chest.

All I can do is obey her command. I walk a circuit around the room while I memorize the posters on the wall. One shows all the muscles in the human body, with the skin stripped off to expose every sinew. My lip curls. Cannae help it. Anatomical drawings always make me feel uneasy. Humans have skin for a bloody good reason. Nobody would want to shag if we all had to see what's under each other's skin.

Five minutes later, Kate whistles and waves for me to go back to her.

"Do you always whistle like that to call your patients back to you?" I ask as I reach her. "Or are you being sarcastic, treating me like an animal because I said ahmno a dog?"

"I don't have patients. You are my client."

"That's what Jack says too. Are you sure you're not a robot programmed by my brother?"

She huffs and points straight down at the blue mat lying on the carpet. "On the floor, Callum. Now."

Bloody hell, she's more than bossy. She's a harpy.

I lie down on the mat, on my back. "You remind me of my cousin Logan, who used to be in the army and MI6. You're sexier than him, but just as demanding."

Kate bends over to aim her sharp gaze straight into my eyes. "Man up, MacTaggart. It's time for straight leg raises."

Bod an Donais. That woman is going to drive me barking mad.

Chapter Four

Hugh

I WALK INTO THE BUILDING AND MARCH STRAIGHT UP TO the reception desk. Why am I here? To save my best mate from a shrew who might also be a she-demon. I expect to see glowing red eyes and small red horns when I finally meet Kate Wagner, considering the way Callum described her. He didn't mention her looks, which makes me wonder if she has green warts too.

The pretty lass behind the waist-high desk raises her head from whatever papers she'd been perusing. Her eyes widen for a heartbeat, then she smiles shyly. "How may I help you, sir?"

"I'm Hugh Parrish." I offer the girl my hand. "Viscount Sommerleigh. And I'm here to meet my best mate, Callum MacTaggart. I believe he's with Kate Wagner right now."

"Oh aye, the fireman." She shakes my hand while fluttering her lashes at me.

Callum hasn't been a fireman for nine months, but I won't correct the girl. She's lovely, and I am always in the market for a sexy companion—for dinner or the night.

"Mr. MacTaggart is with Kate right now," the girl says. "But I'll let her know his friend is here."

I notice the small name tag pinned to her chest. "Thank you, Mary. And what a lovely name you have, though it's not as lovely as you."

Mary giggles, then picks up the phone and punches three buttons. She listens while her gaze goes distant. "Kate, Mr. MacTaggart's friend is here. Should I have him wait?" She listens a bit more while catching her lip between her teeth. "Aye. I'll do that."

She ends the call and smiles shyly again. "Kate says she'll be out in a minute to speak to you, Mister—Viscount Sommerleigh? Or is it Lord Sommerleigh?"

I lean in and wink. "You can call me Lord Steamy."

Mary blushes.

Oh yes, I love making women blush. It's adorable and sexy. Maybe I enjoy telling women the moronic nickname that someone—a female someone, though I don't know which one—invented for me a few years ago. But it does come in handy when I'm trying it on with a woman. I don't want to seduce Mary, though. My flirtation is more of a reflex.

I lean in closer. "Why don't you just call me Hugh?"

"All right." She flutters her lashes again and slants toward me a touch. Then something past my shoulder snares her attention, and she straightens. "Kate is here to speak to you."

I pat Mary's hand. "Thank you for taking such good care of me, darling."

She blushes again.

Then I turn around, getting my first look at the she-demon from the depths of hell. And I freeze. Blimey, that can't be her.

A woman with golden red hair, tied up in a ponytail, stands just outside a closed door, scanning the surroundings as if she's looking for someone. She is looking. For me. I'm a lucky bloke, aren't I? Kate Wagner has a slim body with just enough curves to make any man's mouth water and breasts that make me want to see them naked. All right, I want to see every woman's breasts naked. I love a nude woman, full stop.

Kate notices me and crooks her finger, beckoning me.

Well, it would be rude not to go over there and seduce—ah, *introduce* myself to her. She is the woman who's tormenting my best mate, after all. I need to do in-depth research to determine how best to save Callum from the harpy. Yes, I will sacrifice myself to spare my friend because I'm a valiant knight.

No. I might be many things but chivalrous is not one of them.

I reach the she-demon and offer her my hand. "Hugh Parrish. You must be Kate."

"Uh-huh." She slips her hand into mine for a brief shake. "Callum said you'd be coming for a visit. But I'm afraid you'll have to wait quite a while. We completed his physical therapy for today, but we still need to finish his psychotherapy session. That lasts an hour."

"I see." Can't help skimming my gaze over her body—but only once and very quickly. So it doesn't count. "What sort of psychotherapist are you? MD? PhD?"

"Nosy, aren't you?"

"Cal is my best mate. I need to make sure his therapist is fully qualified and understands his unique needs."

She rests her hands on her hips. "I have PhDs in psychology and physical therapy. Satisfied, Mr. Nosy?"

"My name is Hugh Parrish, Viscount Sommerleigh."

Women always love my title, but Kate just wrinkles her nose. "Viscount? That must be one of those titles that doesn't mean anything because it's given out to rock stars and actors."

"I do not have a meaningless title. I'm the twelfth Viscount of Sommerleigh." I'm beginning to see what Cal meant about Kate. She's...prickly. But I'm excellent at sneaking past the nettles to find a woman's soft, pliant center. So I slant closer and smile. "But you can call me Lord Steamy."

Kate snorts as if she's trying to stifle a laugh. "Lord Steamy? You've got to be kidding."

"Don't you want to know why women call me that?"

"No thanks." Her gaze slides over me from head to toe. "You look like you're dressed for a business meeting."

I am wearing a suit, but no tie, so I can see why she might assume that. "I like to dress well. Unlike my friend Callum, who thinks jeans and a leather jacket are the epitome of fashion."

"Yeah, I bet you're a real fashion whore." She moves toward the closed door, grasping the knob. "Look, I've got to get back to work. It'll be another hour before Callum is done. You're welcome to wait here, but there's a cafe down the street if you get bored."

"Have dinner with me, Kate."

She jerks her head back, chin tucked. "Excuse me?"

I don't normally ask a woman out with no preamble, but she wouldn't let me talk her into it. Maybe I shouldn't ask her out, anyway—at least until I make certain Callum is not interested in her at all. She might be prickly, but she's also beautiful and sexy. So yes, I'd better make sure. My query was a knee-jerk reaction, that's all.

"We can talk about that later," I say. "Better get back to Callum. It was nice meeting you, Kate."

"Uh-huh." She still seems confused, but she goes through the door without looking back.

And I sit down in a ruddy awful chair to wait for Callum. Now that I've met Kate, I can see why she drives Cal mad. A desirable woman who's immune to my charms? That's never happened to me before. I have far more talent in wooing women than Callum does, so I can imagine how much the luscious Kate confounds him.

Bloody hell, the woman confounds me too.

Mary comes over to ask if I'd like some coffee or tea. I decline, and I ignore her fluttering lashes. She's gotten a bit braver, though, and lays a hand on mine for about half a second. Then she blushes again and hustles back behind the reception desk. Well, at least one woman in this place likes me. But no, I don't think I'll unleash my charms on her. Poor little Mary seems far too innocent for my taste.

Since I have nothing else to do, I lean my head back against the window behind me, stretch out my legs to cross them at the ankles, and shut my eyes. I can sleep anywhere, but for some reason, every time the door opens and its electronic chime bongs, my eyes fly open. I wind up chatting to an elderly man who had hip surgery, though mostly I listen to him explaining in detail what's involved in a hip replacement. After he leaves, a middle-aged woman sits down beside me, determined to chat me up. I love older women, but honestly, I'm not in the mood for that right now. Besides, she has brown teeth and smells like cigarette smoke.

At last, Callum and Kate emerge from the depths of the building.

I jump up and rush over there. To see Callum, of course. It's been ages since I saw my best mate. All right, I might actually be hurrying because I want to chat to Kate some more. Or chat her up. Haven't decided which I want to try—conversation or seduction.

As I reach Callum, I slap his arm. "Has the lovely Kate rearranged all your neurons?"

"Neurons?" Kate says, looking more confused than seems necessary.

"Surprised I know what the word means?" I ask. "I do have a degree from Oxford, you know."

"Uh-huh." She turns to Callum. "See you on Friday. Remember, no motorcycle. And keep doing those stretches."

Kate disappears through the mysterious door.

I throw an arm around Callum's shoulders. "So, tell me all about your private session with Kate."

Chapter Five

Kate

I WATCH THE TWO MEN AMBLE OUT OF THE BUILDING AND get into Callum's car. I keep watching until the vehicle zooms out of the parking lot and I can't see it anymore. Those two are going to drive me insane, I'm sure of it. No, I don't want to date either one. Hugh is too full of cocksure charm, and Callum is too grumpy. Both men are attractive and sexy, but I steer clear of hot guys. They always leave a trail of misery in their wake.

Besides, I'm taking a break from dating.

Though I go back to doing my job for the rest of the day, my brain insists on reminding me of Hugh and Callum. Why do I keep thinking about them? I don't like either man, so I shouldn't be musing about them while I'm at work.

I can think about them when I get home.

No, I won't do that either.

During my counseling session with Callum, I struggled to remain calm and professional. But that man is testing my patience and pushing me to my limit. When I asked once again how he gets along with his family, he said, "Fine." When I encouraged him to discuss his friendship with Hugh, he shrugged and tipped his head back to stare at the ceiling. Finally, I broached the subject that seems like the most important one for us to discuss. I asked how he injured his knee the first time.

He grunted. "Everybody knows how it happened. On-the-job injury."

"When you were a firefighter."

"Aye."

"Tell me more about that incident. How it happened, why you quit your job."

He clasped his hands over his belly and stared at the ceiling again.

Oh yes, that man is going to drive me insane—and I'll end up strangling him with an elastic therapy band. Those are supposed to be used for gently strengthening injured muscles, but Callum doesn't need any help in that department. His muscles are already big and strong.

When I get home from work, I contact the one person who might be able to help me get through to Callum. I call Jack MacTaggart.

"Afraid I can't help you," he says when I all but beg for his help. "Callum won't listen to me either. You'll have to find your own way to break through to him."

"Why did you tell me your brother is cheerful and easygoing? He's more like a wounded grizzly bear."

"And he needs you to tend to his wounds."

"Please don't tell me this is some kind of weird matchmaking scheme. Callum and I don't even like each other."

Jack chuckles. "No matchmaking, not this time. You are a talented psychotherapist, Kate. You know better than to let a difficult client commandeer your sessions."

Yeah, I do know better. But Callum... He's impossible.

We chat for a few more minutes, though not about his recalcitrant brother, then we say goodbye. Only after we hang up do I realize exactly what Jack said earlier. *No matchmaking, not this time.* What does that mean? This time? Sounds like some other day he might try to meddle. Jack is a good man and a good therapist, but I don't need anyone messing with my life.

Callum and Hugh seem like they'll be doing enough of that on their own.

But only if I let them. Jack is right. I need to stop letting Callum hijack our sessions. He only got away with that today because I was, um, distracted by, uh...things. His muscles, mostly. And those piercing blue eyes. And okay, I couldn't stop remembering the day we met, when he got a hard-on while I was evaluating his injury. That didn't happen today, but only because I didn't need to evaluate him again.

I don't see Callum the next day, because his therapy is three times a week. But someone does come to visit me. I'm in the middle of eating lunch in my office when Mary, who holds down the front desk, calls me.

"There's a gentleman here to see ye. He doesnae have an appointment, but he says it's important. And he wants it to be a surprise, so I'm not meant to tell ye his name." She giggles as a voice in the background says something I can't hear. "Cannae say that to Kate."

"What can't you say to me?"

She hesitates before answering. "He says you'll know who he is if I tell you it's Lord Steamy."

Oh no, not him. But I'm sure if I ignore Hugh, he'll sit in the waiting room until I come out. I met the man for thirty seconds yesterday, but I can already tell he's the type who won't give up so easily. Might as well get it over with so I can explain to him that nothing will ever happen between us.

"I'll be out in a minute," I tell Mary.

After scarfing down the rest of my lunch, I rinse my mouth out with water and check for gunk stuck between my teeth. I check my hair in the little mirror I keep in my purse. As I march through the exercise room, I can't help glancing at myself in the floor-to-ceiling mirrors just to make sure my clothes look all right. Oh, for heaven's sake. Why do I care what Hugh thinks of me? If I want to shut down his courtship attempts, I ought to make myself look slovenly.

The second I step through the door into the waiting room, Hugh leaps off his chair and trots over to me.

"Good afternoon, Kate," he says with a smile. Then he takes my hand and kisses it. "You look ravishing today."

Overkill much? Sheesh, this guy is laying it on so thick I'll need a jackhammer to dig my way out. "Hi, Hugh. What do you want?"

"To bask in your presence."

"Does that kind of talk usually work for you?"

He shrugs. "Sometimes. I have an arsenal of techniques for seducing a woman, so I'm sure I can find something that will make you randy."

Did he seriously just explain to me that he's a calculating lothario? But he doesn't seem like that kind of guy.

Hugh winks and smirks. "That was a joke, darling."

Thank goodness. "I'm working, Hugh. So why don't you tell me what was so important that you had to stage a sit-in."

"Of course. Here's what I came to say." He moves closer and speaks in a lower, sexier voice. "Have dinner with me, Kate."

"Why?"

"Because we're two single people who have nothing better to do." He tilts his head to the side. "Unless you're married or have a serious boyfriend."

"I'm single. But I don't think it's a good idea. I'm treating your best friend."

"But you are not treating me." He smiles again, and I can't deny that expression is appealing. "Come on, love, give me a chance. I'll pay for dinner. What have you got to lose?"

Oh, that's a loaded question.

But I haven't gone on a date in a long time. Haven't done much of anything for a long time. I work, I go home, I sleep, I go back to work. Maybe I don't want to get entangled in a relationship with Hugh Parrish, but an evening out could be fun.

"Okay, Hugh. I'll have dinner with you tonight."

He grins. "Brilliant!"

"Where's your partner in crime?"

"In the car. He insisted he will not go back into 'the torture chamber' one minute sooner than he has to." Hugh hooks a thumb over his shoulder, toward the windows. "I've been driving Callum around. He grouses about it, but he hasn't shoved me out of the car yet."

"He'd better not be riding his Harley."

"Oh no, I took the keys away and hid them."

A car horn blares right outside the windows.

"That would be the surly Scot," Hugh says. "I should go. But text me your address and I'll pick you up at eight."

"Sure. See you tonight."

Hugh kisses my hand and leaves.

Oddly, I don't think about him all afternoon. But in the evening, I get myself gussied up and wait for my date to arrive. Hugh rings the doorbell at exactly eight o'clock and even offers me his arm as we leave my apartment. It's kind of sweet, but also a bit strange. Does anybody do that anymore? I slip my arm around his, but I don't feel any excitement about our date. Not even a twinge. He's a nice enough guy, under all that Lord Steamy nonsense. Why can't I muster any interest in him? I shouldn't have agreed to a date when I know I don't want to actually date him.

So I stop us at the elevator and turn to face him. "I have to be honest with you. The only reason I agreed to go out with you is because I'm bored with my life. I haven't had a date in a long time. I'm not attracted to you. Sorry, but that's the truth. I'll understand if you don't want to have dinner with me."

He smiles, but the expression falters briefly. Then he reasserts his breezy demeanor. "Of course I want to have dinner with you, Kate. We didn't meet under the most romantic circumstances, so maybe your feelings will change once we're enjoying a meal in a posh restaurant."

"Not sure about that. And I'm actually wiped out after a long day at work."

"You want to reschedule our date."

"Sorry. I know it's last minute, but—"

He pats my arm. "No worries, love. Another time."

"Thank you."

"Although I could cook for you. My mother insisted I learn how to pre-pare a proper meal, so I wouldn't end up living on takeaway foods."

I honestly feel bad about backing out on our date, so maybe I should let him cook for me. What harm could that do? "Okay. Let's eat in."

Once we get inside my apartment, I excuse myself to change out of my dressy clothes and into something more comfortable. When I told Hugh that, he smirked and suggested, "Get as comfortable as you like, pet. I love a woman in fuzzy pink slippers." I told him I don't have any of those, but he just smiled and started to remove his suit jacket.

When I emerge from the bedroom ten minutes later, I'm wearing my favorite sweatpants and T-shirt with a matching hoodie. My slippers are brown suede, not fuzzy and pink. I've washed off my makeup too and tied my hair back in a ponytail. Hugh is standing at the stove whipping up who knows what. I perch on a stool at the island to watch him.

He glances over his shoulder at me, and his brows hike up. "You really did get comfortable."

"Have I ruined your opinion of me with my sweats and slippers? Or maybe it's the fact I'm not wearing makeup anymore."

"No, I don't mind that at all. You are stunning, Kate, with or without makeup."

"Thank you." I try to peer around him, but I can't see the stove top. "What are you making?"

"It's a surprise." He turns around to wave a spatula at me. "Pa-tience, love."

Now I can see he not only removed his jacket but also unhooked the top two buttons on his shirt. Maybe that exposed skin should make me feel...something. I can appreciate his physique and his looks, his personal-ity too, but I don't feel the slightest urge to kiss him. Maybe Hugh is right, though, and the way we met has influenced my feelings for him.

Right now, I have only platonic feelings for him.

A few minutes later, I find out Hugh has made us omelets and toast. I'm not a food snob, so that meal suits me just fine. We sit on the sofa to eat—me at one end, Hugh at the other—and we engage in casual conversation. He doesn't ask about my past with men, and I don't ask about his experiences with women. We avoid the topic of Callum too. So basically, we chat about how beautiful Scotland is, how it compares to England, and then we dis-cuss movies and TV shows. If this were an actual date, it would rate as the most mundane one I've ever had.

But it's not a date. Thank goodness.

When I escort Hugh to the door, he asks, "May I kiss you good night?"

"On the cheek or the mouth?"

"Your lips, love."

I feel the faintest tingle of excitement at the prospect, so I tell him, "Okay."

He cups my face in his hands, leans in, and presses his lips to mine.

That tingle evaporates. It's a nice kiss, but not enough to stir any real desire.

Without trying for a deeper kiss, Hugh pulls away and studies me. "How was that?"

"It was nice." I hunch my shoulders. "But I didn't feel what I'm sure you were hoping I would. I'm sorry, Hugh, but I'm just not attracted to you."

He sighs. "Fair enough. Good night, Kate."

"Good night, Hugh."

He walks out the door.

And for reasons I can't fathom, my thoughts return to Callum.

Callum

YESTERDAY WAS MY DAY AWAY FROM KATE AND THERAPY and all that rubbish. This morning, I get up at my usual time, six a.m., while Hugh keeps on sleeping. He left the door to his room open, so I can see him sprawled across the bed and hear him softly snoring. I take a shower and do some of the stretches Kate taught me on Wednesday, then I check my email. Before I left Loch Fairbairn, Jack had told everyone to email me instead of calling because I need to "concentrate on getting better."

There's nothing wrong with me. I donnae need to "concentrate."

Hugh insists on driving me to the clinic again today, despite my attempts to convince him that's unnecessary. I do not need a babysitter or a chauffeur, but trying to talk Hugh out of doing anything once he's set his mind to it is like telling a dog not to bark. I think he just wants to see Kate again, even after their date last night fizzled out. Aye, Hugh is also as stubborn as a dog with a tasty bone. He won't give up until Kate smacks him on the head with a large hammer. Even then, he might keep at it.

On the short drive to the clinic, Hugh brings up the subject of *that* woman. "Cal, are you sure you're all right with me pursuing Kate? I'd understand if it makes you uncomfortable since she is your therapist. I know you said you're fine with it, but—"

"Donnae care what you and Kate do together."

"You are one hundred percent sure about that."

"Aye, I'm sure. If ye ask me again, I'll skelp ye."

"All right, calm down. No need for violence." Hugh steers the car into the car park at the clinic, pulling into a slot. "You are my best mate, Cal, and I would never want to get in the way if you have feelings for a woman."

I've never liked the nickname Cal, but I let Hugh call me that because he's my best mate. "I don't have feelings for Kate. Unless wanting to strangle her counts."

He chuckles. "She does get under your skin, but I suppose that's a therapist's job."

Aye, it seems to be. Driving me off my head, humiliating me, giving me stern looks... Her therapy method needs work. "If you want Kate, have at it."

Hugh slaps my arm. "You'll find a girl too, don't worry."

"You don't have Kate yet. She told ye she's not attracted to you."

"Do you think I'd be called Lord Steamy if I gave up that easily? Gentle persuasion is the key."

Hugh jumps out of the car while I'm still struggling with my seat belt and opens my door.

When he holds out his hand like he expects me to take it and let him help me out of the car, I scowl at him. "Ahmno an invalid."

"All right, have it your way." He steps back. "I'll be on standby, in case you need emergency support."

"*Falbh dàirich fhèin.*"

Hugh chuckles again. "Considering your mental state, I'll forgive you for telling me to go fuck myself."

"My mental state is fine."

I limp across the car park, limp through the clinic doors, and limp over to the reception desk. Hugh watches me with an amused expression, like he thinks I'm a bloody-minded eejit. Maybe I am. Or maybe I just don't like being tricked into four weeks of double-barreled therapy—mental and physical. Aye, Jack is going to pay for doing this to me.

The sweet lass at the reception desk checks me in, and Hugh and I sit down on the uncomfortable chairs in the waiting room.

Kate emerges from the door on the other side of the room, and her gaze zeroes in on me. "Callum, come with me."

I heave myself out of my chair, groaning.

Hugh smacks my arm. "Good luck, mate."

Luck won't help me survive an hour and a half with Kate. First, she'll torture me with exercises. Then, she'll torture me with psychotherapy rubbish.

I hobble across the waiting room and follow Kate through the door that leads into the hall of "treatment rooms." She called them that once. It's a euphemism for the small torture chamber she's leading me to right now. But we don't stop at the room we'd used on Monday and Wednesday. Instead, she shepherds me around the corner into the exercise room and continues across it to another door. Swinging it open, she waves for me to go through it. Then I follow Kate again, helpless to avoid staring at her backside. The lass shouldn't wear tight-fitting trousers if she doesn't want men to admire her erse. The fact that I don't like her has no bearing on the issue. I'm a man. Cannae resist looking at a woman's body, even if I intensely dislike the lass in question.

The firm, round cheeks of her erse mesmerize me.

We're walking down another hallway that has doors on either side. More treatment rooms? I thought we were done with the so-called evaluation, and I donnae want a repeat of what happened on Monday when she "evaluated" me. Kate might get the wrong idea.

She stops at a door and swings it open. "Here we are."

The room looks like an office, with a desk and file cabinets, an armchair too. But I also see a couch.

Bloody hell. She means to shrink my brain today, and she brought me to her office to do it. That must mean she intends to squeeze me for information until I crack. That will never happen. I've been told my head is made of cast iron, though I'm not sure that was a compliment. My brother said it. Last week.

"You can take the armchair or the sofa," Kate says. "Your choice."

"My choice would be to walk out the door. You're meaning to therapize me, aren't ye?"

"Therapize? That's not a word."

"My sister-in-law invented the term."

"Uh-huh." Kate lays a hand on my back, gently urging me toward the armchair. "Why don't you sit here?"

I limp toward the chair and drop onto it. Well, at least this seat has padding and arms where I can rest my, ah, arms.

Kate sits in the office chair behind her desk. I see a name placard that verifies my belief this is her office. The wee sign reads, "Kate Wagner, PhD."

"Should I call you Dr. Wagner?" I ask.

"Just Kate will do."

"What sort of PhD do you have?"

She leans back in her chair, rocking it slightly while she studies me. "I have two PhDs, in physical therapy and psychology."

"Oh." It's all I can manage to say. Two doctorates? I barely finished university and never even thought of trying for a PhD.

"Let's talk about the first time you injured your knee. Tell me about the fire."

"I told ye already."

"The whole story this time." She rolls her chair forward, resting her arms on the desktop. "Why did you stop being a firefighter after that?"

"Because I was injured. Are ye deaf? I told ye that already too."

"Okay. Let's start at the beginning. Why did you become a firefighter in the first place?"

I shrug. "Seemed like the thing to do. I moved to Inverness because there are no wholetime fire stations in Glencoe. I wanted it to be my career, not work somewhere else and be on call for fires. And a change of scenery sounded good."

"Glencoe? I thought you were from Loch Fairbairn."

"Which is in Glencoe. That's the name of the region in and around Ballachulish and Fort William."

"Oh, I get it." She taps her fingers on her arm, still staring at me. "Must've been hard to be so far away from your family, alone in a new city with no friends."

"Who says I had no mates? My cousin Evan was living in Inverness when I first moved here. He wanted me to be his roommate, but I told him I'd rather get my own place."

"Does Evan still live here?"

"Only part-time. He moved to Utah after he married Keely, though they come back to Scotland for visits."

Kate tips her head to the side a wee bit, her gaze nailed to me. "Why didn't you want to room with Evan? You like him, right?"

"Of course I do. But we aren't best mates. Don't have much in common. I was just a firefighter while he's a tech genius who became a billionaire practically overnight."

"How does that make you feel?"

"I knew you'd get around to that question sooner or later." I lean forward and cannae help growling my words. "Ahmno jealous of Evan. Not jealous of Jack either. I'm happy for everyone in my family who's found what they wanted and needed."

"Didn't say you were jealous. Interesting that you did."

"*Magairlean.*" I grip my chair's arms so hard that my knuckles hurt. "I said I am *not* jealous."

"You should know, I called Jack again last night. He gave me a crash course in Gaelic, so I'll know what you're saying whenever you snarl one of your favorite curses." She squints at me, her lips puckered slightly. "You just said 'bollocks.' If you hope swearing will make me give up on you, think again."

"*Pit air iteig*," I hiss. " *'S e plàigh a th' annad*."

Her brows crinkle in the sweetest way. "Okay, that wasn't in my crash course. What did you say?"

"Doesnae matter." Because I will not tell her. The words flew out of my mouth before I thought about what I was saying.

She reaches for the phone on her desk. "Maybe I should call Jack for a translation."

"Donnae do that." I wince and avoid looking at her. "I said, 'Flying vagina, you are a plague.' "

The lass just stares at me for a moment. Then her lips twitch at the corners. She raises a hand to cover her mouth, but drops it again while her whole body begins to quiver. And she starts laughing. "I love Scottish swearing. It's so inventive."

"Wait till ye hear my Gaelic dirty talk." Why did I say that? Donnae want to talk dirty to her. Well, maybe I want to, but I won't do it.

Kate gets up and walks around to my chair, crouching beside me. "I won't give up on you, and I want you to know that I care about your mental and physical health. I can help you, if you'll let me."

Why is she speaking in a soft, sexy voice? And she's gazing straight into my eyes. This doesn't seem like appropriate behavior for a psychologist. The V-neck of her shirt dives low enough that I get a bonnie view of her cleavage every time I glance down there. Not that I want to look at her tits. I can't do it, anyway, since her eyes have captivated me.

"Therapy is never easy," she says, while with one finger she draws a line from my elbow down to my wrist. "Sometimes you have to slice open a vein and let the blood flow."

I'm breathing harder and squirming in my seat because my trousers are getting tighter. Kate is talking about bloodletting, and I'm getting randy. I'm off my head for sure.

She drags that finger back up to my elbow. "But I'll be here to heal the wound. We'll do it together. "

Her pupils have dilated, and I can see the hard tips of her nipples. We're both aroused, but that's barmy. Arguing shouldn't get us turned on.

I clear my throat and jerk my arm away. "No more psychotherapy today."

She glances at her hand as if she can't understand why it had been touching my arm a moment ago. Then she stands up. "We can put a pin in that for today. Let's go into the exercise room and get you warmed up. Then we'll add two new exercises to your routine."

"Two? Are ye trying to kill me?"

"No pain, no gain."

I groan and follow Kate into the exercise room. We seem to be pretending she didn't just speak to me in a sexy voice while we both got aroused.

After thirty minutes of physical therapy, Kate leads me out to the door that opens into the waiting room. She stops there, one hand on the knob. "I'll see you Monday. Then it will be time to strip your psyche bare."

"Stripping? You need to buy me dinner first." I meant to say that in a cheeky way, but it came out rough instead.

Kate bites her lip, letting it slide free little by little.

Bod an Donais. I cannae stop myself. I back her up to the wall and kiss her. When our lips meet, the lust grips me and willnae let go, not until I've tasted her.

She flicks her tongue out to tease my mouth.

I groan and plunge my tongue between her lips while I tug her hips into me, grinding my stiffening *slat* against her. She moans and wraps her tongue around mine, writhing and rubbing her breasts against my chest. Though I can feel their hard peaks, the taste of her distracts me from that. But it's the way she wriggles that sexy body that drives out all other thoughts. I want to carry her back to her office and shag her on the desk.

But instead, I pull away and stumble backward, breathing too hard to speak. What is wrong with me? Kissing my therapist, who I don't even like, has to be the daftest thing I've ever done. I have only one option now. Luckily, I brought my leather jacket today, so I fold it over my arm and hold that in front of my body to hide my erection. "See you Monday."

Then I walk out the door.

"How did it go?" Hugh asks as opens the front door for me.

I grunt and hobble outside.

"That well, eh? You should try to get on with Kate, since you'll be working with her for three more weeks. She's a lovely woman, Cal."

"*Dùin do ghob.* Donnae want to hear about Kate anymore."

Aye, I told my best mate to shut the fuck up. I'm in no condition to chat to Hugh, especially not about Kate. He can have her. What I did a few minutes ago was nothing more than temporary insanity.

Because I am not attracted to Kate Wagner.

Chapter Seven

Kate

WHAT ON EARTH JUST HAPPENED? I'M STILL LEANING against the wall, a few feet from the closed door to the waiting room, because my muscles won't move and my brain refuses to process the fact that Callum kissed me. I kissed him back and sort of, um, rubbed myself all over him. Jeez, I practically begged him to screw me. Not in words, but in actions.

And God, I wanted him to do that.

I shove myself away from the wall and hurry back to my office, dropping onto my chair. I should never have let Callum kiss me. It's beyond unprofessional, and if anyone found out what we did, I could lose my job. A psychotherapist is not supposed to make out with her client. It was a fluke. An accident. One moment of insanity. It will never happen again.

But a memory of that kiss barrels through my mind, and heat rushes over me from head to toe. The luscious warmth seeps under my skin too, enlivening parts of me that I do not want to wake up right now.

Could I sort of, possibly, be attracted to him?

No, absolutely not. The man drives me insane with his pigheaded attitude and grumpy demeanor. I do not feel that way about him. I'm done with men, anyway. At least I won't see him again until Monday. By then, I'll have repressed that moment and will have no trouble getting back to work.

On Saturday morning, I realize what I need to do. Talk to Callum. Clear the air. So I call him.

"Kate?" Callum says. "Why are you ringing me?"

"We need to talk. Can I come over to your place?"

"Aye. When did you have in mind?"

"Right now. Is that okay?"

Silence follows for several seconds. "Aye."

"Great. Text me your address."

Half an hour later, I knock on the door to his apartment.

It swings open two seconds later, and Callum moves aside, waving for me to enter. "*Madainn mhath*, Kate."

"What?"

He chuckles. "I said good morning."

"Oh. Good morning, Callum."

Why do I feel like a criminal? Kissing a man is not a felony.

As I follow Callum into the living room, I try so hard not to notice he's wearing snug jeans and a snug T-shirt that show off his muscular physique. I wish he'd worn loose-fitting clothes. Not that it matters. I refuse to allow lust to override my willpower, so it makes no difference what he wears.

Maybe I shouldn't have worn a skirt. It's a casual, swishy one that hangs just past my knees, not a miniskirt. I felt like being feminine after five days of wearing sweats and T-shirts at work.

"Sit wherever you want," Callum says.

I shuffle over to the armchair positioned kitty-corner to the sofa and settle onto it, dropping my purse on the floor. Callum takes the sofa, sitting at the end closest to my chair.

"Where's Hugh?" I ask.

"Getting the messages. That means groceries."

"Yeah, I know that Scottishism."

I bite my upper lip, glancing around the fancy apartment with its floor-to-ceiling windows and open kitchen. The view out the windows overlooks the River Ness. The apartment has a clean, modern design with white walls and ceilings as well as gorgeous wood floors, and a dining table stands halfway into the kitchen. I don't see any artwork on the walls, but I do notice an array of picture frames on a table in the corner, and I bet those are family photos, though I can't see them well from over here.

A hallway to my left accesses two rooms that have their doors shut. To my right, another doorway hangs half-open. It looks like a bathroom that's discreetly tucked into a corner.

"Feel free to walk around and explore," Callum says. "I can wait while you satisfy your curiosity."

"No, that's okay. I've never seen a swanky apartment before. Didn't mean to be rubbernecking."

He shrugs. "Doesnae bother me. But I'm wondering why you're here."

"After what happened yesterday, I feel like we need to clear the air." I wriggle in my chair and set my hands on my thighs. "The way I behaved was highly inappropriate. I apologize. From now on, when we're at the clinic, we both need to stick to our roles as client and therapist."

"I agree."

"Good." I blow out a sigh, relieved beyond belief that he didn't argue. Had I hoped he would announce he wants me so badly that he can't agree to my terms? No, of course not. "I'd like us to get to know each other better so you'll feel more comfortable sharing your thoughts and feelings with me. I think part of the problem we've been having is that we're strangers. Away from the clinic, we can be friends."

"Sounds reasonable."

He looks and sounds reasonable, for sure. After his grumpy, growly behavior, I can't help feeling slightly unnerved by his calmness today. But this isn't the clinic, and I'm not acting as his therapist right now, so that's probably why his behavior has changed.

My gaze flicks to the coffee table. "Is that a bowl of condoms?"

"Aye." Callum winces. "It was, uh, Hugh's way of telling me I need to get laid. The cheeky sod."

"It's nice you have a friend who cares."

Callum scratches the back of his neck. "I should apologize. My mother taught me to treat women with respect, but I haven't done that with you. I'm sorry."

"Thank you, Callum. I appreciate that. But I know your behavior has very little to do with me and everything to do with all those things you haven't wanted to talk about yet." I raise a hand when he seems about to speak. "Let's not go into that today. I came here so we can get better acquainted. Ask me anything you want."

He lifts his brows. "Anything? That could be dangerous."

"The peril goes both ways. Assuming you let me ask you questions."

"Aye, ye can."

"You go first."

He studies me for a moment, then relaxes into the sofa. "What is a bonnie American doing in Scotland? Do you have family here? Or a boyfriend?"

"None of the above." I want to tell him that's too personal and not his concern, but getting to know each other was my idea. "I got divorced. It was finalized fifteen months ago. My husband had cheated on me repeatedly, and I kept forgiving him—until I couldn't forgive him anymore. He slept with my boss. I had to find another job, and getting as far away from my ex as possible sounded like a good idea. Then I saw an ad in a journal for a psychology conference in London, which seemed like the perfect getaway. I met Jack there. He told me about the Inverness clinic and that they'd been looking for someone like me, a combination physical therapist and psychologist."

"Jack helped you get the job?"

"He provided a reference. Two months later, I was living and working in Scotland."

"That's quite a change. How are you getting on in a new country?"

I cross my legs and rest my arms on the chair. "Sometimes I get confused by the things you Scots say, but I love it here. The land is beautiful, the people are kind and welcoming, and I'm far away from the ghosts of my past."

"Have you dated anyone since your husband?"

"No. I've decided to be celibate for a while."

"Celibate?" He sounds surprised. After our kiss yesterday, I can't blame him. "You're a bonnie, passionate woman. Cannae let one bleeding ersehole put you off men." He eyes me with a touch of suspicion. "But you went on a date with Hugh."

"No, I almost went on a date with him. He charmed me into saying yes, but I quickly realized I'm not ready for that. He said he understood."

"I'm sure he did understand. Hugh's not a *tolla-thon*." Callum smirks. "Not like me."

"What is a *tolla-thon*?"

"An ersehole."

"You are not an asshole, Callum." I sit forward, gazing straight at him. "I can tell you've got issues, and I think some of them involve your accident, but I won't push you on that today. I have a different question for you. Why don't you like to talk about your brother? Seems like you two get along well."

"We do. But Jack is..." Callum bows his head. "I was always the one the lasses liked the best. Jack didn't have many girlfriends. He was never spontaneous or impulsive like I am. But then he married a woman he met in Las Vegas and had known for twelve days. They got divorced, but now they're together again—married and having a bairn."

"It's natural to feel a little jealous, especially when you're struggling with your own life."

"Ahmno jealous, and ahmno struggling." He shuts his eyes and scrunches up his face. "All right, maybe I am a wee bit jealous. I'm happy for Jack and Autumn, but... Donnae know. Maybe it's just that I haven't been with a lass in almost nine months."

"You haven't had sex since just after your accident?"

He nods, his mouth tight and his fingers curled into his thighs. "Tried to shag a girl a few weeks after my injury, but I, ah, couldn't perform."

"Do you mean you couldn't get an erection?"

Callum flashes me a scowl. "No. I am not *breallach*. I meant I couldn't do it because my bloody knee hurt too much. Can't expect a bloke to perform when he's in pain."

Breallach must mean impotent, based on what he said after that.

I think about what he just told me, and something occurs to me. "Were you on top?"

"Of course." He sounds only a touch irritated, despite the fact he's frowning—at the wall, not me.

"Why not let the woman take control? Your knee wouldn't be an issue if—"

"Tried that too. The lass suggested it, but it didn't work." He crosses his arms over his chest and finally looks at me. "Let me guess. You're the sort who always has to be on top and in control."

"No, but I can't understand why you're so stubborn about this. There are a lot of submissive positions for a man that might alleviate the pain issue during sex."

"Submissive? I am not letting a lass tie me up."

"I didn't mean it that way. Letting your partner take control, so you can relax and enjoy it without causing yourself pain, that's what I meant."

Though I wouldn't mind tying him up and taking command, maybe gagging him too so he can't gripe at me. He is gorgeous, and I'm so far past pent-up. Celibacy sounded like a good idea until I met Callum. My gaze wanders over his hot body and all those muscles... *No sex with the grumpy Scot. Got it?*

Callum slumps into the sofa. "I'm sorry. You're trying to help, and I'm acting like a *bod ceann*." He gives me a wry smile. "That means I'm a dickhead."

"No, you're just frustrated. And I'm starting to understand the reasons for that." I walk over to the sofa and sit down beside him. Not sure why, but I feel the need to console him. "I shouldn't have pushed you to talk about sex. I want to help you, and I feel like I'm failing at that."

"You aren't." His gaze shifts to my mouth. "That kiss yesterday helped a lot."

"We shouldn't do that again."

He sighs. "Aye, it wouldn't be right."

But I'm so damn sick of doing the right thing. Giving my ex-husband chance after chance to reform his ways had gotten me nowhere. I haven't slept with anyone in so long. And Callum knows how to kiss.

He slides a hand up my arm, his rough palm exciting my skin. The short-sleeve blouse I'm wearing lets him slowly glide that hand up almost to my shoulder. Our gazes connect, and suddenly I can't catch my breath, mesmerized by his pale blue eyes.

Callum drags his hand over my shoulder, up my neck, to cradle my nape.

What's the harm in one little kiss? Nobody will ever know I did it.

But it's wrong. I should move away from him.

Callum leans in, his mouth a hair's breadth from mine.

I swear I can taste his breaths as they tickle my lips, and the scent of his aftershave teases my senses. I can't stop staring at his mouth or stop myself from dragging my tongue across my lips. Maybe I can indulge in one kiss, just to get it out of my system.

He wraps his free arm around me, tugging me into his body, while with the other hand he keeps hold of my nape. "Need to taste you again."

"Yes, please."

Callum presses his mouth to mine, groaning deeply. I moan and sag into him. He slips his tongue between my parted lips, teasing me with light flicks while he slides his hand down to grasp my ass. He tastes so damn good. My pulse races as a sensual heat rushes through me, and I can't catch my breath.

Then it happens.

A switch flips inside me, one that shuts down all common sense and self-control. I swing my leg over to straddle his lap, my sex now poised above his hardening dick. We keep kissing, the passion erupting like a fire doused with gasoline, and we begin to grope each other wildly while our tongues lash and the kiss grows deeper and hotter. He clamps his hands onto my ass, tugging me into his erection.

I tear my mouth away from his, breathing hard, and gaze into his eyes.

Then I grasp the zipper on his jeans and yank it down.

Chapter Eight

Callum

KATE IS UNZIPPING MY TROUSERS. AM I STILL ASLEEP AND dreaming? The woman who dislikes me and seems to relish torturing me three days a week just took hold of my zipper and dragged it down. All the way down. My swollen cock, though trapped inside my boxers, bulges out to graze her groin. Is she about to fuck me? Here on the sofa? In my cousin's apartment? No, Kate wouldn't do that. I should stop this before she does something she'll regret.

But she doesn't seem to be regretting it right now. The look of sheer hunger on her face makes my *slat* throb.

I push my hands under her skirt, curling my fingers around her hips. My brows lift. "Where are your knickers?"

"Don't wear them."

"Never?"

She makes a frustrated noise and shoves a hand inside my boxers, pulling my cock free. When she drags her tongue over her lips and strokes my length, I suck in a sharp breath.

Aye, she means to fuck me.

I should stop this. Shouldn't I? Kate said she wanted to talk and clear the air, not hold my dokey in her hands. But I cannae make myself tell her to stop. I want her so much that I can't think anymore. Well, my lack of brainpower might have more to do with her stroking my *slat*.

"Condom," I growl, my fingers digging into her hips. "Hurry."

Kate leans back to snatch a packet from the bowl on the table. She tears it open with her teeth, then rolls the latex onto my cock. Her breasts rise and fall as breaths bluster out between her parted lips. She's so bonnie, so sexy, and I need to get her naked. But I can't move. The sight of her flushed cheeks and the peaks of her nipples jutting against her blouse strips away all my self-control.

I shove my hands under her erse and tug her forward until the hairs on her mound brush against my *slat*.

She wraps her fingers around my length and sinks onto it.

My cock is buried inside her lush body.

With a throaty moan, she starts to move her hips, rolling them into me in a slow and steady rhythm. The scent of her cream surrounds me, making me hunger for more of her, for everything, but I can't even see her tits. I want to flip her onto her back on the sofa and drive into her hard, but that would blow my knee out for sure. So instead, I wrap my arms around Kate and pull her close to kiss her.

Someone knocks on the door. "Callum, I forgot the key."

Who the bloody hell is that? What key? Donnae care. I plunge my tongue deep into Kate's mouth while she rides me faster.

"Callum!" that annoying voice shouts. "Wake up and let me in, please. These bags of groceries are getting heavy."

Kate jerks her head back. Her eyes go wide. "That's Hugh."

Pit air iteig. She's right. My best mate is outside that door while I'm inside shagging the woman I swore to him I didn't want.

The lass in question leaps off my lap and races into the bathroom, slamming the door shut.

"Oh, wait," Hugh says. "The key was in my trouser pocket. Never mind."

I hear the sound of a key being inserted into the lock. And I'm sitting here with my trousers undone and my dokey hanging out—with a condom still sheathing it. Muttering a slew of Gaelic curses, I strip off the condom and shove it into my pocket, zipping up my trousers as the door swings open. Hugh has his head down as he enters the apartment, so I just have time to grab a throw pillow and, ah, throw it over my lap to hide my raging erection.

Hugh sets his grocery bags on the coffee table. His gaze drifts to the armchair where Kate had sat earlier. His lips kink into a smirk, and his gaze veers to me. "You have a girl on the premises."

"What? No." *Of course ye do, ye bloody eejit.* Why did I lie? I'm panicking, I suppose.

My best mate chuckles. "Does your brother carry a purse now?"

I glance at the chair. Kate's purse lies on the floor beside it. But I don't have a chance to explain.

Kate walks out of the bathroom, snatching up her purse. "I should go. You guys have, um, guy things to do, I'm sure."

Guy things? I've got no sodding idea what she's on about.

"Don't leave on my account," Hugh says. "We can all chat to each other."

"No," Kate and I say at the same time.

She bites her lip.

I clear my throat. "Kate stopped by to clear the air between us."

Hugh drops onto the sofa. "I hope you apologized and showed Kate how much you appreciate everything she's done for you."

"Aye." Not sure a halfway shag counts as showing my appreciation, but I have no idea about what to say to Hugh. He seems oblivious of the sexual tension between me and Kate. My *slat* still throbs, and I cannae think clearly. "But I'm sure Kate has someplace else to be."

She grips her purse strap tightly and glances at the door.

Before she can speak, Hugh announces, "We should go for a walk. The three of us. It's a lovely day."

Kate glances at the door again. "I should go home. Callum needs to rest his knee, anyway."

Hugh leaps up. "You and I can go for a walk, then."

Shut your bloody mouth, Hugh. But he won't. I swore to him I can't stand Kate, so he assumes I'll have no problem with him spending time with her. I have no choice. I have to tell him, "Aye, you two should do that."

"I can't," Kate says. "Sorry."

And she bolts out the door, slamming it shut.

Hugh settles onto the sofa again, angled toward me, and lays an arm across its back. "What did you do to Kate?"

"Nothing." She did it to me, which means I'm not lying. Technically.

"Come off it, Callum. She was upset."

No, she was highly aroused and on the verge of climax. "Kate wants us to be friends. She was here to talk, nothing more. We did not argue."

"Hmm." Hugh narrows his gaze on me, drumming his fingers on the sofa's back. "I hope you didn't cock it up with her."

No, my cock was working very well.

Luckily, Hugh gives up on interrogating me. He sighs and stands up. "Kate is a challenge, but I'm up to the task."

He carries the messages into the kitchen while humming a cheery tune.

I am lying to Hugh, aren't I? He believes I have no interest in Kate other than physical therapy. I believed it too—until yesterday. That kiss had changed everything, and our half a shag a few minutes ago made it impossible for me to pretend I don't want her. But should I date her? Or do I want only sex? Either way, I'm buggered.

Hugh likes her. That means I cannae touch Kate again.

Mhac na galla.

"What would you like for lunch?" he calls out to me. "Your servant awaits instruction."

"*Pòg mo thòin*, Lord Sommerleigh."

"Kiss your arse? Ah, the ogre is back. I thought for a moment you might be the old Callum again."

The old me? Donnae recognize that man anymore.

Hugh goes back to humming.

I push up off the sofa. "Going for a walk."

"Let me finish putting away the groceries and I'll go with you."

"No," I snap, sounding even grumpier. Bloody hell, what's wrong with me? "I'd rather go alone."

"What if your knee gives out? Besides, walking is more fun with company."

"I said I'd rather be alone." I grab my keys and my mobile, then march to the door and settle my hand on the knob. When I glance back at Hugh, he's staring at me blankly. "What's fashing you now? Wanting to go for a walk alone is not a crime. I willnae fall into the river and drown."

Hugh points at my leg. "You're not limping."

"What?" I look at my leg too, but it seems no different to me. So I walk to the sofa and back to the door. *Bod an Donais*, it doesn't hurt at all. "The physical therapy must be working, I guess."

"You were limping when I left for the store." Hugh's gaze narrows as he scans me from head to toe, and his lips pucker slightly. "Did Kate give you a new exercise to try?"

Oh aye, she gave me a "new exercise." But a poke with Kate couldn't have cured my knee. Could it? Maybe it was hormones or...something.

"Well, I'm away," I tell Hugh as I pull the door open. "Be back later."

"At what time, dear? Your wifey needs to know when to start lunch."

I cannae stop myself from growling at the cheeky sod. "The day I marry you is the day I hack off my own leg."

He chuckles as I shut the door behind me.

A few minutes later, I'm walking out of the building to head for the walking path along the river. But I stop just as I reach the curb in front of the apartment complex. I let Kate run away without even talking to her about what happened between us. Though I know I can't touch her again, I do need to clear things up between us and make sure she knows I don't expect anything from her. Will she still be my therapist? I don't want her to hand me off to someone else, but I wouldn't blame her if she did.

I rush back into the parking garage, intending to drive to Kate's place. But as I climb into the car, I realize I don't know where she lives. Since she had given me her mobile number, I dial it and hope it's not a number she only checks when she's at work. I get her voice mail. Cannae leave a message. I disconnect the call and try to think of what to do. I need to see Kate—to explain, to apologize, to do whatever it takes to convince her not to dismiss me as her client. Maybe I can find her in an online phone directory. Can't be that many Kate Wagners in Inverness.

A quick search gets me her address.

Maybe I drive a wee bit too fast, but that doesn't mean anything. I'm enjoying the freedom, that's all. I haven't driven in almost a week thanks to my British nanny.

Fifteen minutes after I pulled out of the parking garage, I'm standing at the door to Kate's flat on the first floor of a quaint building. Evan's apartment is posh and modern, and it's located in a complex designed for holiday travelers, so it doesn't have the homiest ambiance. But Kate's building feels welcoming. After a few minutes of staring at the door to her flat, I finally ring the bell.

Thirty-seven seconds later, she opens the door. No, I wasn't counting. I just happened to look at my watch—for thirty-seven seconds. What a ruddy eejit I am.

Kate blinks rapidly, and her lips fall open. "Callum? What are you doing here? How did you even know where I live?"

"Phone directory. That's how I found out where you live." I wince and grasp the back of my neck. "Could I come in? To talk. I think we need to...straighten things out."

"Um..." She bites her lip. "Okay."

I follow her into the flat. It's not large, but the space feels like a home. And it's definitely occupied by a woman. The sofa has a floral pattern, just like the throw pillows. I also see flowers in a vase and family photos on a table in the corner. The coffee table in front of the sofa holds magazines about home decorating alongside journals dedicated to physical therapy and psychotherapy.

Kate sits in the puffy chair across from the sofa. She tucks her hands under her thighs and bites her lip again.

Christ, I've made her uncomfortable just by coming here.

I settle onto the sofa, perched on the edge, and clamp my hands over my knees. "Are you all right, Kate?"

"Sure, fine, yeah," she says with a panicked wee laugh.

"This is all my fault. I'm sorry. If I hadn't kissed you yesterday—"

"I wouldn't have climbed onto your lap this morning and unzipped your pants?" She squeezes her eyes shut, her whole face pinched. Then she blows out a breath and looks at me. "It wasn't anybody's fault. We both participated in the, um, event."

Now having a poke is an "event." Whatever she wants to call it, I'll go along.

"Do you regret it?" she asks.

"Well..." Should I lie? I came here to sort things with her and apologize, but suddenly, I realize the truth. "No. I don't regret anything except that we had to stop."

Chapter Nine

Kate

"WHAT?" THAT'S ALL I CAN MANAGE TO SAY. IS MY MOUTH gaping open? Maybe I misunderstood what he said, because Callum could not have just announced he wishes we hadn't stopped screwing each other when Hugh walked into the apartment. "I'm confused. Are you saying you don't think it was a mistake for us to, um, do what we did?"

"Aye, that's what I'm saying."

"But we agreed we should never do that again."

"When did we agree on that? Donnae remember you saying anything when you ran out of my apartment."

Okay, he has a point. I fled like my hair was on fire. Well, parts of me were on fire, though not literally. I burned for Callum like I've never burned for any man, and I did not want to stop. The way he kisses drives me crazy, but to feel him inside had been so damn good that I never wanted it to end. Great sex is not a proper foundation for any kind of relationship. Of course, I can't be sure it would've been great. I shut my eyes and groan. It had been amazing, and if Hugh hadn't interrupted, I know I would've come harder than I ever have in my life. Which is insane. Because I don't even like Callum.

"Are you in pain?" he asks.

My lids pop open, and my gaze lands on his face. "Huh? No, I'm fine."

"You had your face pinched up."

"I'm not in pain." I kind of am. It's the pain of a thwarted climax. Even before Callum turned up at my doorstep, I hadn't been able to shake the memory of that moment on the sofa in his apartment. Now we're in my place, and he's sitting on the sofa. Jeez, it's not like I'll screw him again just because he sits on a particular piece of furniture. "We shouldn't ever do that again."

"What? Shag?"

"Yes. We can't go there. It's wrong."

"Because I'm your client."

"No. Yes. Ugh, I'm so confused." I sink into my chair, letting my head fall back against it. "Sleeping with a client can't be ethical."

"We haven't slept together. We had half a poke."

I lift my head to squint at him. "You are not helping."

"Sorry. What can I do to make things right?" He gazes at me with such earnestness that I feel a twinge of empathy for him. "Donnae want to find another therapist. I want you, Kate."

"As your physical therapist slash psychotherapist."

"That too." His focus drops to my lips, then shifts back to my eyes. "Thought the right thing to do was to come here and promise I'll never touch you again. But now that I am here, I know I can't make that vow. It would be a lie."

"We don't get along. And I'm not interested in a relationship."

He skims his tongue over his bottom lip, and his eyes seem darker, as if the pupils have dilated.

Oh God, he wants to have another "poke" with me. And I can't swear I'll say no if he suggests it. The man drives me insane with his grumpiness and his unwillingness to share his feelings, even in a therapeutic setting. Maybe his growliness makes me kind of hot. But that's no excuse for my total loss of control with him this morning. And yesterday. Two wrongs don't make a right. Isn't that what people say? Doing the wrong thing with Callum sounds too damn appealing. A mature woman with a serious job should not be thinking the things I'm thinking right now.

A memory rushes through me, setting off a wave of tingling heat. Callum's rough tone when he whispered, "Aye, it wouldn't be right." The scent of his aftershave. The softness of his lips when he kissed me. The velvety feel of his tongue coiling around mine. Then I'd mounted his lap, unzipped his pants, and ridden him like I hadn't gotten it on with anyone in over a year. Well, that's because I hadn't. It was sexual frustration, right? Not a genuine desire for him.

I'm not kidding anyone, not even myself. I lust for Callum Mac-Taggart.

"Doesn't matter if we like each other," he says, his voice a sexy rumble. "We need to get this out of our systems. Aye?"

Can I get him out of my system? I've only ever slept with guys I cared about, but what he suggested sounds like casual sex. "What happens on Monday? You said you don't want a different therapist."

"That's why we need to deal with our desire. Then we can go back to the way things were."

Forget I did the deed with him? Not sure I can do that. But I'm also positive that I'll go even crazier if I don't at least try to get him out of my system. On Monday, if I feel weird about it, I can refer Callum to another therapist. Yeah, that sounds like a good plan. Not desperate or nuts at all.

I clear my throat. "Okay. Let's do it."

He freezes. "You're saying yes? To one more shag to get it out of our systems?"

"Yes. Let's do that right now." Before I lose my nerve and run into the bathroom to hide again, like I'd done in his apartment.

A slow, sexy grin spreads across his face. "Just tell me where ye want me."

I'm breathing harder, almost breathless, as a tingle sweeps over every inch of my skin and dives deep into my sex. Where do I want him? Every-where. I want him on the sofa, in the chair, on the floor, in the bedroom, in the shower. I want him, period.

"What about your knee?" I ask.

"Feels good. But maybe you should be on top, to be sure I donnae injure myself."

How he makes injuring himself sound erotic, I can't explain. He hadn't wanted a woman on top earlier, but now he's suggesting just that. He has a twinkle in his eyes I haven't seen before, and he keeps smiling, his cheeks dimpled. That makes me crave him even more. Is this the old Callum his brother mentioned? The one I've known this week was grumpy. This version of him seems playful. As much as I wanted grumpy Callum, to see the sexy, playful version of him has me so turned on that I can't think anymore.

"Do ye have condoms?" he asks, wagging his eyebrows at me.

"Shit. No, I don't. I was planning to stay celibate."

"*Bod an Donais.*" His shoulders flag. But then he straightens and grins again. "I saw a chemist just down the street. Donnae move. I'll get what we need."

He leaps off the sofa and sprints out the door.

I stare at it. Callum wasn't limping.

While I wait for him, I go into my bedroom and strip off my clothes, then pull on the only piece of sexy lingerie I own—a pink nightie with spaghetti straps that hangs just low enough to cover my bottom. I brush my teeth too. And fluff up my hair. I know I shouldn't be doing this, especially with Callum, but I won't change my mind. More than a year without sex, only getting off with my vibrator? That ends today.

I've just sat down in my chair when the door bursts open.

Callum dashes inside and slams the door. He's breathing hard, his chest heaving, but he holds up a box of condoms. "Ahm ready."

"Better sit down and catch your breath first."

He flops onto the sofa. His gaze travels over me, and his lips curve into a sensual smirk. "Are you wearing that for me?"

"No, I thought the mailman might like it."

"Cheeky lass." He licks his lips and groans. "I love that thing you're wearing."

"It's called a nightie. And I'm glad you like it." Since I've surrendered to my lust for him, I crawl onto the coffee table. When he reaches for the zipper on his jeans, I shake my head. "Uh-uh-uh. I want to do that."

Sliding off the table, I kneel between his legs and grasp his zipper, dragging it down inch by inch while I gaze into his hooded eyes. His lips have parted. His chest rises and falls like he can't catch his breath. When I glance down at the bulge of his cock, still hidden inside his boxers, my mouth waters. That's not hyperbole. It actually happens. I hunger for his body that much. My sex has been wet ever since he walked through my door, and I keep getting slicker and hotter every second.

Once I've unzipped his pants, I slip my hand inside his boxers to tug his cock free.

Callum groans, the deep sound resonating in his chest.

The box of condoms lies on the cushion beside him. I tear it open and grab a packet, then slowly roll it onto his length. Holy shit, the man has a gorgeous dick. I can't take time to admire it, though. I need him inside me right now, which means no foreplay. So I climb onto his lap, grasp the base of his erection, and sink my body onto his cock until he's nestled deep inside me. I can't help moaning because it feels amazing. *He* feels amazing.

"Ah, lass," he purrs, "yer so wet for me, ah can feel yer cream dripping onto mah *bagais*. That means my balls. They're aching for ye."

He grasps my hips and urges me to move.

I rock my hips, rising a little with every backward swing, burying him deep inside me every time I tip forward. My breasts graze his chest, but though he glances down at my tits twice, he keeps his gaze pinned to mine the rest of the time, like he can't bear to look away. The fullness of him inside me feels so delicious that I moan again and clutch his shoulders, riding him faster. He slings his arms around me to pull me into him, my breasts smashed to his chest and the zipper of his pants scraping on my thighs. I rock faster while he grunts and gasps and I let out sharp cries and dig my fingers into his shoulders.

Callum claims my mouth, the kiss ravenous and as wild as the pace of our bodies colliding. I can't help making hungry little noises. This isn't enough. I need more.

I tear my mouth away from his, though I keep thrusting my hips. "Bedroom. Now. Please. Need you naked."

"Aye." He seizes the hem of my nightie and flips it up and over my head. The flimsy thing flutters to the floor. He stares at my tits for a moment, dragging his tongue over his lips, his expression rife with hunger. Then he hoists himself off the sofa while cradling me in his arms. "Where's the bedroom?"

I hook a thumb over my shoulder. "First door on the left."

He veers around the coffee table, bumps into the armchair, and staggers toward the hallway. But we crash into the wall. He starts thrusting into me while he strips off his shirt, muttering words that must be Gaelic curses. His cheeks turn pink, and he's gasping for breath, but somehow he manages to kick off his boots and shimmy out of his pants while still fucking me up against the wall.

Damn, he's got skills.

I whimper when he grasps my ass and his longest fingers slip between my cheeks. "Hurry, Callum. The bed. I need you to do me hard on a soft mattress."

"Bod an Donais."

He staggers down the hall and into the bedroom, swerving toward the bed, and leaps onto it while our bodies are still entwined. Without even half a second's pause, he raises onto his straight arms and rolls his hips with a rotating motion.

I clutch his biceps. "Oh God, Callum, yes!"

Grunting with every thrust, he locks his gaze onto mine again while the mattress bounces and the bed creaks. My cream dribbles down my thighs, and the wet slapping of flesh echoes inside the room. He grits his teeth, sucking in a breath every time he withdraws and the air gusting out of him when he punches into me again, every exhalation punctuated by a guttural grunt. I'm teetering on the verge of climax, my body on fire, when he reaches down to rub my clit.

A cry explodes out of me. My neck arches, my back flattens into the mattress, and I come so hard I swear my eyes roll back in my head. I can't breathe, move, think, or do anything except revel in the pulsating waves of my release as my body clenches him over and over. He punches into me several more times and shouts when he comes, but by then, I'm lying here limp and so damn satisfied that all I can do is close my eyes and smile.

He rolls off me, snuggling up to my side. "Feeling good, eh?"

"Yes, yes, holy shit, yes."

"I know I'm good, but I've never seen a lass actually look blissful after I shag her."

Am I doing that? Yeah, I think I am.

Maybe it's the afterglow making me do it, but I can't resist rolling onto my side to face him and cuddle up close. He drapes an arm around me. I nuzzle his chest and sigh, loving the way fine hairs tickle my skin. When I look at him, he's smiling.

Until today, I had never seen him do that. All week, he'd been grumpy, growly Callum, the difficult client. But when I agreed we should have sex, he grinned. It was the sweetest, sexiest expression. Maybe he's not a jerk after all. Back in his apartment, he opened up to me like he never had before. Gazing at his smiling face now, I wonder if maybe...

No. I cannot date him.

Chapter Ten

Callum

I'M FAIR CERTAIN I'M GRINNING LIKE A BAMPOT. KATE AND I had sex, all the way this time, and it was bloody incredible. So of course I'm grinning. I feel better than I have in months, maybe better than I have in years. Kate and I have shared personal things today, which means this shag meant more than just a way to get each other out of our systems. Aye, that had been my idea. But now I don't want it to end.

My knee still doesn't hurt, though I imagine I'll suffer for this later. Shagging her like a madman cannae be good for my knee, but I donnae care. Maybe getting my end away has made me a wee bit barmy, because I suddenly announce, "Have dinner with me."

She goes stiff, her eyes wide. "What?"

"Let me take you on a date."

"No, Callum. I do not date anymore."

I smirk and pat her erse. "Aye, you're celibate. I thought that word meant no sex, but apparently, it means 'shag a Highlander like there's no tomorrow.' Is that right?"

"No, it—Well—" She flips onto her back, covers her eyes with her hands, and moans pitifully. "I can't date you, Callum."

"Sure you can. Put on a bonnie frock and let me take you to a restaurant. It's simple."

"You don't understand."

"Explain it to me. Please."

She lowers her hands. "One disastrously failed marriage was all I could take. No more relationships, not for a long time."

"Letting fear hold you back isn't healthy, is it? You're a therapist, Kate. You should know."

"I can't date you, and I can't ever have sex with you again. One time only. It's over, and you are out of my system."

"Am I?" The lass is full of rubbish, for certain. I spread a palm over her belly and tease her navel with my thumb. "What does 'one time only' mean? One orgasm? One hour? One day?"

"One time means *one time*."

"Well, I think it means we can shag all we want today. That counts as one time. Aye?"

Her lips curl up at the corners, though only a touch. "You are so stubborn."

"It's a family trait." I trail my fingers up her belly and close my fingers around her breast. "Our one time isn't over yet."

She sucks in a breath when I flick my thumb over her nipple. "Okay. Anything we do before noon counts as a single sexual encounter."

"Ye came round to my way of thinking, eh?"

"Just shut up and do me."

For the next two and a half hours, I obey her command. We make love in every way we can think of until we're both too jeeked to do it anymore. Kate is inventive and sensual, though I never would have guessed she could be this way. At work, she acts rigid and uptight, but I guess she needs to be that way with her clients—assuming I'm not the only pigheaded eejit on her roster.

After our two and half hours of "one more time," I try to kiss her goodbye at the door.

She holds a hand up between our mouths. "We are not dating, Callum. A goodbye kiss is not required."

I shake her hand. "Ring me later when you get randy again."

"Not going to happen. I'm over it. See you Monday."

The bloody-minded woman seems to honestly believe she can forget about our morning of cracking sex and act like my therapist again on Monday. *Mhac na galla.* I don't know if I can do that. Everything changed between us today, even before she climbed onto my lap in my apartment. We got to know each other a wee bit, just enough that I need to know more about her. I need to date her.

But she's having none of it.

While I'm driving back to my apartment, I suddenly remember what's waiting for me there—or rather, *who* is waiting for me. *Magairlean.* Hugh will be there. I cannae tell him what Kate and I did this morning. After vowing I didn't like her and had no interest in the lass outside of therapy, now I've gone and shagged the woman for two and a half hours. I should confess to Hugh, but not without talking to Kate first.

Aye, procrastination sounds good. And aye, I've become a bleeding coward.

When I walk into the apartment, I still haven't decided what to do about Hugh and Kate. He has a crush on her, or whatever people call it these days, but Kate has said she's not interested in him. They're mates, that's all. Despite that, Hugh plans to work his magic on her and win the lass's heart.

The lass I just fucked repeatedly.

Well, it was only the one time, according to my definition of the term. That doesn't make me feel like any less of a *cacan*. I had a poke with the girl my best mate likes.

Hugh rushes out of the kitchen wearing an apron and holding a large wooden spoon. "Where have you been?"

"I went for a walk."

"That was hours ago. I rang your mobile, but you didn't answer. Left you voice mails too."

Aye, my phone had been in my trouser pocket—and I'd left my trousers in the living room of Kate's flat when I carried her into the bedroom. I hadn't thought to check my voice mail later.

"I'm sorry," I tell Hugh. "Didnae think I was gone that long."

"What were you doing for hours? That must've been the longest bloody walk in history." He squints at me. "Isn't it bad for your knee to walk that far?"

"I had other things to do too." That other thing is called Kate, but I can't tell him what I did with her.

"Other things?"

"Aye, and it's none of your business, Hugh. I'm not married to you, which means I donnae need to explain myself."

He frowns and stalks back into the open kitchen. "At least you deigned to return in time for lunch. It will be ready in ten minutes."

"I said I'm sorry, Hugh. Christ, you're turning into a nagging wife." I head for the hallway. "I'm changing clothes, if that's all right with you."

"Yes, do that. Your shirt is on backwards."

No, it can't be. But I look down and realize Hugh is right. *Bloody hell.* Despite my clothing issue, I don't think Hugh has guessed what I did this morning. Why would he? He believes his best mate would never lie to him, but that's exactly what I have to do. Since I will never kiss or shag Kate again, there's no point in upsetting Hugh by telling him what happened.

In my bedroom, I change clothes and then sit down on the bed. What have I done? Kate will probably pass me off to some other therapist, and Hugh will murder me when he finds out I had a poke with her. I know he will figure out the truth sooner or later. Hugh is too clever, and he knows me too well.

When I walk back into the living room, Hugh is setting plates and silverware on the kitchen table.

He smiles when he sees me. "Sit down, mate. I've whipped up a gourmet meal for you."

I shuffle over to the table. "Bangers and mash? That's your gourmet meal?"

"Of course." He lifts the lid on a bowl, revealing what's inside. "But I did lower my standards to make this dish. Anything for my best mate."

The bowl contains haggis.

I clap a hand on Hugh's shoulder. "You're a good friend."

But I'm a rubbish one.

"Can't let you cook for yourself," he says. "Your idea of gourmet is to serve Scotch pies you stole from your mum's refrigerator."

There's another lie I've told him. Well, I never actually said I can't cook. I let him believe it and never corrected his misconception. I can cook, but I usually prefer not to bother. But for Hugh, his culinary skills are a badge of honor.

I sit down to enjoy a meal with my best mate, telling jokes that make Hugh laugh so hard his eyes water. Better enjoy whatever time I have left with him. When he finds out what Kate and I did, he will never speak to me again.

Chapter Eleven

Kate

MONDAY MORNING HAS ARRIVED. I DIDN'T SLEEP WELL last night, knowing what awaits me this morning. I will see Callum for the first time since we had sex, and I'll probably see his best friend too. That explains why I'm standing at the door to the waiting room, staring at it blankly while I clasp my hands to my stomach and fight the urge to run back to my office and hide under my desk.

Yeah, I'm a big old chicken.

But I suck it up, roll my shoulders back, and walk out there.

I stop just outside the door and glance around to look for my client. Callum is sitting by the windows with one leg stretched out, rubbing his knee. Hugh sits beside his friend, leaning his head back against the window with his hands folded over his belly.

Did Callum tell Hugh what happened on Saturday? No, he wouldn't do that without consulting me first. Right? I haven't known Callum long, so I can't be sure of anything he might do.

No, he wouldn't tell Hugh.

"Callum," I call out, waving when he lifts his head to look at me.

Hugh leaps up and tries to help Callum get out of his chair, but the Scot shoves the Brit's hand away and makes a grumpy face. Hugh throws his hands up in surrender. Both men walk toward me. Well, Callum hobbles toward me. Hugh follows his friend, flashing me a grin.

Oh, God. He doesn't know.

I'd been terrified Callum might've told Hugh our secret, but now I feel horrible because he doesn't know. This is such a mess. But I behave like a professional.

"Good morning, Callum," I say. "Good morning, Hugh."

The Brit aims a sexy smile at me.

Callum avoids looking at me and winces the tiniest bit as he glances sideways at his friend.

Hugh claims my hand, kissing it. "Good morning, Kate. You look scrumptious as usual."

"Uh, thanks."

"Did you have a good weekend?"

"Sure, yeah." I resist the urge to bite my lip and pray I don't start to blush. I've never been prone to that, but I've also never secretly screwed a guy while his best friend is trying to woo me against my will. I've become such a horrible person.

"Glad to hear it," Hugh says. He sandwiches my hand between both of his. "Let's have lunch together. A picnic along the River Ness."

"Um, sorry, I can't. There's a staff meeting, then I need to...catch up on paperwork." Not a total lie. But the staff meeting isn't until three o'clock, and my paperwork is not urgent.

"Maybe tomorrow." Hugh releases my hand, hitting me with another sexy smile. "I'm available anytime—for you."

Callum clears his throat. "Could we, ah, get on with my therapy now? Not in the mood for blethering."

"We're not gossiping," Hugh says. "I believe you meant 'havering.' I've known you long enough to have learned some of the Scots' bizarre language."

"Haud yer wheesht, Hugh."

"My, you are in a mood this morning." Hugh slaps Callum's back. "Have fun being tortured by a beautiful woman. Kate, try not to work him too hard."

Fortunately, Hugh ambles back to the chair he'd sat in before and drops onto it. I know his interest in me is kind of my fault, since I agreed to a date with him and then backed out. But I've told him several times that I am not interested in him. When he suggested a picnic, I should've told him I do not want to date him because I'm not attracted to him. But I got anxious and experienced a sharp pang of guilt over what Callum and I did, so I babbled about not having time for a picnic.

I pull the door open and gesture for Callum to go through it first. He refuses to look at me, keeping his head down. I shut the door and lead him into the exercise room. This time, he doesn't gripe about warming up on the stationary bike. I catch him admiring my ass, and when he sees me noticing that, his lips curve into a smile so sensual that my nipples tighten. He shouldn't be acting that way. One time only, that was our agreement. Sure, our "one time" lasted two and a half hours, but that is not the point.

After the warm-up, I have Callum start his recovery routine. First up, straight leg raises. He doesn't unbend his knee very far, and he winces when he makes that small movement.

I crouch beside him. "Power through the pain, Callum. That's how you get better."

"My knee is too bloody stiff." He averts his gaze. "You know why."

Oh, he means his knee got sore from the incredibly athletic, mind-blowing sex we enjoyed on Saturday. My nipples get even harder when I think about that. I don't want to think about it, but he just had to mention it, indirectly. Today, I'm at work, not tangled in the sheets with him. Time to act like a physical therapist.

I hop over him to crouch alongside his bad knee. "Lay your leg flat on the mat."

"Cannae."

"Yes, you can. Put your leg down as flat as you can." I wait until he does that, but his knee is still mostly bent. "Now take a deep breath, hold it for a count of three, and exhale it for a count of ten. Ready? Go."

I can tell he's trying to follow my instructions, but seems to be so afraid to use his knee that he can't manage even to do the breathing exercise I gave him. Instead of letting it out gradually, he blows the breath out and scowls at me.

"Doesnae work," he says. "This is rubbish."

"No, it's not. But you need to relax." I rest one hand on his kneecap and the other on the underside of his calf. "Stop tensing up. Just do the breathing exercise and let me move your knee. Okay?"

"Aye."

He does what I said, and as he slowly releases the breath he'd held, I feel his muscles relaxing and ease his knee into an almost straight position on the mat.

"Very good," I say. "Now do the leg raises. And try not to tense up again."

"Afraid my knee will hurt too much."

Wow. He actually admitted to being afraid of the pain. That's progress.

After the leg raises, we do some of the other exercises I've taught him. Then it's time to add another new one. Naturally, Callum complains about that.

"I overworked my knee the other day," he says. "Adding another torture exercise willnae be good for my recovery."

"Trust me, this won't make things worse. But if you experience any sharp or shooting pains, let me know."

"All right," he sighs. "Show me the new torture exercise."

"It might help if you stopped thinking of this as torture. It's a therapeutic workout."

He grumbles, but I can't understand what he said. If it was even words.

"Roll onto your stomach," I say, "with your legs straight. You can prop yourself up with your elbows if you like, but make sure your hips and legs remain flat on the floor."

Callum gets into position. "Now what?"

"Tighten your glutes and raise your injured leg. Keep it straight."

He barely lifts his leg, then drops it onto the mat again. "Cannae."

"Yes, you can." I crouch near his hips and rest my hand on his bottom. "Tighten your gluteus muscles. That means your ass, Callum. You need those muscles to support the prone leg raise. Go on, tighten those glutes."

He gives me a strange look, then tightens those muscles and lifts his leg.

I already knew he had strong glutes, but damn, feeling them work makes me want to—No, I will not finish that thought. No more sex with Callum. I keep my hand on his bottom only to make sure he keeps doing the exercise the right way. It's not because I love feeling those muscles move while I remember the way he had driven into me hard and deep while those glutes flexed with every thrust.

My grumpy client groans miserably and lets his forehead fall onto the mat along with his leg.

I remove my palm from his bottom and lean over to get a peek at his face. "What's wrong?"

"Donnae want to talk about it."

"We're done with the exercises, which means it's time for your psychotherapy session. You'll need to talk to me."

"Not about this...problem."

I stare at him while I try to figure out what his "problem" is. Then I suddenly realize what's going on here. I had my hands on his butt. We got it on two days ago, so having me touch him, even in a therapeutic setting, must have given him a hard-on.

"Tell you what," I say as I stand up. "I'll meet you in my office. Take as long as you need."

"Thank you, Kate."

"No problem."

Five minutes after I get to my office, Callum walks into the room. Even in sweats and a plain blue T-shirt, he looks hot and thoroughly lickable. I *had* licked that body two days ago. I remember how his skin tasted and how his muscles flexed under my fingers when I felt him up. Yeah, I memorized every inch of his body, including that gorgeous cock. Though I had licked his skin, I hadn't tasted his dick. I wanted to take him in my mouth and make him come, but he wouldn't let me do it. Callum said it "wasnae necessary." I wanted to ask why, but he started kissing me again, and I forgot what I'd meant to say.

Callum sits in the chair across the desk from me with the cutest little smile dimpling his cheeks.

"You seem happier now," I say. "Ready to get back to work?"

"Aye."

"I will be asking questions that you won't like. That's my job. Are you going to growl at me today?"

He wriggles in his chair, that smile faltering. "I'll try not to, but I can't promise I won't."

"Fair enough." I lean back and rock my chair absently. "Tell me about the accident that injured your knee."

"Ask me something easier first."

"No. I've let you get away with not talking about it until now, but today you need to tell me."

He opens his mouth, then shuts it again. Starts to lift his bad knee as if to prop it on the other one, then drops his foot to the floor. Screws up his mouth. Then blows out a breath and slumps in his chair. "What do you want to know?"

"Tell me about the accident."

"It was a house fire. I was on the team that responded, but by the time we got there, the house was engulfed in flames. Four of us went inside because a neighbor told us the resident, an elderly woman, might still be inside." He shuts his eyes, rubbing his forehead. "We found the woman on the second floor, and my mate carried her downstairs while I followed him. Then a beam started to fall, and I pushed them out of the way. The only injury I had was to my knee. I came limping out of the house. The other firefighters had already left the building."

He told me what happened, but not how it affected him. I doubt he did that on purpose. Seems more like unconscious avoidance. I get the feeling he also left out pertinent facts.

"You were a hero," I say. "Your friend and the woman might've been seriously hurt or died if you hadn't stepped in."

He grunts. "Some hero I was. Limping out with—Doesnae matter."

Oh yeah, there's something he's holding back. I'll set that aside for the moment. "Let's talk about what you felt during that experience."

"I felt hot. It was a fire."

"Don't do that. I need you to talk to me."

He scrunches up his face. "Isn't that enough for today?"

Maybe I should cut him some slack. He shared more than ever just now, and I don't want to force him back into his shell by pushing for answers he's not ready to give. "Okay. Your session is over. But next time, I do want to delve into your feelings a lot more."

"Aye," he all but moans. Then he pushes up out of his chair. "I'll see you on Wednesday."

He looks so dejected that I want to hug him. I shouldn't do that. After our fling on Saturday, I need to keep my distance as much as possible. Fling? We made love for two and a half hours. We laughed, we teased each other, we touched and kissed, and we lay in each other's arms. And yes, we gave each other fantastic orgasms. No matter how hard I try, I can't forget about that. But if it had been only hot sex, I wouldn't be in this mess. I could put it behind me.

I can't forget the intimacy of what we did. Wish I could, but I can't.

Without thinking about the ramifications, I approach Callum and pull him into an embrace. He remains stiff at first, probably stunned that I'm hugging him. I rest my cheek on his chest. He tentatively drapes his arms around me, then his entire body relaxes and he holds me snugly in his arms. This feels so good, almost better than sex.

"Kate, I—"

My desk phone rings.

"Sorry," I say as I pull away from Callum. "I can't ignore that."

"It's fine."

Turning away from him, I pick up the phone. "Yes?"

"Kate? Is your session running late?" Mary asks. "Hugh wants to know how much longer it will be. He says it's almost lunchtime, and he's starving."

"We just finished. Callum will be out in a minute."

"Oh, there he is. Thank you, Kate."

Mary hangs up.

I drop the phone back into its cradle and turn around.

Callum is gone. The Scot sneaked out while I was on the phone. Maybe our hug rattled him. Why I felt the need to comfort him baffles me, but I'll have plenty of time to mull over that issue later. Right now, I have another client to help.

Even while I do that, I can't stop thinking about Callum.

Chapter Twelve

Hugh

SOMETHING STRANGE IS GOING ON AROUND ME, BUT I can't put my finger on what it is. The strangeness began on Friday, escalated over the weekend, and has reached its zenith today. Yesterday when I drove Callum to the clinic, he didn't speak until we got there, and then he only spoke to inform me he didn't want to "haver" with me. So we slouched in uncomfortable chairs in silence until Kate called for him. He seemed much happier then.

But after his therapy session, he raced out into the waiting room like his trousers had caught fire. He wasn't limping either. I'd noticed his lack of limping on Saturday too. But after he went on his secret mission for several hours, his knee had clearly gotten worse.

I won't even think about the car trip back to the apartment. Let's just say that I realized within thirty seconds of getting into the vehicle that trying to talk to Callum was not worth the trouble. I suppose if a bloke likes responses that consist entirely of grunts and huffs, then it was a fruitful conversation. The second we walked into the apartment, Callum hurried into his bedroom and shut the door. He emerged for lunch and dinner, but otherwise, I had an invisible roommate.

What on earth is going on? I feel like I'm missing something very important.

The next morning, Callum emerges from his cocoon seeming more relaxed, though he limps a bit.

"Good morning," I say. "Ready for a new day? I was thinking we should do something fun today."

He drops onto the sofa, at the opposite end from where I'm sitting, and groans. "Stop trying to be my cruise director. I came to Inverness for physical therapy, not to have a good time."

"There's no law against having fun, even when you're getting medical treatment."

"Leave a body alone, Hugh."

He's telling me, in his charming Scottish way, to shut up.

Yes, I definitely smell a whiff of weirdness. The time has come to grill my best mate. "What happened on Saturday?"

"Nothing."

"That's bollocks. I'm not blind, deaf, or stupid. Something happened, and you've been behaving oddly ever since."

He grunts.

"Use your words, Callum." I turn toward him, resting my arm on the sofa's back. "I can't translate grunts and huffs into meaningful syllables."

"Donnae want to talk about it."

"Ah, so there is something to talk about, then."

He throws me a sideways glare. "Leave a body alone, Hugh."

"That's the second time you've said those words. Repetition is a definite sign of something being off."

Callum growls. I am not exaggerating. He actually growls, like a wild animal. I've never heard anyone make a sound like that.

"Might as well confess," I say. "You know I'll get the truth out of you sooner or later."

"Aye, you're a bloody-minded *cacan*."

"Call me whatever names you like. It won't help." I jump up and grab his arm, trying to haul him off the sofa. "Get up. We are going out for breakfast, then we'll find something to do other than watching the telly. This is not optional. Get off your arse and come with me now."

He makes an annoyed face.

I pull on his arm hard. "Off your arse. Now."

Callum finally stands, though he flashes me another irritated look.

But he does follow me out of the apartment.

Neither of us knows Inverness very well, so I drive us around in a fashion that might seem sort of...aimless. But no, I have an aim—to find a place where we can get breakfast.

"Why donnae ye use that map thing on your mobile," Callum says, and naturally, he sounds grumpy. "Driving down every street in Inverness until we stumble onto a restaurant is not my idea of a good time. I'm starving."

"It's an adventure. Where's the fun in looking things up and knowing precisely where you're going?"

He grunts. "You're a bloody annoying *bod ceann*."

Ah, the Scottish insults have begun. Fortunately, I spot a cafe up ahead, so Callum stops griping about my driving. He orders enough food to satisfy an entire football team after a grueling match. And he eats most of it. Is that stress eating? I need to convince him to tell me what in the name of heaven is going on, but I can't seem to get through to the stubborn Scot. I need to put on my detective hat and puzzle out the answers on my own. Yes, that's right, I am a detective. Maybe I've never actually tried to solve any mysteries, and maybe I have no training in how to do that, but I have one thing on my side. I'm a bloody-minded *bod ceann*.

Callum threatens to "make a run for it" if I don't drive him back to the apartment after we finish our meal. I give in. For now.

But I have a plan.

Callum plants his arse on the sofa and turns on the telly. I inform him I will go for a walk on my own. And of course, he grunts. My "walk" consists of me trotting across the street to sit on a bench along the River Ness.

To ring Kate.

She answers on the third ring, sounding sleepy.

"Kate, darling," I say, "it's Hugh Parrish. How are you this morning?"

"Hugh?"

"Yes, it's me." I said that already, but she still sounds not fully awake. "Did I rouse you from a steamy dream?"

Silence. For three seconds. Yes, I counted.

"Are you all right, love?" I ask. "Should I not have called?"

"No, it's fine. I overslept, that's all."

"Ah, I see. I hope Callum isn't causing you too much stress. He's a bit of a bear lately. That's actually why I rang you."

"Why?"

"Because of Callum."

Silence again. For several seconds Then Kate coughs in the way people do when they're uncomfortable. "What about Callum?"

"He's behaving strangely. I thought you, as his therapist, might have some idea why."

"No. Sorry. Can't help."

Kate is being terse, just like Callum. Next, she'll probably grunt and growl at me. They're both behaving strangely now, which suggests something happened between them. Could they have... No, Callum and Kate don't like each other, and he swore he has no interest in her other than as his therapist. Besides, he would've told me if he'd changed his mind about her. They must've had an argument.

"How about a picnic for lunch?" I ask. "Callum refuses to leave the apartment, so I'm in need of a new partner in crime."

"I don't know. That sounds romantic, and I've told—"

"No romance. Yes, I remember. You are depressingly celibate." Maybe I can change her mind about that. Kate is a lovely woman, and I honestly want to get to know her better. "I promise not to seduce you unless you beg me to do it."

She coughs and splutters as if she's choking on something. "Please stop saying things like that. No sex. Not interested."

"It was a joke, darling. Relax. I only want to share a meal and chat to you."

"Well...okay."

Bloody hell. I've never had so much trouble convincing a woman to spend time with me. It's like pulling an elephant's tooth.

I sit on this bench, alone, and wait for the woman who won't date me to arrive for our platonic picnic.

Kate turns up fifteen minutes later. I'd told her to park in the garage for the apartment building, so she appears from that direction. She is the most beautiful woman I've ever seen, with her golden red hair hanging in loose curls around her face, and those green eyes glittering in the sunshine. Yes, the weather god of Scotland gave us actual sunshine today. It's a miracle.

The woman of my dreams halts alongside the bench, and her brows wrinkle. "Where's the picnic? Don't see any food."

"Bollocks. I knew I forgot something."

"Why don't we just go to a restaurant?"

"It's such a lovely day that I thought a picnic would be nice." I grimace. "But food is a requirement for a picnic, isn't it? I'm a ruddy moron."

"You seem distracted."

I seem like that? She and Callum are the ones having focus issues today. Maybe it's contagious.

Kate glances at the river and hunches her shoulders. "How is Callum doing today?"

Her question stops me. It shouldn't. Kate is Callum's therapist, so for her to ask about him shouldn't feel odd. But it does. I wish I could put my finger on what about her question bothers me—and what about the way she and Callum are behaving bothers me. Am I blind to something that would be painfully obvious to everyone else?

Time to play detective.

"Why don't you come to the apartment?" I ask. "I'll make lunch for the three of us."

"Three?" Kate's eyes almost bulge, but she clears her throat and shakes off her surprise. "You mean Callum will be there. Not sure he wants to see me right now."

"Rough day at the office? I hope he isn't getting under your skin too much."

"Um..." She rubs her arms and stares down at the ground. "Don't think it's a good idea, that's all. I need to reassert the line between client and therapist."

"Reassert?"

She freezes, not even blinking. "I meant, um, well, that being friends with a client isn't professional. I know I suggested that, but, uh... It's just a bad idea."

I might be getting a sliver of an inkling about what's going on here. But no, it can't be that. Callum wouldn't hide the truth from me. If he realized he's attracted to Kate, he would tell me.

"Lunch with a client isn't a crime," I tell her. "Come on, Kate. Say yes."

She chews on her bottom lip. Then she sighs. "Okay. Yes."

Finally, I've convinced Kate. Now, if I can just get one or both of them to tell me what happened on Saturday...

Chapter Thirteen

Callum

At last, I have some peace and quiet. Hugh has been bloody annoying lately, asking intrusive questions about things that are none of his concern. I don't have to tell him everything. Aye, he's my best mate. But even friendship has its limits. I will never tell him what Kate and I did, because it will never happen again. Why upset him for no reason?

I stifle a groan. No reason? I shagged the woman he wants to date after I told him I have no interest in Kate. I am the worst sort of *tollathon*. Hugh should call me an ersehole, in English or Gaelic, because I have become one. A selfish, lying, cheating bastard. That's me.

The door swings open, and Hugh walks into the apartment.

Kate walks in behind him.

I jerk forward, twisting my neck around to gawp at the pair of them. Why the bloody hell would Hugh bring Kate here? I thought he went for a walk alone, but he comes back with her.

"Relax, Cal," Hugh says. "I invited Kate to have lunch with us. She's not here to torture you, though if you ask nicely, maybe Kate will give you a massage."

Kate goes pale, her jaw drops, and she gapes at me.

Brilliant. That won't make Hugh suspicious at all.

My best mate gets an odd look on his face as he glances between me and Kate. "Am I missing something here? Did you two have a massage-related argument? If Callum got grumpy with you, Kate, about the erection incident—"

"It's not about that," I snap. "Kate doesn't do massage. There was no incident and no argument."

"Calm down. I was only trying to be helpful."

Kate glances at the clock on the wall in the kitchen. "I don't have time for lunch with you guys, anyway. Need to get back to the clinic. I'll just order something to be delivered there."

"Eating alone at your desk?" Hugh says. "That's not acceptable."

"It's acceptable to me."

Kate rushes out the door, slamming it behind her.

Hugh stares at the door, his brows furrowed. "What was that about?"

"She has work to do."

"Yes, I figured that out on my own." He sits on the edge of the coffee table directly in front of me. "I can't understand this, Callum. Not your behavior, not Kate's. You and I are meant to be best mates, but I feel like you're hiding things from me. What happened to the days when we would go to a pub on Saturday night and chat up girls?"

"Donnae feel like chatting up anybody. And I thought you were dead-set on Kate."

"I am, but—" He rubs his forehead. "Would you rather I went home? It seems like you don't want me around."

"Of course I want you around, Hugh. But donnae invite Kate over anymore."

"Why not?"

Because I can't watch while he works his magic on the lass I want to...date. *Pit air iteig.* I should tell Hugh my feelings have changed, but the words won't come out. I think I've got situational laryngitis. It only flares up when Hugh asks me questions about Kate.

"Just don't invite her over," I say. "Please, Hugh. I can't see her outside of therapy, and I'm not even sure I want to continue with that, anyway."

"You're quitting your rehab? But it seems to be working. On Saturday, you weren't limping at all. At least, not until after you returned from your mysterious disappearance."

"It wasn't mysterious." I need to end this conversation now. "Why don't you go...do something. I'm sure you can find a way to entertain yourself."

"Yes, I can." He studies me for a moment, his lips puckered slightly. Then he slaps his hands on his thighs and stands up. "I will leave you to your brooding, if that's what you want."

"Aye, it is."

"Maybe I should stay to make lunch, then abandon you."

"I can feed myself, Hugh. Do it all the time when you're not here."

He raises his hands, palms out. "I surrender."

Then he walks out the door.

My best friend might not believe it, but I *can* manage to feed myself. Maybe I wind up eating Scotch pies I nicked from my mother's refrigerator, but Hugh will never know that. Though I try to relax by watching television, I can't stop thinking about Kate. We still haven't cleared the air between us. She hugged me, and I hugged her back. That doesn't seem like a proper client-therapist thing to do. I need to talk to her. I need to see her. Maybe she meant what she said about not wanting a romantic relationship. The only way to know what Kate wants is to ask her—in person, not on the phone.

I drive to the clinic and walk up to the glass door, grasping the handle. But I cannnae move a single muscle in my body. I stand here holding the metal handle, staring into the space beyond the glass.

Kate and Hugh have just walked out of the door into the waiting room. They're laughing. Kate lays a hand on Hugh's upper arm and leans in to say something to him. Then he leans in to whisper in her ear. She grins and wags a finger at him.

Are they flirting? *Bod an Donais.* I shouldn't have come here.

Kate glances toward the front windows, where I'm standing.

What do I do? Run away like a bleeding coward. I jump into my car and speed away. Cannae explain why. Maybe because it's dead obvious that, yes, Kate and Hugh were flirting. She's attracted to him after all, despite saying she has no interest in him beyond friendship. Her feelings changed, like mine have. But she changed her mind about wanting Hugh, which leaves me out in the cold.

I have no one to blame but myself.

Kate couldn't have seen me. I ran away just as she looked in my direction, and she could've gotten only a brief glimpse of someone standing at the door.

When I get back to the apartment, I go straight into my room and drop onto the bed to stare up at the ceiling. Jack was right. I do need psychotherapy. What sort of ersehole behaves the way I have? Well, at least there's no need to tell Hugh I had a poke with Kate. He's won her affection, and I'm out of the picture. It's just as well. Kate deserves a man who isn't afraid to confront his fears.

My mobile rings.

I dig it out of my pocket and answer with a grumbled hello.

"Are you okay, Callum?"

That's Kate speaking. I spring into a sitting position, my heart pounding. "What?"

"I asked if you're okay. Saw you outside the clinic. Why did you drive away without coming inside?"

"Well, I—You were busy."

"Busy? No. My next client had canceled at the last minute. We could've talked, alone. We need to do that, Callum."

"Aye, but you weren't alone."

She says nothing for a few seconds. "You mean because Hugh was here. He was just leaving."

"I'm happy for you. Hugh's a good man, and you're a good woman."

"What are you talking about?" She pauses. "Do you think I'm dating Hugh? I'm not. We had a nice talk, but it was purely platonic."

"You were leaning in and touching him."

She sputters like she's trying not to laugh at me. "That's your big evidence that I have the hots for Hugh? He's a nice guy, but not my type."

"But he's charming. Women love him."

"I thought you guys were best friends, but it sounds like you're—" She falls silent again, and I swear I hear a clock ticking in my head, counting the seconds until she tells me I'm a sodding moron. "Callum, are you jealous?"

"Of who?"

"Your best friend. You clearly don't like that Hugh came to see me."

"No, I—" Cannae stop the frustrated noises that erupt out of me. "Can we talk in person? Need to sort things with you."

"Okay. Why don't you come to the clinic? I have the rest of the afternoon free. Doing paperwork is mind-numbingly dull, so you'd be saving me from going cross-eyed."

Well, I suppose that makes it all right. I'm helping her, not running over there to beg her to want me instead of Hugh. Not that I want a relationship with Kate. It wouldn't work.

"I'm on my way," I tell her.

Then I hang up and rush back to the clinic.

Kate meets me at the door. She ushers me into the private area of the clinic and straight to her office. I take the chair I've sat in before, while she perches her bonnie erse on the desk's edge in front of me. Since that day when we shagged, whenever I look at her, I picture the lass naked. More than that, I imagine her writhing beneath me and begging me to make her come.

And now my *slat* is getting stiff. *Bollocks.*

I want to hook an ankle over the other knee, but that would make my injury act up. So I try to casually drape my hands over my lap, over my groin.

Kate glances at my lap, and her lips twitch as if she's trying not to smile. Her gaze lifts to my face. "What's bothering you, Callum? You said you wanted to 'sort things' with me, but I don't know what that means."

"It means I need to, ah, make sure there aren't any misunderstandings between us."

She shakes her head, almost smiling. "If you beat around that bush for any longer, you'll get dizzy. Why don't you just tell me what the problem is?"

"We fucked, Kate. That's the problem."

"Oh. I didn't realize having sex with me was a problem you needed to solve."

"No, I didnae mean it that way." What a numpty I am. Kate does this to me. With other lasses, I never get tongue-tied. "We haven't talked about what we did."

"It was sex. That's all." She smiles. "Hot, amazing sex. But still, just a physical thing."

"We could try going on a date."

She shakes her head, her smile fading. "No, Callum."

"But—"

"You're right, though. We do need to clarify things. I'm not interested in dating anyone. Not you, not your best friend, nobody."

Did I honestly think she could have feelings for me? No, a woman like her couldn't want a relationship with me, the man who quit his job because it got too tough. And I've behaved like a *bod ceann*.

"We'll be seeing each other three days a week," I say. "Donnae know about you, but I can't erase what happened from my mind. Can you?"

Kate gazes at the wall past my shoulder and chews on her lip. Then she pushes away from the desk. "I can't be your therapist anymore. It's inappropriate and unhealthy for us to continue our professional relationship. I can refer you to someone else."

"Donnae want anyone else."

"I'm sorry. This will be the last time we see each other." She marches to the door and swings it open. "Goodbye, Callum."

"But Kate—"

"Goodbye." She points at the open doorway. "That means leave, Callum."

I walk out the door, and she slams it shut.

Chapter Fourteen

Kate

I HAVE BECOME A DAMN COWARD AND A HARPY. KICKING Callum out of my office and slamming the door in his face? That's not like me at all. I know I can be tough with my clients, but I don't act like I did yesterday with him. Okay, maybe I slammed the door on his ass, not in his face. Jeez, like it matters which direction he faced when I booted him out.

All night, I tossed and turned in the most clichéd way. Guilt will do that to a person. Getting a good night's sleep requires a clear conscience and a heart that knows what it wants. I haven't got a clue.

So yeah, I won't be getting much sleep for a long time.

Hugh calls me just as I'm scarfing down the last of my unhealthy breakfast of frozen waffles drenched in syrup and a pile of microwave sausage links. I answer while still chewing the last bite, so my hello sounds like I've got cotton balls in my mouth.

"Did I catch you at a bad time?" Hugh asks. "I wanted to talk to you before you go to work."

"Why?" Oh no, that didn't sound rude at all. *Sheesh, woman, get a grip.* "I meant why before work."

"Because you've left Callum out in the cold."

"I referred him to a colleague at another clinic."

"Yes, I know. You're sending him to Edinburgh." Hugh sighs. "Honestly, you should know by now that Cal doesn't like being far away from home. Edinburgh is on the other side of Scotland."

"He's a big boy. He can handle it."

"What's happened to you, Kate? I know you care about Callum. Why are you banishing him?"

"Not banishing anyone. I can't work with him anymore."

Hugh says nothing for a moment while I drum my fingers on the kitchen counter. "Has Callum done something to upset you? I know he's been a bit of a bear lately, but I can tell he trusts you. Switching to a new therapist might set his recovery back. Please reconsider, Kate."

"I can't. My decision is final."

Okay, I know I shouldn't let Hugh believe I dumped Callum as a client because he's too grumpy. Not correcting his assumption will have just that effect. But maybe it's for the best. If Hugh tells Callum that I can't stand his attitude anymore, he might accept that I don't want to see him again.

"All right," Hugh says. "Have it your way. Though honestly, I think you're making a mistake."

"Goodbye, Hugh."

Finally, the call is over. So is my acquaintance with Callum and his best friend. I have no reason to see either of them again.

Work takes my mind off everything, but only as long as I'm with my clients. Paperwork gives me too much time to think about Callum. My life would be so much easier if he had stayed a grump, but no, he had to show me his sweet and sexy side, his humor, and his bedroom skills. I've never laughed so much during sex. He would tickle me until I started laughing so hard my abdominal muscles hurt, then he would make love to me until the pleasure robbed me of breath. Those two and a half hours with him had been the hottest, most intimate experience I'd ever had.

No, I do not have feelings for him. I refuse to fall for another screwed-up man who will wind up screwing me over. I let my husband tie a blindfold around my psyche for years, unwilling to rip it off and see the truth. Callum doesn't seem like the cheating type, but I met him less than two weeks ago. How much can I really know about him?

Then there's Hugh. No matter how often I tell him I do not want to date him and I'm not even attracted to him, the stubborn man still believes he can charm me into wanting him.

My life is one big steaming, stinking mess.

Avoidance is my best option, and I try my damnedest to do that. It's not working. The next day, I realize no one has taken the time slot left empty by Callum's absence, which means I will think about him every morning at ten o'clock until someone takes that slot. By afternoon, I feel like I'm losing my mind. Can't focus. Can't think. Can't stop flashing back to those hours with Callum in my bed.

I don't have feelings for him. He's stuck in my brain because we had amazing sex, and I haven't been with anyone since my divorce. Only Callum. I will go insane if I don't do something. Like what? Taking him back as a client is out of the question.

Maybe...

No, don't you dare think about that. Be strong. Resist the Scot and his big sexy body.

Yes, I can do that. I have willpower. No man is so good in bed that I can't stay away. My resolve lasts until six thirty on Friday evening. That's when I knock on the door to Callum's apartment. Yeah, okay, I'm hopelessly addicted to the Scot.

His brows hike up when he swings the door open. "Kate? I thought you were never going to see me again."

"This doesn't mean anything, okay?"

"What doesn't mean anything?"

I raise onto my tiptoes to see if the Brit is in there, but I can't tell with Callum's body in the way. "Is Hugh around?"

Callum's entire posture sags. "No, he went to get some takeaway for dinner."

Does he think I asked about Hugh because I want that man instead of him? But I'm not seeing either one. I need one thing and only one thing tonight. "How long do you think Hugh will be gone?"

"Knowing him, it'll take an hour, maybe longer. He likes to drive around until he sees a restaurant that interests him."

"Good. We have time."

"Time for what?"

I square my shoulders, lift my chin, and just do it. "I need you to fuck me. Right now."

His expression goes blank, and he stands there like a statue.

"Did you hear me?" I ask. "I said I need you to—"

"Heard ye the first time. Cannae believe it, though."

"Well, start believing." I slap a hand on his chest and push, walking into the apartment while he backs up. I kick the door shut. "This is not a sign I want a relationship with you. Sex only. One more time to get you out of my system."

One side of his mouth kicks up. "Thought last Saturday was the only time, and you got me out of your system already."

So did I. No such luck.

I grab a handful of his shirt. "Are you going to shut up and fuck me already?"

Callum grins. "Aye. Any way you want."

He scoops me up in his arms and carries me down the hall into a bedroom. His bedroom, I assume. He slams the door shut with his ass and sets me down, then starts stripping off his clothes. "Undress, Kate."

I obey his command, but only because I want to do it. Besides, he spoke in a deep, rumbly tone that makes every inch of my body tingle with anticipation.

He gets naked first and leaps onto the bed, landing on his back. As he clasps his hands under his head, he drags his gaze over my half-naked body. "You are the sexiest woman on earth. I love being with you, Kate, and I'm glad ye knocked on my door tonight."

I shimmy out of my jeans, then dig several condom packets out of the pocket and toss them onto the nightstand. "You're not *with* me. All I want from you is orgasms."

"Donnae worry. I'll give ye plenty of those."

Finally naked, I crawl onto the bed to lie beside him. "I want it hot and hard. Let's make the bed shake."

He rolls on top of me. *"An toir thu dhomh pòg?"*

"What?"

"Do I get a kiss?"

"That's not appropriate. Sex only, remember?"

He reaches between my thighs to caress my folds. "Anything for you, *mo leannan."*

No idea what he just called me. Don't care. His erection feels hard against my belly, and the heat of his body covering mine gets me so turned on that I grow even wetter than I'd been when I arrived at his apartment. Just the thought of him inside me again got me hot. But the sensation of all his muscles pressing down on me and his evening stubble rasping against my cheek drives me insane with a need I will not examine, not tonight.

Callum slithers down my body, kissing and licking a path from my throat down to my hips. He nuzzles my mound. I suck in a breath, my heart racing. He pushes his mouth between my folds and seals his lips around my clit, suckling it so gently that my pulse speeds up and I can't pull in a full breath. Then he shifts his mouth down to lap up my cream like he can't get enough of me, scraping his tongue along both sides of my folds. When he takes my clit into his mouth again and nips at my flesh, I jerk and shout. Everything he does fires the most delicious shocks down my nerves, straight into my sex.

He thrusts a finger inside me, and I gasp. But when he pushes two more fingers into my opening, I let out a sharp cry, fisting my hands in the sheets. "Yes, Callum. Oh God, please."

He sucks my clit harder, thrusting his fingers deeper and faster. The orgasm hits like a bomb blast. My back flattens into the mattress as I throw my head back, unable to scream or even gasp.

Callum rises to his knees.

I shut my eyes and try to recover from that climax, or at least recover the ability to breathe. When I look at Callum again, he already has a condom covering his dick. I want him so fiercely that I can't speak. All I can do is stare at his cock and lick my lips.

He palms his erection. "Want something, lass?"

I nod, and a strangled whimper bursts out of me. This man turns me into a pathetic puddle of lust.

Callum chuckles. "I love how excited ye get when ahm about to fuck ye. Spread your legs for me, *mo leannan*."

My brain has shut down, so I can't question his orders or consider the consequences of my need for him.

I spread my legs.

He kneels over me, his gaze locked on to mine, and plunges his cock deep into my body.

The firmness of his length, the way it fills me up, feels better than words can describe. While he thrusts into me with deliberate slowness, we keep gazing into each other's eyes. He bends his arms to kiss me, loving my mouth the way he's loving my body, and I tunnel my fingers into his hair. The sensation of his hard cock consuming me does something strange to me. Though he rises onto his straight arms again, I can't tear my focus away from his blue eyes. Will one more time be enough? The way he takes me, it's intimate and personal, more than hot sex.

"Faster," I plead. "Harder and faster."

He increases the pace little by little, and the bed starts to creak. I grip his biceps, and the way they flex under my hands heightens my arousal even more. I can't stop the desperate noises that erupt out of me as he punches into me harder, deeper, quickening the pace until I feel like I'll shatter if I don't climax right now.

"Come for me, *mo leannan*," he growls as he reaches down to rub my clit.

I go off just like that, my body convulsing and curling into itself while pleasure rockets through me, devouring every last shred of my self-control. I dig my nails into his biceps and open my mouth, but I have no breath to scream. My heart pounds so hard I can't hear anything except the thundering of my pulse in my ears. My knees draw up toward my chest like a string has been pulled taut inside me, and my inner muscles clench him again and again.

Callum lets out a hoarse shout and blows apart inside me.

For a moment, we stay frozen in that last moment. I manage to breathe again, but I can't make my muscles work. My hands stay clamped around his arms. Our gazes remain bound.

A door slams. "Your wifey is home."

Hugh. Oh shit, he's home—and Callum is still buried inside me.

The Scot who just gave me the best sex in history spews a string of Gaelic curses and leaps off the bed.

Hugh knocks on the bedroom door. "Are you awake? I brought take-away for dinner."

Callum glances at me, his eyes wide and his chest heaving.

I yank the covers over me, pulling them above my head so I'm co-cooned beneath the sheet and blanket. Then I hear Callum open the door. When I peek out from under the covers, I realize he only opened the door a sliver.

"Not now, Hugh," he hisses. "Ahm busy."

"Have you got a girl in there?"

Callum glances at me again, then snatches his jeans off the floor to pull them on. He rushes out, slamming the door shut.

Chapter Fifteen

Callum

BREATHING HARD, I STARE AT HUGH AND TRY TO THINK OF A believable explanation for the fact I have a woman in my bed. I cannae tell him it's Kate. She wants this to be "one last time" for the second time. Tomorrow, she'll probably suggest a third "one last time." If I have any chance of convincing her to have a real relationship with me, I need to get rid of Hugh. Not permanently. I donnae plan to murder him—unless he gets too nosy about the lass in my bed.

"Just finished, eh?" Hugh says with a smirk. "Still can't catch your breath. Must be an athletic woman."

"What do ye want, Hugh?"

"I went to all the trouble of getting takeaway for us. The least you can do is eat it." He rises onto his toes to peer around me, but the eejit can't see anything with the door closed. "Invite your girl to join us. I'd love to meet the woman who finally got you to break your celibacy vow."

"There was no vow, ye erse." Kate won't like it if I let on she's here, so I attempt to be creative. "Ye donnae know I have a girl in there. Maybe I was rubbing one off."

Hugh tries to stifle a laugh, which makes him snort instead. "You were shouting and making the bed creak while you masturbated?"

"Aye. It was, ah, very invigorating."

"I don't believe you. Just admit you've got a girl."

Hugh isn't the sort to give up, especially when he knows he's right. "Fine. I have a lass in my bed, but you are not going to meet her."

"Why not? You must really like her."

"No." I might have barked that word. *Bloody hell.* "She doesn't want anyone to know about us."

Hugh squints at me. "Are you shagging a married woman?"

"Of course not. She likes her privacy, that's all."

"I see. I've never known you to date secretive lasses. You always tell me about them, and introduce me to them when I visit." He peers around my shoulder again, as if he thinks the door will magically disappear so he can glimpse the woman in there. "I'm here. She's here. You're here. At least ask the girl if she wants to join us for a meal. She must be starved after the way you shagged her relentlessly."

"How would you know if I shagged her that way?"

My best mate smirks again. "I have a confession. I got here a few minutes before I shut the door loudly. Must've shagged the girl relentlessly or she would've had breath left to scream in ecstasy."

"Haud yer wheesht. No more talking about who I shagged or how I shagged her. She does not want to have dinner with us."

I open the door just enough to slip through it and slam the bloody thing in Hugh's face.

Kate has her clothes on.

"What are you doing?" I ask. "Hugh already knows I'm with a woman, so we might as well have a few more pokes."

"No poking with you ever again," she says in a hushed voice. She bends over to look under the bed, and I cannae help admiring her bonnie erse. "Where are my shoes?"

"Behind you."

She whirls around and almost falls over, but catches herself just in time. Then she grabs her shoes and tugs them on. "This was absolutely positively the last 'poke,' so don't try to seduce me again."

"Cannae resist me, eh?"

Kate flashes me a halfhearted scowl. "Help me escape without Hugh seeing me."

"We should tell him about us. I don't like lying to my best mate."

"No, you can't tell him," she hisses, a wee bit louder than she had been speaking. "This has to stay a secret. Since it's over, you won't need to lie to anybody."

"Since what's over? You kept telling me we don't have a relationship."

"I meant the sex is over."

"Until the next time ye beg me to shag ye."

Kate plants her hands on her hips. "I didn't beg. I ordered you to do it."

"Ah, of course. That makes it less like a relationship."

She thrusts an arm out to point at the door. "Get rid of Hugh. Lock him in the bathroom or something."

"You are a difficult lass. But I can handle you."

"Stop flirting with me."

"Cannae."

"I won't do what you want, Callum. I can't get involved with you." She covers her face with her hands and moans pitifully. When she looks at me again, she seems so distraught that I want to pull her into my arms. "Don't you get it? I've become like my ex-husband—a cheater."

"We're both single. It's not cheating."

"But it feels that way because Hugh thinks he can win me over, but I'm sleeping with you."

I rub the back of my neck, trying to think of a way to make her feel better. I come up with nothing. "Kate, I—"

"Just get Hugh out of the way so I can leave. Please." She gestures at her body, then mine. "This whatever it is between us, it's over for good. I'm sorry, Callum. I know you want something else from me, but I can't give it to you. A relationship that starts with secrets can't bring anything but pain."

Though I want to point out she kept saying we don't have a relationship, I haud my own wheesht. Kate doesn't want me. She only wanted my body. Now she means to run away. Trying to keep her with me when she doesn't want that will only make her hate me.

A sigh gusts out of me as I walk out and shut the door behind me.

Hugh is still standing in the hallway, but now with his arms crossed over his chest. He lifts his brows.

"No, you won't meet her," I say. "Go into your room so she can leave without you seeing her. It's what she wants."

"Is this woman a secret agent? Or perhaps a fugitive?"

"Enough, Hugh," I growl. Then I grasp his shoulders and force him to turn toward his room on the opposite side of the hall. "Go in there and shut the door. No peeking. Understand?"

"Yes, yes. I vow not to sneak a look while your mysterious lover scurries away."

Hugh ambles into his room and shuts the door.

I open the door to my room and wave for Kate to come out.

She does what Hugh said. She scurries past me and out of the apartment like a fugitive evading the police. A poke with me isn't a crime, but Kate seems to think it is. I want to hunt down her ex-husband and give him a right skelping for what he did to her.

Once Kate is gone, I knock on Hugh's door. "You can come out now."

He cracks the door open and peers out with a worried expression that's pure sarcasm. "Are you sure it's safe? I wouldn't want to be assassinated by your secret agent lover."

"Just get your erse out here so we can eat dinner."

After our meal, we watch rugby on television. I prefer shinty, but I know Hugh likes football and rugby. Maybe I'm letting him have his way because I feel guilty about secretly shagging Kate. But why should I feel guilty? Kate told Hugh repeatedly she doesn't want to date him, but she also said being with me makes her feel like a cheating slag. Well, I paraphrased that. Being American, Kate wouldn't use the word slag. She isn't like that, anyway. How can I convince her we haven't done anything wrong?

I shouldn't bother trying. Plenty of lasses out there. I don't need to keep struggling to change Kate's mind since I can get a date with someone else anytime I want. I need to stop acting like a numpty because of my knee and get back out on the dating scene.

The next day, I realize what I need to do.

Hugh and I are watching some rubbish reality show on television when I inform him of my plan.

"Let's go to a pub tonight," I say, "and find some lasses to have a pint with."

"I hope that's a pint of beer, not Irn Bru."

"Have you ever seen me drink orange soda?"

"Good point. All right, I'm in."

We go to a pub that night, but I have trouble focusing on the plan. Every lass I see doesn't seem quite right, no matter how bonnie and charming she is. Hugh keeps giving me a look I know well, the one that means "you're ruining my chances, you pillock." I don't mean to wreck his evening, but I have no interest in the women we meet. Once, I catch a glimpse of reddish hair, and for a moment, I experience a bloody stupid rush of excitement. But it's not Kate.

After an hour at the pub, Hugh leans in to whisper to me, "Why are we doing this? Neither of us wants to be here."

"Let's go home, aye?"

We abandon all the lasses who might have wanted us and head back to the apartment to share a bottle of single malt whisky. We had both sipped our pints at the pub, not actually drinking much of it. Hugh hadn't behaved like he usually does when women approach him, but I don't want to ask why. He might tell me he's in love with Kate.

Hugh takes a sip of his whisky and turns partway toward me, leaning back into the sofa's corner. "Hunting for girls was your idea, but you barely spoke to any of them."

"You weren't trying very hard either."

"Guess we both had other things on our minds." He swirls the whisky in his glass, staring down at the amber liquid. "You're traumatized by your injury, and I want a woman who's determined to be celibate."

I almost choke on the mouthful of whisky I just swallowed. Celibate? Kate commanded me to fuck her. Though I want to confess to Hugh that I've had multiple pokes with my therapist, I cannae figure out how to tell him. Since Kate insists we will never have sex again, I suppose it doesn't matter.

"Do you honestly like Kate?" I ask. "Or is it the thrill of the chase, trying to win a lass who doesn't want you?"

"I genuinely like her. She's an amazing woman." He swigs the last of his whisky and sets the glass on the end table. "But something in her past has clearly left her bruised and afraid to take a chance. Wish I knew what it was."

"Kate is divorced." *Mhac na galla.* Why did I tell him that? Well, it's not a state secret—as far as I know. At least I didn't blurt out that her husband cheated on her.

"Divorced?" Hugh says. "Kate told you that?"

"Aye, she told me last Saturday when she stopped by to talk. I think she did that only because she thought I'd be more cooperative during our sessions if she shared something about herself."

"Kate is a clever woman." Hugh smiles a little, almost wistfully. "Maybe I have a chance with her after all. A painful divorce would explain her reluctance."

Oh, bollocks. I've just convinced him he can win Kate over, though I didn't mean to do that. Well, she will probably tell him to bugger off anyway, so I won't have to watch him charming her the way he does with every woman he sets his sights on.

"Things are looking up," Hugh says with a smile. "You've got a girl to shag, and I have hope for Kate."

I feel slightly nauseous when he says that. Donnae want him to charm Kate. If I have to watch her fall in love with him...

Heaving my body off the sofa, I announce, "I'm going to bed."

"Cheer up, mate. Your girl won't want to stay undercover for long, mark my words."

I barely manage to stop myself from wincing. His girl and my girl are the same lass.

Bloody fucking hell.

Chapter Sixteen

Kate

DID I ACTUALLY THINK HUGH PARRISH WOULD GIVE UP ON his plan to date me? *Ugh.* Of course he hasn't given up. Maybe if Callum had told Hugh about us—not "us" as in a couple, but rather the fact we had sex—then he might stop trying to talk me into going out with him. But I told Callum not to tell Hugh. I made him sneak me out of his apartment. At the time, stealth seemed like the best option.

Today, I'm rethinking that choice.

I've been at work for thirty-two minutes when Hugh marches into the building. I saw him arrive. Mary had needed some help sorting out the schedule for this week, so I'd been at the front desk giving her pointers. I know the moment Hugh arrives because Mary gets that dreamy look I've seen every time the Brit walks through the door. Though I'm facing away from him, I swear I can feel his gaze land on me.

Mary giggles. "Lord Steamy is back."

Aw, shit. Since I sex-dumped Callum, I do not want to see his best friend. Maybe I spent the entire weekend fighting the impulse to sneak over to Callum's place and order him to fuck me again. And maybe I dreamed about him doing that. But I will never get naked with him again, and I'd hoped never to see him again. If I talk to Hugh, I'll feel like I'm cheating or...something.

Yeah, okay, my head is so messed up when it comes to men that I can't trust my own judgment.

I do the cowardly thing and try to escape before Hugh realizes I've seen him. I know he already saw me, but this is desperation, not a sensible plan. I hurry toward the door to the treatment area while pretending I haven't noticed the Brit sauntering across the waiting room.

"Kate," Hugh calls out. "Wait, please."

Damn, damn, damn.

I halt inches from the door and turn toward the man I cannot avoid anymore. "Good morning, Hugh."

"Are you trying to get away from me?"

"Why would I do that?"

He touches my arm. "I just want to talk, love. Do you have a moment?"

The answer is, unfortunately, yes. I still haven't found another client to fill Callum's empty slot on my schedule. Just thinking about him gives me a strange pang in my chest. But I don't want to be rude. Damn, I wish my parents hadn't raised me to be a good girl.

"Okay, fine," I say. "Come into my office."

"Thank you, Kate."

I lead him down the hall and into my office, though I leave the door open. Why? No idea. I'm not worried I'll go wild and throw myself at Hugh. He's attractive and charming, but I just can't muster any romantic interest in him. But I am intensely attracted to the grumpy Scot.

Hugh sits in the chair Callum had occupied the last time he came here, while I take the one behind my desk.

"Nice office," he says, glancing at the windows. "Nice view too. But I don't see a couch. Thought that was required for a psychotherapist."

"Feel free to lie down on the floor if you'd be more comfortable that way."

"Only if you lie down with me."

Even his sexy tone doesn't stir any interest in me. If Callum had spoken those words in that way... Oh, damn it all to hell. I need to stop thinking about him.

"That was a joke," Hugh says. "I apologize if I've offended you."

"Not offended. I was thinking about something else." Some*one* else. Maybe I should tell Hugh what Callum and I have done, but I don't want to hurt his feelings. It's nobody's business, anyway.

"Please have lunch with me," Hugh says. When I start to balk, he raises a hand to silence me. "Not a date. Just two friends having a meal together. I'd like us to get to know each other, as mates. If something else develops after that, it will happen naturally. I won't push. You are an incredible woman, and I want to know you better. No pressure."

"That's very sweet, Hugh. But I don't think—"

"It's only lunch." He raises a hand, palm out. "I swear on my father's grave."

His father died? I didn't know that. I suppose he had to inherit the title of viscount of whatever-it-is from his father, which means his dad must have died. I wish he hadn't told me that because now I feel bad for him. Not that I worry I'll suddenly develop an urge to date him or sleep with him simply because he told me about his father.

"Okay," I tell Hugh. "Lunch. But only lunch, and nothing else. This does not mean I want to date you."

"I love it when you get tough and tell me not to get any cheeky ideas. It's adorable."

"Uh, whatever. You're a nice guy, Hugh, but I am not going to fall head over heels for you. Got it? I do not date anymore."

"Not for now. You said it was a temporary celibacy vow."

Did I say that? Can't remember. "It's a long-term moratorium."

There. That should stop him from wanting to date me. *Yeah, right.*

Hugh and I do go to lunch, at a cafe he suggested because "it has windows everywhere, so I can't seduce you." Jeez, that guy never lets up. He isn't pushy or annoying about it, but he finds sneaky ways to slip flirting into every conversation. Maybe I've gotten kind of uptight. My husband is partly responsible for that, but I let his cheating mess me up when I didn't have to do it. Spending time with Hugh gives me a chance to relax, without worrying when he'll try to get me into bed and what might happen after we do the deed because I don't want to do that with him.

No, I want Callum.

Great, that's just what I need. An emotionally damaged man who gets testy whenever I ask about his accident. I need a nice long break from all that shit.

But I do have a good time with Hugh. It's nice to have a friend.

After work, I go for a walk with Hugh along the River Ness. He talks about his family, but I can't make myself talk about my life with him. It feels weird. Hugh is easy to talk to, but every time I think about sharing something with him, Callum's face flashes in my mind. No, no, no, I cannot be falling for him. I just met Callum last week. I don't love him, but I feel...something. The fact that I want to share things with him instead of Hugh seems like a bad sign. I shouldn't spend time with either of them. It's too dangerous. Eventually, either Callum or I will blurt out the truth, and Hugh will know what we did.

It shouldn't matter, but it does.

Our walk takes us back to the apartment complex where Callum lives. I had parked on the street in front of the building, and Hugh accompanies me to my car. He kisses my cheek, then says goodbye and ambles away with a satisfied smile on his lips. Movement above draws my attention to the window of Callum's apartment—the big picture window in the living room. I see a figure there. It has to be Callum. He stares down at me for a moment, then turns away, disappearing from view.

Did he see Hugh kiss my cheek?

I feel a touch nauseous again and unconsciously lay a hand over my belly. Callum must think I'm dating Hugh, but that's not true. *Dammit.* These are exactly the kind of complications I wanted to avoid by moving far away from everyone back home to live in a country where nobody knows me. That plan had worked perfectly until Callum MacTaggart became my client.

How can I fix this mess I've gotten myself into?

I swear an actual light bulb pops on above my head. Oh yes, the solution is right in front of me.

The next morning, I enact my plan. Nobody, not even Callum, will seduce me into changing my mind.

Chapter Seventeen

Callum

HUGH HAS BEEN DISGUSTINGLY HAPPY EVER SINCE HE WENT to see Kate yesterday. They went for a walk too—a romantic one along the banks of the River Ness. I wish Nessie would have snatched him up for a snack. No, I don't really wish that. Hugh told me he planned to talk to Kate at the clinic and try to convince her to go for a river walk with him, and he asked if I minded. I couldn't say yes, could I? I might be lying to him about what I've done with Kate, but I won't tell him to stay away from the lass. It's her choice, not mine.

So I act like a good mate and listen while Hugh relates every last ruddy second of his time with Kate yesterday. The look on his face tells me everything I need to know. He has feelings for her. *Bod an Donais.* I have feelings for her too, but Kate threw me over so fast I got whiplash. I know Kate said she's not interested in Hugh, but he has a way of changing women's minds.

Hugh always gets the girl.

That never bothered me until now, until Kate. I need to get to know her better, to find out if we could have something real and lasting. But now that my best mate has set his sights on her, I don't stand a chance. I've never been as good at dating as Hugh. I did well enough, but the accident knocked me back on my erse. I know that's my fault. I've let fear control me.

And I realized too late that I want Kate, for more than sex.

"So Callum, do you think I have a real chance with the lovely Kate?"

"You're trying it on with a woman who doesn't want to date."

He makes a dismissive noise and a matching hand gesture. "Tosh. I never let a little thing like that stop me."

No, he never does. That's why they call him Lord Steamy. It's a bloody stupid nickname, but it fits him. Hugh Parrish knows more about satisfying women than anyone I know.

But Kate loved being with me. She came back for more.

Aye, and then she threw me over.

"You're looking glum again," Hugh says. "What's bothering you?"

"My knee hurts."

"Go to the clinic and get Kate to give you a massage."

I laugh, but there's no humor in it. "She'll toss me out the door. I'm not her client anymore."

"Why is that? You never did tell me."

"She—Well, it's—" I rub my forehead and try to think of a believable lie. Aye, now I'm reduced to deceiving my best mate. What a scunner I've become. "Her type of therapy wasn't working for me."

"Well, go over there and talk to her. Fix whatever the problem is."

"Bugger off, Hugh."

He raises his hands. "Calm down. I won't mention the K-word again."

I want to see Kate, but I cannae tell Hugh that. Donnae give a fuck about therapy. I need to let her know how I feel.

So I get my erse up off the sofa. "I'm going for a ride on my bike."

"Thought Kate told you not to do that. It's bad for your knee."

"I cannae sit here watching rugby with you anymore. I need to do something that will relax me. A good ride will do the job."

"Don't go overboard."

"Are you my mother or my best mate?"

Hugh smirks. "A bit of both lately."

I rush down to the parking garage and rev up the Harley. Aye, a ride will make me feel better. But I'm not just going sightseeing. I mean to find Kate. When I get to the clinic, I ignore the stab of panic that hits me when I think about what I plan to say to her and instead push through the doors, heading straight for the reception desk. That sweet lass, Mary, glances up from rifling through papers and smiles when she sees me.

"Mr. MacTaggart, how are you this afternoon?" she asks. "Donnae see you on the schedule today."

"I'm fine. And I don't have an appointment, but I need to speak to Kate."

"Oh, I'm sorry. She isn't here anymore."

"Is she ill?"

"No, she just doesn't work here anymore."

"Why not?"

Mary gives me a sympathetic smile. "Donnae know what happened, but she came in this morning and handed in her resignation, effective immediately."

No, she wouldn't do that. Kate loves her job. That's been my impression of her, anyway. The stubborn lass wouldn't quit because of me, because we had sex and it scared her. Well, maybe she might. Her fears have her tied up in double knots with a steel chain wrapped around them.

"Could another therapist help you?" Mary asks.

"No. I need Kate."

Without another word, I race out to my Harley and roar toward my destination—Kate Wagner's flat. I drive too fast, but miraculously don't get arrested or have an accident. My heart pounds as I park my bike, rushing to the elevator and tapping my foot on the floor so fast it makes my knee start to ache a wee bit, but I donnae give a shit.

The doors slide open.

I sprint—all right, I mostly hobble—to Kate's door and thump my fist on it three times. I'm breathing hard, so I force myself to take several slow breaths.

The door swings open, and Kate gawps at me. "What are you doing here?"

She doesn't need to sound so bloody shocked. Well, maybe she has good reason for feeling that way since she essentially told me to sod off.

"I need to talk to you," I say. "Please."

"There's no point. I'm moving back to America."

"What?" I swear all the blood in my body has suddenly evaporated, leaving behind a powerful chill. "No, Kate, please don't do that. Let me in so we can talk. I'll beg if that's what it takes."

"I quit my job and gave up my lease on this apartment. Tomorrow, I'm flying home." She shakes her head, but her eyes glisten as if she might cry. "I'm sorry, but I can't do this."

"Running away isn't the answer." I inch closer, but though I need to touch her, I don't do it. "Just let me talk to you."

She gnaws on her lower lip, staring into my eyes for so long that I start to wonder if time has stopped moving. "Okay. But only for a minute."

"Aye. Thank you."

I follow her into the apartment, but I don't sit down. She doesn't either. We stand several feet apart, gazing at each other like neither of us knows what to say. I had a speech worked out in my head, but now I've forgotten all of it. Donnae need a speech. I just need to tell her how I feel. "Please don't leave, Kate. I want to spend more time with you and figure out if we could have something together."

"I told you from the start, I can't give you that. Sex only." She lashes her arms around herself. "You're a good man, Callum, but I can't go down the relationship road again. Even if I wanted that, it's way too complicated with Hugh and the lying. I told you I feel like a cheater, and it's killing me."

"But it doesnae have to. I'll tell Hugh about us. He won't be happy, but he'll get over it."

"Hurting someone is the last thing I want to do."

The lass means to hurt me, but I know she doesn't want to do that. How can I convince her?

I walk up to Kate and take her face in my hands. "Give me a chance, *mo leannan*. That's all I'm asking."

She shakes her head as tears roll down her cheeks. "I can't."

"Aye, ye can. Please don't run away without at least finding out if we could have more between us." I bend my head to gaze into her eyes, and my lips brush hers. "I haven't wanted anyone since the accident. But I want you. I need you. Please let me show you how good we can be together."

"Even if I want to, I just can't—"

I crush my lips to hers without even considering what I'm doing or why. The thought of losing Kate before we gave ourselves a chance pushes me to do the only thing I can. I kiss her. She sags into me, pushing her tongue into my mouth, and I wrap my arms around her. Our tongues collide, our teeth bump into each other, and we both make grunting noises while we grope each other mindlessly. I know desperation drives this kiss, but I donnae care.

She peels her lips away from mine, breathing hard. "We need to say goodbye. In the bedroom."

"Ye want me to help ye pack your bags?" Aye, it's a bloody stupid thing to say. I cannae think straight after that kiss.

"No, I want you to fuck me."

"Oh, aye."

She mashes her mouth to mine again, and I carry her into the bedroom with one eye cracked open just enough that I won't crash into the wall or the door. I shouldn't let this happen, not when we're both upset. But I cannae resist this woman. Tomorrow, I'll think of how to talk her out of running away. But for tonight, I'll show her what she means to me in the only way I know she'll accept—by making love to her. We do that for an hour. It's hot and wild and a wee bit desperate. Then we fall asleep with our bodies tangled up in the sheets.

In the morning, before I've even opened my eyes, I stretch and yawn and smile. My only task for today is to convince Kate to stay, and I know I can do it. I believe that until the second I open my eyes.

And realize I'm alone in Kate's bed.

Maybe she went to the kitchen to make breakfast. Or she's in the shower. Or... I freeze when I see a small folded sheet of paper on the nightstand. Sitting up, I swallow against a tightness in my throat and force myself to pick up the paper and unfold it. I recognize Kate's handwriting even before I start to read the note. As the words sink into my brain, I crumple the paper and let it fall out of my hand.

"I told you I couldn't stay," the note reads. "Please forgive me. I never meant to hurt you. The landlord is giving you until noon to leave."

For a moment, I sit here without moving. Kate is gone. The clock tells me it's after nine, but I have no idea when her flight leaves. Should I go to the airport to find her? The lass told me several times she wants to go home. No, she said she can't stay and she can't do this. Maybe I do still have a chance if I hurry. But I don't know where her home is in America, so I have no sodding clue what flight she'd be on. Will they even let me into the airport if I don't have a ticket? I'll buy one. Donnae care how much it costs.

The sound of three solid raps on the front door jerks me out of my thoughts.

Is it Kate? She said she gave up her lease, so she must have handed her keys over to the landlord. At least she hasn't left me here to get arrested for trespassing. I know I'm an eejit for doing it, but I can't stop myself from sprinting to the front door and tearing it open.

Hugh stares at me, his brows raised, and glances at my body. "Why are you naked? And what are you doing in Kate's flat?"

Bollocks. I forgot I don't have any clothes on. "What are you doing here?"

"Came to see Kate, of course."

"She's not here. I don't have time to haver with you." I try to push the door closed, but Hugh jams it with his foot. "Get out of my way, ye *cacan.*"

"Not until you tell me where Kate is."

"She's not your girlfriend. Sod off, Hugh."

I kick his foot away and slam the door. Then I rush to get dressed and get out of the flat, but when I open the front door again, Hugh is still standing there.

"Tell me what's going on," he demands. "Right now, Callum. Where is Kate?"

"Donnae care about why I was naked anymore, eh?"

His gaze narrows, and his lips flatten. "I called the clinic this morning to speak to Kate, but she isn't there. Did you know she quit her job? And she's flying back to America."

"Aye, I know. It's your fault."

"My fault? Kate likes being with me, but you've been a complete arse to her. Tell me what you did to chase her away."

"Ye really want to know?" I yank the door shut, leaving us standing in the hallway where anyone might hear or see us. "I had sex with Kate Wagner last night. It wasn't the first time. Now get out of my way before I skite my fist on your face."

"You're lying. Kate wouldn't do that."

"Aye, she would, and she did. We shagged so many times I lost count."

His eyes bulge, and he grits his teeth so hard a muscle pulses in his jaw. "You fucking bastard. You knew I wanted Kate, but you seduced her anyway."

"She begged me to do it, Hugh. The lass wants me, not you." I try to walk past him, but he blocks my path. "Out of my way. Move your erse or I'll move it for you."

He plants his feet wide. "Go on and do it."

I slug him in the gut. While he gasps and doubles over, I dodge around him. Minutes later, I'm on my Harley racing toward the airport.

Chapter Eighteen

Kate

WHY DIDN'T I BOOK A FLIGHT IN ADVANCE? BECAUSE I panicked, and that state of mind doesn't lend itself to critical thinking. If I had at least called to check on flights before fleeing to the airport, I would've saved myself a lot of time. But I didn't do that either. Get away from Callum and Hugh, that was my only objective. Now I'm stuck in this country, in this city, where both men are currently in residence. *Fantastic plan, Kate. You escaped from them good, didn't you?*

As soon as I arrived at the airport, I found out flights are all booked up through the afternoon. I can't get anything until seven o'clock this evening. I gave up my flat, so I can't go there to wait. I have no luck getting a hotel room either. Turns out somebody decided to have Highland games here in Inverness this week, which means all those caber tossers and stone-throwers have gobbled up every available accommodation except for a teeny, by-the-hour room in a motel on the outskirts of town.

Well, thank goodness for that much.

I watch TV for a while, but I keep thinking about Callum. Damn, I can't get away from him physically or mentally. I'm stuck in the same city with him, though he doesn't know that. He must assume I flew away already. Good. I don't want him to track me down and try to sweet-talk me into staying so we can find out if we "have something" together. If I see him, I know we'll wind up naked and sweaty again, just like last night. So what if he's incredible in bed? That is not a valid reason to stay. He's also sweet and fun and smart. But no, even that isn't enough.

Uh, what would be enough? No idea.

After a nap and a quick snack that consists of junk food from a vending machine, I catch a taxi back to the airport. My flight doesn't leave for an hour, so I now get to sit in the waiting area with nothing to do but think about that damn Scot. I'll forget about him as soon as I get home. Yes, I will for sure.

I'm slumped in my chair, with my head resting on its back, when I hear someone sit down beside me. Oh great, that's just what I need. A chatty passenger.

"Hello, Kate."

My lids fly open, and I jerk upright to gape at the pretty blonde woman who sits beside me. "How do you know my name?"

She laughs softly. "Don't freak out. I'm here to help."

The woman sounds American.

"Help me how?" I ask. "I don't even know you."

She holds out her hand to me. "Emery MacTaggart."

"Kate Wagner," I say as I shake her hand. "But you already know that. Did you say MacTaggart?"

"Yep. I'm married to Callum's cousin Rory."

"Oh. I see. Not to be rude, but what on earth is going on? How did you find me?"

She smiles and pats my leg. "Relax, honey. I honestly am here to help. How did I find you? It's simple. Hugh called Jack, who called Callum, who called Rory."

"That doesn't explain anything."

"It's the MacTaggart grapevine at work. Apparently, Hugh and Callum had a tiff when the Brit found the Scot naked in your former flat."

Oh shit. Hugh knows everything now, I assume. Not that it matters because I'm leaving the country in less than an hour.

Emery grins. "You look baffled. Let me clear things up a bit. You see, Callum punched Hugh, so he called Jack to report the 'assault' from Jack's 'lying knob of a brother.' Apparently, a knob is a dick. Anyway, Jack immediately hung up and got hold of Callum, who said Hugh is 'the biggest *blaigeard* on earth' and had it coming. I gather that Gaelic word means 'bastard.' Well, being a therapist, Jack understood what needed to be done. He called my hubby to tap into Rory's connections and make it happen."

Precisely nothing she said makes any sense. I feel dizzy just thinking about it all.

But Emery isn't done talking. "It's all set, except for your part."

"My part? I'm not involved in whatever you guys are plotting."

"It's called meddling, sweetie, and the American Wives Club knows what to do when these things happen."

"The what club?" I'm sure I sound completely baffled. I can't understand anything Emery said except for the part about Callum punching Hugh. "Look, the last thing I need to do is get tangled up in ruining a friendship."

"What happened is not your fault."

"You don't understand. I told Hugh I wasn't interested in Callum, then I slept with his best friend anyway."

"The way Callum tells it, the whole thing is his fault. You were caught in the middle. But I don't know all the details, and I don't need to know." Emery clasps my hands. "Listen, sweetie, we want to help. If you care for Callum in the way I think you do, then help us help him—and Hugh. Their friendship won't be ruined if you stay. While we sort out the guys, you can figure out whether you want to be with Callum or not."

"I don't know if I can see either of them again. I'm a coward."

"Oh, I doubt that. You're confused and scared. Believe it or not, I understand what you're going through."

Yeah, I do doubt that. But she seems like a nice person, and I appreciate that she wants to help.

"Here's the deal," Emery says. "I'm going to tell you a story that no one else knows, except for me and my hubby. I think it might help you understand and decide whether you still want to go back to America."

"Okay."

"I met Rory in New Orleans, and we had what was supposed to be a one-night stand, except it turned into more than one night. Rory had been so badly damaged by his ex-wives that he couldn't trust any woman or his own feelings." Emery leans closer, lowering her voice to almost a whisper. "I married him a few days after we met and came to Scotland with him, living in an old castle in the middle of nowhere. He resisted his feelings for me, which made him a grumpy bear a lot of the time. I wasn't in the best place either, emotionally, since my ex-boyfriend had posted naked pictures of me online without my permission. I had to fight like hell to get through to Rory and get past my fears, but it was worth the struggle. We're happily married and have two beautiful twin babies, a boy and a girl."

"That's a neat story, but I don't see how it relates to me."

"I never gave up on Rory. I stuck with him because I felt in my soul that we could be happy together." Emery gives my hands a light squeeze. "Do you want to walk away from Callum before you've given it a real try? Will you let your fears run your life?"

When I think about Callum, I get a lump in my throat. Why did I have sex with him last night? I should've slammed the door in his face. But he spoke with such earnestness and tenderness that I couldn't shove him away. I needed to be with him one last time.

Oh no. I understand what that means. My feelings for him are deeper than lust.

But I still don't want to become the wedge that pushes Callum and Hugh apart forever.

"I get what you're saying, I do," I tell Emery. "But I don't see how Callum and I could ever sort out our feelings for each other when we've both hurt Hugh. They've been friends for years. I couldn't be happy knowing I'm the reason their relationship fell apart."

"That won't happen. Trust me."

"Because you and your club have a plan or something."

"Yep. The American Wives Club is an informal group consisting of the American wives of the MacTaggart men along with the American husbands of certain MacTaggart women. We've made it our mission to ensure no one in our family wrecks a chance at love out of fear."

Callum never mentioned that club. It sounds weird. A group that exists solely to meddle in people's lives? Well, maybe I do need that. I've screwed things up royally on my own. "What is it you want me to do?"

"We want you to come to Dùndubhan."

"Dun-what?"

Emery laughs. "Dùndubhan. It's the castle Rory and I own. We don't live there anymore, and part of the castle is a museum now. But we've arranged to close the museum for a while to help you, Callum, and Hugh settle things between the three of you."

"You want me to stay in your castle?"

"As a guest, yes. Will you do it?"

I stare down at our hands. This woman who has never met me before came here to convince me to give Callum a chance. Why would she do that? I don't know much about the MacTaggarts, but I'm starting to see that this family isn't like any other. Though I've only met Callum and Jack, they are two of the best people I've ever known. Maybe I should trust Emery and the American Wives Club and all the MacTaggarts. Maybe I need to give this a shot.

Normal hasn't worked out so far. Might as well try a holiday in crazy town.

Can't believe I'm doing this. But I clear my throat and say, "Okay. I'm in."

"Yay!" Emery releases my hands to clap hers three times. "You won't regret it."

"If Callum and Hugh are so mad at each other, how do you plan on getting Hugh to stay at your castle?"

"Oh, you just leave that to us."

"Your club."

"Mm-hm." Emery stands up and waves for me to do the same. "Come on. There's no time to waste. We've got a three and half hour drive to Dùndubhan."

I stop at the desk to cancel my plane ticket, then Emery helps me carry my luggage out to her car—a Jaguar convertible. Holy crap, Emery and Rory must be stinking rich. At least I can rest easy knowing I won't wind up sleeping in a drafty castle that has a leaky roof. I bet Dùndubhan is a spiffy place.

As we zoom down the road, leaving Inverness behind us, I have to ask a question. "When will the meddling start?"

She laughs again. "Oh, honey, it's already underway."

Chapter Nineteen

Callum

A KNOCK ON MY DOOR WAKES ME AT SIX O'CLOCK THE next morning. I'd gone to the airport but couldn't find Kate, and she wasn't at her flat either. The lass is gone. I know I should forget about her, but I can't do that. Crawling out of bed to answer the door at least takes my mind off Kate for a wee bit—about thirty seconds, but I'll take what I can get. My thoughts drift back to the American lass as I pull the door open.

Jack eyes me up and down. "Put on some trousers, would you? I got enough of seeing you naked at Alex and Cat's wedding extravaganza."

"It was at a nudist resort. Most of us went naked, including you."

"Aye, but cover up anyway. Donnae want to be shanghaied without any clothes on, do you?"

Shanghaied? My brother is off his head. Maybe his wife has done that to him. Autumn likes to watch documentaries about UFOs and monsters in the forest. She's a sweet and bonnie lass, though, and we all love her.

But I'm confused. "What are ye doing here, Jack?"

"Evan wants you out of his apartment. We all do."

"Why? He said I could have it for as long as I wanted."

"As long as you needed it, that's what he said." Jack strides across the threshold, forcing me to back up, and shuts the door. "You stopped your physical therapy, which means you don't need this apartment anymore. Get your things. I'm driving you home."

"Donnae need a chauffeur. I have my own car and my bike."

"Aye, and I'm driving your car with your Harley towed behind it."

"What about your car?"

Jack claps a hand on my shoulder. "I took a taxi to get here, and it took three bloody hours. Evan paid for the fare. He is a billionaire, after all, and he wants this to happen as much as I do."

"Wants what to happen?" No one can blame me for sounding suspicious. My family has a habit of interfering in other people's lives. "I should never have answered my mobile when you rang me yesterday."

"But you did. Too late to fight it. The plans are in motion, and nothing short of an asteroid hurtling toward Scotland will derail the plan." He squeezes my shoulder. "The American Wives Club is taking care of everything."

I do not want to know what they have planned, but I realize I'll have no choice in the matter.

"Get dressed," Jack says. "Unless you want me to bring out the handcuffs."

"What?"

He pulls a pair of cuffs out of his trouser pocket—lavender-colored, fluffy ones. "Autumn suggested I bring these. She borrowed them from Keely."

No, I will never in a billion years ask why Evan's wife has handcuffs.

"Fine," I growl. "Wait here while I get dressed."

"Pack your bags too."

I hurry into the bedroom to dress and throw all my rubbish into the two suitcases I'd brought with me. I follow Jack into the elevator and down to the parking garage, where we stash my things in the boot, including my motorcycle helmet.

Just as I'm about to shut the boot, Jack dangles the lavender handcuffs from one finger. "Might come in handy later."

He tosses them at me.

I jerk out of the way as the cuffs drop into the boot. "No, I will not need those."

He chuckles.

Aye, my brother is off his head for sure.

"Where are ye taking me?" I ask. "Not to your house, I hope. It's cramped."

"Insulting my home? I should dump you on the side of the road for that." He's smiling, so I know he isn't annoyed. "But no, you won't be invading our house, though Autumn would love that. You're staying at Dùndubhan."

Rory's castle? Well, that won't be too much of a trial. It's posh and spacious.

We get on the road, with Jack driving, and I count the miles until we reach Dùndubhan. It's a long trip, but I feel more relaxed with every passing mile that takes me closer and closer to my home. I was born in Loch Fairbairn, grew up in Loch Fairbairn, and still live in that village. I left for a while to become a firefighter in Inverness, but I never felt as at ease there as I do at home. I gaze out the window at the lochs and trees and houses that speed by outside my window, feeling a sense of peace that had slipped away from me while I was in Inverness.

Except when I was with Kate.

I offer to drive part of the way, but Jack won't let me. He says I need time to think about what I really want. I haven't got a clue what he means by that. Maybe he's talking about my job. I like working as a carpenter, so I don't need to consider my options. Jack can't mean Kate. She flew back to America.

Aye, I want her. But it's not meant to be.

The landscape starts to look familiar, and I know we're getting close to Loch Fairbairn. Dùndubhan is half an hour past that, in the back of beyond. I suggest we stop at our parents' house in Loch Fairbairn before heading to the castle, but Jack dismisses that idea with a shake of his head and an enigmatic smile. I've never known my brother to be mysterious. I'm starting to feel a wee bit anxious about what's waiting for me at Dùndubhan.

No, it won't be anything bad. They'll probably throw a ceilidh to cheer me up. I wouldn't mind a good party.

The closer we get to the castle, the fewer houses I see. Soon, we're driving down tree-shrouded roads that segue from asphalt to gravel. Once we turn onto the long driveway that accesses our destination, even the gravel disappears. The dirt path guides us through the forest, but it transitions to gravel as we go through the metal gate that marks the halfway point. The gate is open since we've been expected. How many of my relatives will be waiting for us? I'll try not to get grumpy with them, but I haven't had the best time lately. The woman I want in my life ran away to another continent. But I'll try to muster some enthusiasm for whatever kind of party or activity they've arranged.

I've lost the girl and my best mate. Yesterday, I tried to ring Hugh but only got his voice mail. Will he ever forgive me for slugging him? I think he's most upset about me and Kate, though he knew she didn't want to date him. But Hugh has always gotten the girl, so he probably needs to process the fact he lost this time. We both did.

At last, the trees open up, and the castle comes into view. Dùndubhan is a traditional medieval stronghold, with turrets and a massive wall surrounding the whole complex, not to mention two bloody huge wooden gates that stand open now, the halves spread wide to greet us. Jack navigates through the gates to park in the gravel courtyard near the main door to the castle. The compound also includes a large garage that had once been a carriage house and a walled garden with an attached cottage. No one lives in the cottage anymore. Mrs. Darroch, the housekeeper here, used to live in that wee house, but she moved into Loch Fairbairn when she married her second husband, Tavish, and became Mrs. Brody.

I don't see anyone milling about in the courtyard. No one came to greet us? That's unusual. I start to feel uneasy about what's waiting for me inside, but that's rubbish. The worst my family might do is drag me into a round of Highland games.

Jack shuts off the engine and aims that strange, enigmatic smile at me again. "It's time."

"To go into the house? Aye, I knew that."

He shakes his head slowly. "No, that's not what I mean."

"What, then?"

"We've arranged a sort of intervention."

I roll my eyes. "Ahmno a drug addict or an alcoholic. Donnae need an intervention."

"Oh aye, ye do." Jack swings his door open and steps out, leaning down to peer at me. "Donnae blame the lass for this. The American Wives Club did all of it for you, so try to be gracious."

"Have you joined the club? Maybe your wife has infected you with the meddling virus."

"Be as cheeky as you want. It won't spare you."

Why do I feel like my brother wants to scare me? I donnae get anxious that easily. "Your bum's oot the windae, Jack."

"Everything I've said won't seem like nonsense anymore once you find out what we've done."

"Ye helped? Aye, you've definitely caught the illness. Meddling is terminal, ye know."

Jack shuts his door and moves in front of the car, where he stands with his arms locked over his chest, facing me.

I climb out and follow him up the path, through the main door of Dùndubhan. It opens into the vestibule. A spiral staircase winds its way up the four levels that include three floors above our heads. I turn toward the doorway to the ground floor, but Jack plants a hand on my back and pushes me toward the staircase.

"Up, Callum," he says. "Nothing to see down here. It's all on the third floor."

That would be the fourth level of the castle. For reasons I've never understood, the ground floor is not the first floor. What bloody stupid medieval architect decided to name the levels that way? But I've gotten used to it since Rory has owned this castle for several years.

We wind up in the long gallery. I can see the door to the tower bedroom at the right end of the huge space that makes up this floor. MacTaggarts love to hold a ceilidh here when the occasion calls for it. And in my family, any sort of occasion qualifies for a party. Jack leads me into the middle of the room and stops.

"Are we waiting for something?" I ask.

"You'll find out soon enough."

"Donnae like the secrecy, Jack. What are you lot scheming to do now?"

His mysterious smile returns, but he says nothing.

My skin starts to itch. Jack plotting? I know he's conspiring with all those American lasses who married MacTaggarts, but I donnae like it. Their plotting might have helped a lot of my cousins, including Jack, but there is nothing for them to engineer for me. Kate is gone. Hugh is gone. It's all over.

"I'm hungry," I say. "Let's go downstairs and have a piece in the kitchen."

"No eating until after."

Cannae help growling. "After what? Getting bloody sick of your mysterious act."

Jack's mobile rings, and he digs it out of his trouser pocket to answer. "Hello, Luke. Aye, it's time. Donnae worry about Callum. I've got him, and he won't be getting away no matter how hard he tries. No, I haven't done that yet. Thought I should wait until you're sure you and the lads have the package in hand." Jack grins and gives me a thumbs-up sign. "Brilliant. I'll take care of things at my end."

What in the name of heaven is my brother doing? Luke must be Luke Turner, the fiancé of our cousin Kirsty. But what are he and "the lads" doing? What sort of "package" did they get in hand? Ahmno liking the sound of this.

"Think I'll jump on my Harley and go for a ride," I say. I'm leaving out the bit where I plan to drive back to my house and lock all the doors and windows. "Need fresh air after the long car trip."

"Oh no," Jack says, clamping a hand on my shoulder. "You're going nowhere."

I try to back away, but he pulls out those ridiculous lavender handcuffs and secures one around my right wrist. Then, before I realize what he's about, he moves behind me to secure the other cuff around my left wrist. I hadn't seen him retrieve those restraints from the car boot, but we had stopped to get petrol and use the bog. He must've gotten the handcuffs while I was in the restroom.

"What the bloody hell do ye think you're doing?" I snarl through my clenched teeth. "Let me go, Jack. Right now."

"Sorry. Cannae do that." He pushes me until I give in and start walking. "We assumed you'd be wanting some time alone to think before the intervention begins."

"What fucking intervention? You're all off your heads."

"Aye, it's a family trait. Even the Americans in our clan have developed that problem."

"How did you convince Luke Turner to help you with your meddling scheme?"

Jack swings the door to the tower bedroom open. "He volunteered. Now, go into the bedroom, Callum."

"No."

My brother takes a step back, then raises his leg to plant his boot in the middle of my back and shove.

I stumble across the threshold and spin around to glare at Jack.

He smiles in that secretive way yet again, which is starting to make me very angry. "Take this time to relax and reflect."

Jack removes the cuffs and shuts the door.

When I try to open it, the thing won't budge. Jack locked it from the outside. I hurry over to the other door, the one that accesses the stairs that lead up to the top floor, but that one is locked too.

"Relax and reflect," Jack shouts through the door.

I kick the door and shout, "'*S e plàigh a th' annad*, Jack!"

Aye, he is a plague, the sort that will drive me barking mad.

Jack chuckles, the sound fading as he walks away.

My own brother has imprisoned me.

Chapter Twenty

Hugh

AFTER A NIGHT AND MOST OF A DAY REFLECTING ON THE events of late, I have reached a conclusion. I need to get the hell out of Scotland. Yes, that's my brilliant idea. What a genius I am. I groan, which makes the taxi driver glance at me in the rearview mirror with an odd look on his face. Sod the driver. Sod the world. My best mate betrayed me and slept with the woman I'd been trying to court. Sure, Kate told me repeatedly she had no interest in dating me. She also claimed to be celibate, but then she shagged Callum. They both betrayed me. I've been cuckolded twice over.

Bloody hell. Now I'm feeling sorry for myself.

My hours of self-reflection have brought me to the Inverness airport. The taxi driver pulls up to the curb and does not offer to help me get my bags out of the trunk. The bloke must not want a tip. Well, I only have one bag, so it's not an ordeal to get it myself. I do tip the driver, strictly because my parents raised me to believe that even the worst worker deserves a tip. We are, as my mother still likes to say, blessed with good fortune and inherited opportunity.

I stand at the curb and watch while the taxi drives away. It's possible I am partly responsible for the disaster that happened this week. Only a tiny bit responsible. Almost zero culpability. How can it be my fault when Callum and Kate sneaked around behind my back? Maybe I should work it out with Callum, but I need a break from all that rubbish before I can even consider the idea. Yes, my wounds need to heal. That's why I'm going home to Sommerleigh, not because I'm a ruddy coward.

Sighing, I pick up my bag and turn toward the entrance to the building.

A vehicle drives up, stopping right behind me. Peripherally, I can tell it's a van of some sort.

I take one step away from the curb.

The van's door slides open, and a pair of brawny arms lock around my torso, pinning my arms. I drop my bag and kick my feet out, but that does no good. I'm hauled backward into the van while a second bloke grabs my bag and shuts the vehicle's door. In the gloom within the space, I can't make out anything more than humanlike shapes. While I blink rapidly and try to sort out my surroundings, the bloke who had seized me lets go, and the vehicle begins to roll down the street.

Bright sunlight glares through the windscreen, blinding me for a moment.

"What the bloody hell are you lot doing?" I demand. "Kidnapping the Viscount Sommerleigh is a rubbish idea. You'll end up in prison."

"You aren't that important," an American male voice says. "Now, if you were the Prince of Wales, we might worry. But you're just a low-level aristocrat."

Low-level? Oh, that's it. I've had enough of these twats.

I spring to my knees and reach for the van's door, yanking it. The blasted thing does not move.

A deep voice chuckles behind me. "Ye willnae get out that way. It's locked, ye *cacan*."

That can't be—No, he wouldn't abduct me. But it sounded like… "Logan MacTaggart? Is that you?"

Someone switches on a large torch, and the lantern-like bulb illuminates the interior of the van's cargo area. I kneel here surrounded by men I recognize, men I've chatted to many times, men I called mates. Well, they won't be getting any Christmas cards from me this year. Logan squats near the back of the van, while Luke Turner perches on a small wooden crate. Nick Hunter sits cross-legged on the floor. Now that my eyes have adjusted to the light, I can see the two men who occupy the seats in the front. The driver is Chance Dixon, and the other occupant is Damian Petrescu.

What on earth? Damian is American, but he didn't marry a MacTaggart. His wife, the lovely Heidi, is as American as he is. I met them last year at the wedding of Alex Thorne and Catriona MacTaggart, which they held at a rural nudist resort in Oregon. Damian is a gypsy. Did my mates all conspire to get him to cast some sort of spell over me? I can't imagine why else he would be here. I don't believe in that magic bollocks, which means he can't hypnotize me.

"Aye, it's me," Logan says. "Who did ye think it was, the tooth fairy?"

"With you lot, who knows." I maneuver myself into a sitting position with my knees bent in front of me. Kneeling on the floor of a van is not terribly comfortable. "Why have you abducted me?"

"Because you're being an erse, and we don't appreciate that."

"Did Callum put you up to this? He punched me, not the other way round."

"We know what happened," Luke says. "That's why we're here. To stop you from hightailing it back to England when you know you should deal with the issue at hand."

I glare at Luke. "The issue at hand? Callum betrayed me. That's the issue, and unless he means to apologize to me with a great deal of groveling involved, there's nothing to deal with."

Nick Hunter finally speaks up. "I don't see that happening anytime this century. Why do you think Hugh and Callum are such good mates? They're both bloody-minded prats."

"You lot are meant to be my mates," I say. "But you're all on Callum's side, aren't you? Perfect. I've been kidnapped by agents of the enemy."

"No," Logan says with a chuckle that I'm sure he thinks is menacing. "We're agents of the American Wives Club."

"Oh, I see. You gents are doing this because your wives won't let you get a leg over with them unless you do their bidding." I shake my head. "It's pathetic when men hand their testicles over to women."

"Best get comfortable, laddie. We have a long drive ahead of us."

I glance around at the five men who are holding me hostage. "Where are you taking me?"

"Dùndubhan," Nick says. Then he looks at Logan. "Hope I pronounced it right this time."

"Aye, ye did well." Logan squints at me. It's the expression the Mac-Taggarts call his deadly calm stare. "But you're needing more therapy than even Jack could give you. So we've arranged an intervention."

"No thank you."

"Did I say ye had a choice, laddie?"

Luke reaches into a tote box that was hidden behind him and hands me a blanket and a pillow. "Take a nap. You'll need your strength."

These men, my former mates, are trying to intimidate me. It won't work. I'm not that stupid.

But I take the blanket and pillow, then lie down to pretend I'm sleeping. At least they might leave me alone for the entire trip to Dùndubhan. I've been there before. But I imagine this time the full complement of the American Wives Club will be present, including the British Branch. Oh, that's just lovely. I lose the girl of my dreams, my best mate assaults me, and now I am a prisoner.

Amazingly, I do fall asleep. Nick wakes me sometime later and informs me we have arrived at Dùndubhan. Logan opens the van's door but won't let me out yet. He insists on tying my wrists with a slender length of rope to stop me from "fleeing like a *cacan*." I see no point in arguing with these men, not yet, so I let them haul me away. But they don't drag me into the castle. No, they take me on a forced march through the walled garden to the door in the outer wall that leads onto the green. They stop me at the closed door.

"Since we cannae trust you to keep your eyes closed," Logan says, "we devised an alternative method."

Chance Dixon produces a canvas hood from inside his jacket and hands it to Logan.

The Scot tugs it down over my head. "Now you're ready."

My pulse has sped up, but that is not anxiety. It's...exertion. They've dragged me through the castle compound at a brisk pace.

I hear a thump which I recognize as someone opening the door to the green. Then a hand settles on my back, between my shoulder blades, and the owner of that hand pushes me through the opening. I keep walking, at my captor's insistence, until I am finally allowed to stop. The warmth of the sun penetrates my hood, and I feel a cushion of grass under my feet. We have reached the green.

Now what? Not sure I want to find out.

Someone whisks the hood off my head.

I blink several times until my brain at last understands the change in my environment. I see lots of MacTaggarts as well as Dixons and Hunters. Then I notice a familiar figure standing a dozen yards away, maybe a bit more, and my pulse accelerates for a different reason.

Kate Wagner stands at the front of the crowd. When she sees me, she waves and gives me a tight smile.

Did these twats abduct her too?

Logan grasps my shoulders and turns me away from the crowd. That's when I see it.

Callum stands several yards away with his cousin Lachlan beside him. Lachlan holds a canvas hood in his hand, which I assume he just removed from Callum's head. What these people have in mind,

I can't even guess. Kidnapping, manhandling, and now...who knows what.

"Please don't kill each other," Kate shouts.

I glance back at her, and she winces. Why would she do that? Perhaps she knows what this lot has planned for me and my former best mate. Wincing doesn't bode well, does it? Not that I'm worried. These blokes don't scare me, and their wives certainly do not.

"Now that you're both here," Lachlan says, "we can get started with the intervention."

Jack MacTaggart emerges from the crowd, taking up a position between me and Callum but off to the side a bit. "This is a radical intervention. Lachlan and I are the referees."

"Referees?" I say. "You'd better explain, or I'm leaving."

Behind me, Logan chuckles. Yes, I know it's him, though I can't see the man. No one else laughs the way he does. "You aren't leaving until we say so. Do ye think ye can get away from all these people? They're the hunting party, if it should become necessary to retrieve you. That will only happen if you try to run. I donnae recommend that."

"Yes, you're so terribly frightening, Logan. Get on with it, would you? Whatever rubbish you have planned doesn't scare me."

"Just be glad Magnus isn't here. He would snap your neck for what you've done."

"Me? What about your lying arse of a cousin?" I flap a hand in Callum's direction. "This is all his fault."

"Haud yer wheesht," Callum snarls. "Not my fault Kate didn't want you."

Before I can respond, Lachlan announces, "Here are the rules of the match. There are no rules."

"Match?" I say. "What are you on about?"

"The wrestling match."

"I don't know how to wrestle."

"Neither does Callum. That makes it a fair competition."

This is insanity. They want us to fight?

Lachlan takes a deep breath and shouts, "Ready! Set! Go!"

Oh, bloody hell.

Chapter Twenty-One

Kate

THIS IS NOT GOOD. EMERY AND JACK BOTH EXPLAINED TO me the theory behind this so-called radical intervention, but I still worry the whole thing will end in catastrophic failure. Jack is a psychotherapist, so I'm trusting his instincts and experience. Callum, Hugh, and I can't go on like this. The American Wives Club is right about that. But will a wrestling match help?

We're all about to learn the answer.

Callum and Hugh have been circling each other for a minute or so, both squinting their eyes and holding their fists up. I thought Lachlan said they should wrestle, but these two look more like they want to pummel each other's faces.

Lachlan shakes his head. "Wrestle, ye eejits. This isn't a boxing match.

Callum smirks. "Aye, but Hugh knows I'll trounce him. He's afraid to wrestle me."

"Like hell I am." Hugh lowers his fists and bends his knees, shifting his weight from one leg to the other, kind of like a sumo wrestler. "I'll have you on the ground in five seconds flat. Might as well concede."

Callum trips over something and almost falls, but catches himself.

Hugh freezes for a second, distracted by Callum's problem. That tiny delay gives the Scot an opening. He rushes at Hugh, ramming his head into the Brit's gut and knocking him to the ground. Callum throws his body onto Hugh's, pinning him to the ground, but the Brit rolls out of the way with a triumphant shout. Then he leaps to his feet and tries to kick his friend in the side. Callum grabs Hugh's foot, though, and pushes the Brit away before he even grazes the Scot. Hugh staggers backward but stays on his feet. Callum jumps up, bares his teeth, and barrels toward Hugh. The two tackle each other to the ground and start rolling around, though they move so fast that I can't keep track of who's doing what to who. Lots of grunts and hollers accompany their bizarre wrestling match.

How is any of this helping?

Emery comes up beside me and hooks an arm around my shoulders. "This is what happens when we let the men decide how to handle a situation like this. Don't worry. We ladies have our own ideas."

"Uh-huh." I know she's trying to make me feel better. But more secret plans? That doesn't sound good. "Was kidnapping Hugh an idea the ladies came up with?"

"That was a group decision. We all voted on it—women and men alike, including the MacTaggart boys." Emery gives me a light squeeze. "This must all seem like total lunacy, but there is a method to our madness. The American Wives Club has been saving the day ever since Jamie and Gavin. I'll tell you their story sometime. It's a hoot."

"What's going on over there"—I nod toward the two jackasses rolling around on the grass—"is not a hoot. I don't get how this is supposed to fix anything."

"Not fix. Facilitate."

"Um, what does that mean?"

She smiles. "You'll see."

Emery walks away, leaving me alone with a crowd of Scots, Brits, and Americans behind me. Okay, I'm not literally alone. But I feel weird about standing here with all these strangers who for some reason want to help me and Callum work out our issues. Naturally, they started their meddling with a ridiculous display of machismo.

Hugh shoves Callum off him, and the Scot flips over backward while the Brit scrambles to his feet. Both men sport grass stains, and their hair has gotten so mussed that I expect mice to crawl in there soon to nest. Both men are also breathing hard, and sweat sheaths their skin.

Sweaty, gorgeous men brawling ought to turn me on. But it doesn't.

Until Callum whips his shirt off.

Oh damn, that chest. I can't stop myself from getting warm and tingly all over because I've memorized every inch of that torso and licked his skin too. He tastes like Scottish man. Okay, that's not actually a flavor, but to me, it is. The taste of his skin made me even wilder for him. No man has ever gotten me as hot as Callum does.

He notices me ogling him and smirks.

And of course, his best friend seizes the opportunity to rush at Callum and catch him in a headlock.

This has gone on long enough.

I march over to the morons and lodge my hands on my hips. "Stop right now."

They ignore me. Callum kicks Hugh's shin, and Hugh tightens his headlock while both men grunt and growl at each other.

All right. No more polite suggestions.

I suck in a big breath and holler, "Cut that out right now!"

My voice echoes off the castle wall.

Everyone freezes. All eyes turn to me while silence falls over the green.

Hugh releases Callum. Both men stare at me.

I seize Callum's arm. "Come with me now."

The half-naked Scot winks at me. "Anything you want, *gràidh*."

"Don't get cute with me." I stab a finger toward Hugh. "I will deal with you later."

He twists his lips into an annoyed slant, but then sighs and nods.

"The show is over," I tell the crowd. "For now, at least."

Emery shouts, "There are refreshments in the great hall!"

Refreshments? Wow, they do treat this like a big party.

I keep hold of Callum's upper arm while I half walk, half jog back toward the castle compound, though I let him grab his shirt off the ground along the way. I don't slow down as we rush through the garden and across the courtyard. He keeps giving me sly sideways looks, but I will not let him seduce me into forgetting what I need to say to him. When he seems like he might speak, I throw him a sideways scowl.

He smirks, but doesn't say a word.

We burst into the vestibule, and I veer us toward the spiral staircase.

"Do I get to know where you're taking me?" he asks.

"No. Shut up and keep walking."

We march up the stairs, passing the first and second floors to head straight to the third and final level. I drag him down the hall and into the bedroom where I slept last night. Then I shove Callum through the door and slam it shut.

I fold my arms under my breasts.

His gaze veers down to my tits, and one side of his mouth kicks up.

"Don't be looking at my breasts," I say. "You won't see them again anytime soon."

"You are dead sexy when you're angry."

"We will not have sex, Callum."

"Then why bring me to a bedroom? One that has a large bed."

"No sex. Understand?"

"Aye. But ye do have a habit of jumping on me and begging me to shag ye."

I nail my gaze to his, leaning forward slightly, and speak with knife-like precision. "We will not have sex today. Nod if you understand."

He nods—and then grins. "I can wait until tonight."

This is pointless. I give up and move on. "What are you doing? Hugh is your best friend."

"Not anymore. He's a *tolla-thon* who can't handle the fact I got the girl this time, not him."

"You must be talking about some other girl, because nobody has gotten me."

He bows his head. "I know."

Why does he have to look so pitiful? I suddenly feel like a jerk who drove right past a lost puppy sitting along the side of the road in the rain. Well, I probably feel that way because I caused this mess. I made Callum lie about our sexual relationship and kept hanging out with Hugh even though I knew he wanted more than friendship with me. I told him repeatedly I don't want that. But still, I feel responsible.

"It's not your fault," Callum says. "I did this."

"No, you didn't. How is it your fault, anyway?"

"Because I expected you to want me for more than sex, but you made it clear you didn't want that."

Playing the blame game won't fix anything. I brought Callum up here so I could tell him... I don't know what. The speech I had worked out in my head has suddenly evaporated. All I can do now is speak from the heart.

"I like you, Callum," I say. "You're a sweet, thoughtful, smart, sexy man. Being with you made me feel better than I have in years. And I'm not just talking about sex. Even during our therapy sessions, when I had to push you to open up, I felt something I hadn't experienced in a long time."

"What's that?"

"After years of holding everything inside and denying myself what I really needed..." I move closer, tipping my head back to gaze into his eyes. "You make me feel alive, Callum."

He stares at me.

Maybe I shouldn't have said that. It's too much too soon, isn't it?

Callum cradles my face in one hand. "You make me feel alive too."

"Oh. Good." Was that the dumbest thing I could've said? Probably not. But it felt pretty damn stupid.

"It's time I answered all your questions."

Did he actually say that? I didn't hallucinate it, right? Callum said he wants to open up to me at last, all the way. Excitement tingles over my skin, which is ridiculous. It's not like he asked me to marry him.

"Why don't we lie down on the bed?" I say. "You'll be more comfortable sharing everything with me if you're relaxed."

"You said 'we' should lie down."

"I know. Got a problem with that?"

"No." He sweeps me up in his arms and tosses me onto the bed. "Do we keep our clothes on?"

"Yes. This isn't sex therapy."

I scoot over to make room for him, then he lies down beside me. I cuddle up to him and rest my head in the hollow of his shoulder. He curls an arm around me.

"Whenever you're ready," I say. "We've got all the time in the world."

"Aye. As long as I'm in here with you, those lunatics out there won't harass me."

"Forget about everyone else. Just talk to me."

"You want to know why I resigned from the fire station."

"Anything you want to tell me, I want to know."

He absently strokes a finger up and down my arm and focuses on the ceiling. "I didn't save that elderly woman. My mate did. When we got into the bedroom, the fire was all around us, all around the bed. We had seconds to save that woman, and I froze."

"Had you been in a burning building before?"

"Aye. Been in all sorts of fires and always got the job done. I never froze." He scrubs a hand over his face. "Until that day."

"What changed?"

"Not sure." He groans and shuts his eyes. "My mate rescued her and shouted for me to follow him out. That beam did almost fall on my mate and the woman, and I did push them out of the way. But I tripped going down the stairs. That's how I injured my knee. The woman was sobbing, havering about 'the kittens in the living room.' While my mate carried the woman outside, I found the kittens and brought them outside."

He twists his features into a pained expression.

"Why are you scrunching up your face like that?" I ask. "You did a good thing."

"Saving kittens? I'm glad I got them out, but I was no hero. I almost got that woman killed."

"How long were you frozen?"

"A few seconds. That's what my mates at the fire station all told me."

"Seconds? That's nothing, Callum. You have no reason to feel embarrassed about it." I push up onto one elbow so I can look straight into his eyes. He has them squeezed shut, so I tickle his lips until he peels his lids apart. "Why did you let me think you hurt your knee when the beam fell?"

"Because the truth is humiliating."

"Is that why you quit your job? Embarrassment?"

"No. I quit because I'd lost the respect of my mates at the fire station. They called me Super Kitten Man and put stuffed kitten toys in my locker. Even gave me a cape—a pink one—and a matching mask."

"That's what guys do, right? Harass each other. It's how all you macho men show your affection."

He screws up his mouth. "My picture was in the newspaper. Well, it was a photo of my mate carrying the woman out of the burning house. But you could see me too—carrying the kittens."

"Come on, Callum. Tell me the real reason that bothered you so much."

He sighs—and tells me.

Chapter Twenty-Two

Callum

"IT'S BLOODY STUPID," I SAY. KATE HAS CONVINCED ME TO tell her the truth, and I'm starting to regret it. No, that's not true. I need to share more with her if I expect her to become my girlfriend. "They put me on desk duty after the fire, because of my knee. I hated it. Sitting around answering the phone and doing paperwork is not the sort of work that suits me. I like to be active. With the kitten humor and the fact I froze during that fire, I knew I couldn't stay at the fire station. So I quit."

Aye, Kate will want me now for sure. Super Kitten Man is the sort of title that makes the lasses swoon.

"Thank you, Callum," she says. "I appreciate how hard it was for you to tell me that. But you don't need to be embarrassed about anything. Everyone makes a mistake now and then. Yours didn't hurt anyone."

"But it could have." I groan and growl. "The kitten thing I could've let go. But being injured, not being able to work with my mates... That was the worst part."

"You're a hands-on guy, aren't you?"

"Aye."

"So you quit because manning a desk frustrated you."

"Aye."

Kate taps my nose with one finger. "Good boy."

Cannae help smirking. "Am I a dog now?"

"No. You're a big, sexy Scottish bear."

"Suppose that's better than being a kitten."

The lass leans over me, her lips close enough that I could kiss her if I moved a wee bit. "Kittens are adorable. Women love to cuddle with them, just like I love to cuddle with you."

"Well, maybe being a kitten isn't a horrible insult after all."

"You're finally catching on." She rolls half her body on top of me, folding her arms on my chest, and rests her chin on her hands. "Did you love being a firefighter?"

"Aye."

"Do you love being a carpenter too?"

"Is there a point to this interrogation?"

"Can't you just answer the question?"

"Aye, I do love being a carpenter. I'm a hands-on man like you said." I palm her erse to prove my point. "Do you love your job?"

"I did. But I'm unemployed now, remember? Not sure if I want to go back to the clinic in Inverness, even if they'd let me."

"Of course they would. You're the best therapist they've got." I slide my hand up to the small of her back, rubbing it in slow circles. "You helped me, that's a fact. Though I don't think you should give anyone else the kind of physical therapy you gave me."

"Sex is not physical therapy."

"For me, it is. Every time we shagged, my knee stopped hurting."

Her lips curve into a knowing smile. "Told you so."

"Even when you're smug, I want to shag you."

"Ditto." She wriggles against me, which I'm sure she does on purpose as an attempt to distract me by rubbing herself on my *slat*. "When I suggested your injury might have a psychosomatic component, you said that was 'bollocks.' But you just admitted I was right."

"No, I did not."

"You said your knee doesn't hurt when we have sex."

"I—Well—Gah, yer trying to trick me."

Kate pushes herself up with two hands on my chest. "It's okay. I'm a therapist, which means I can be very patient. Let that information sink into your steel-reinforced brain and let me know when you realize I'm right."

"Are all psychotherapists raging bampots? I thought it was only Jack."

"Ha-ha." She climbs over me to hop off the bed. "Let's do something fun."

"Shagging is lots of fun."

Kate sets her hands on her hips and shakes her head, though her lips curve up in a sweet smile. "Something that doesn't involve sex. Please. Come on, get off your hot ass and show me a good time—with our clothes on. I want us to get to know each other better, so we can find out if we could have a future together."

"You do?"

"How can it be such a shock? Yes, I want that." She puckers her lips and narrows her eyes, but it seems like fake irritation. "Want me to change my mind? You have five seconds to comply with my order. Five, four, three—"

I leap off the bed and throw my arms around her, tugging the lass close. "Donnae need a countdown. Whatever you want to do, ahm ready. So, what's your pleasure, Kate?"

"Not sure. I assumed it would take longer to convince you, and I'd have time to think of something."

"No need. I already have several ideas."

"I hope it doesn't involve wrestling with Hugh again." She slips her arms around my waist and rubs those bonnie tits against me. "Though it would be kind of hot to watch you two wrestling in the nude."

"Ahmno doing anything with him in the nude. My idea is just for us, you and me."

"I was kidding."

"Glad to hear it." I pull away from her. "Meet me in the courtyard in ten minutes. Wear jeans or khakis or something like that. A jacket and boots too."

Her brows knit together over her nose, and it's the most adorable expression of confusion. "Where are you taking me?"

I smirk. "Anywhere I can."

"You know what I meant, you sneaky Scot."

"Aye, I do know." I slap her erse. "Get changed. I'm assuming your clothes are in here. Mine are in the room at the end of the hall."

"I know. Emery told me. And yes, mine are in here." She sashays over to the door to the walk-in closet, pausing with her hand on the knob. "This might surprise you, but I liked you even when you were being a grumpy jerk. Though I like you best when you're this way."

Kate walks into the closet.

And I head for my room.

She liked me when I was being an erse? Oh aye, she's definitely a bampot. Only a lunatic would enjoy listening to me growl and complain about my life.

I swap out my clothes and head down to the courtyard. The sounds of laughter and chattering voices emanate from the green, so it seems like my family means to hang around for a good while. Whatever they have planned, I donnae care anymore. Let them plot and haver and blether. Kate has come back, and that's all I care about right now. I need to show her I am not a grumpy Scottish bear and that we can have something good together if she'll give us a go.

Never in my life have I needed to win a lass's heart more than I do now.

Kate walks out the vestibule door a few minutes later, but she doesn't notice me until she's well past the door. Her focus had been on her clothes, which she seemed obsessed with straightening. Then her head came up—and she froze. She still stands there gawping at me like I'm sitting astride a unicorn instead of a motorcycle.

I crook a finger at her. "Hurry up, lass. Your chariot awaits."

"That's a Harley, not a chariot. And you cannot ride your motorcycle." She marches up to me, shaking her head while giving me a disapproving look. "It's bad for your knee, remember? Sex hasn't cured your injury, you know."

"Well, maybe if we have a poke right here, it'll give me the strength to take you on a tour of the area." I sling an arm around her waist to pull her close. "Let me show you my home—Loch Fairbairn. If you're sweet to me, I might show you Ballachulish too."

"You want to show me around?"

"Of course I do. We don't need to lie and hide anymore. Hugh knows about us, and you said you want to give us a chance. Aye?"

"Yes, I do want that." She bites one side of her lip while her gaze travels to the castle wall beyond the garden. "What do you think they're doing with Hugh?"

I chuckle. "They willnae torture him, if that's what you're worried about. Might keep him in the dungeon for a wee while, but they'll make sure he gets bread and water regularly."

Her eyes flare wide, but then she gives me a fake scowl and punches my shoulder. "Very funny. Do all you MacTaggarts have a twisted sense of humor?"

"Most do. It's genetic." I grab the two helmets I'd set on the back of my bike and hand one to Kate. "For the record, there is no dungeon in this castle. They turned it into a wine cellar."

"Oh, how nice. I can drink wine that came from a former torture chamber. It's probably full of haunted chardonnay and cursed merlot."

"Donnae forget the enchanted single malt whisky."

She takes the helmet I offered her, turning it in her hands while her lips curl up in a teasing smile. "Must take a lot of girls for motorcycle rides if you have a pink helmet on hand."

"I have. But none of them got the grand tour, and none of them ever met my parents."

Kate stops rotating the helmet. "Are you saying you want me to meet them?"

"Aye. If you want to, and if we have time. They live in Loch Fairbairn."

"I think I can handle meeting your mom and dad."

"Today?" I hold up a hand to stop her from responding. "Sorry. I know, it's too soon."

"Actually, I was going to say yes. I'd love to meet them today."

She pulls on her helmet and climbs astride the bike, molding her front side to my backside, her arms locked around my midsection. "Let's go."

I pull on my helmet and start up the engine, gunning it, and we roar through the castle gates.

Kate whoops and hugs me tighter.

Aye, today is the best day of my life. But I have a feeling even better ones are coming.

Chapter Twenty-Three

Kate

WE SOAR DOWN THE ROADS THAT BROUGHT US TO DÙN-dubhan, speeding away from the castle as we begin our journey toward Loch Fairbairn. Emery had told me a few things about that village when we drove through it on our way to Dùn-dubhan, but now I have the best tour guide to show me around. Callum grew up here. This is more than the place where he lives and works now. It's also his birthplace. I can't believe he wants to introduce me to his parents, but as soon as he suggested it, I knew I wanted to do that. Maybe I haven't known Callum for long, but I need to give him a chance and find out if hot sex and banter are all we have, or if this could turn into something far more meaningful.

Yeah, I'm still scared. My previous marriage had wrecked me. But Callum is a good man, not the kind who would cheat and deceive me. We both lied to Hugh, but that was my fault, not Callum's. We will make it right with Hugh sooner or later, I know it. He needs to cool down first.

Which gives us the perfect excuse to go for a ride on a wicked cool Harley.

I rest my chin on Callum's shoulder as I enjoy the scenery whizzing past us. I haven't experienced this kind of easy intimacy with any other man. Something about Callum relaxes me deep down in my soul. He looks damn sexy in a leather jacket. When we stop to get gas, he fingers the lapel of my denim jacket and says, "We need to get you some leather. A biker's girlfriend should look the part. If you are my girlfriend."

"Of course I am. Will you teach me to ride your motorcycle?"

"Maybe. But not yet." He winks. "I like having you plastered to my backside, especially that bonnie erse."

"I like having you nestled between my thighs while all that horsepower growls and vibrates under me."

"Are ye trying to make me randy? Keep talking that way and I'll shag you on my bike while we're going sixty miles an hour down the road."

"Hmm, that sounds not quite plausible."

Callum pulls me into his body. "I'm a very creative sort. Very strong too."

"Oh, I'm totally aware of how powerful your body is."

We don't have sex on the Harley while driving down the road, but we do have lots of fun. Callum stops at every tourist destination and some places that only locals know about, and I love getting the secret tour of Glencoe. Callum had told me when we first met that Glencoe is the name of the region that includes both the village of Ballachulish, where his cousins live, and the village of Loch Fairbairn, where his parents and brother still live, not to mention his cousin Kirsty. She's a Wiccan, along with her two sisters. Their brother Logan is not a Wiccan. He's a former MI6 agent. I met Logan today but didn't get a chance to talk to him—or any of the MacTaggarts except Callum.

Emery told me, or maybe warned me, that the family has a lot of "events" planned to help me, Callum, and Hugh. Should I be afraid? No, they're nice people. They wouldn't do anything too crazy.

I mention that assumption to Callum, and he laughs. We're having lunch at a little seafood restaurant in Fort William, the town just north of Ballachulish.

"They won't do anything crazy?" Callum says while still chuckling. "Ye donnae know the MacTaggarts, *gràidh*. Going overboard is in our DNA."

"Yeah, Emery kind of hinted at that. But they'll tone things down because I'm here. Right? Wouldn't want to scare me away."

"My family is canny enough to realize you aren't the sort who will panic because they surprise you with one barmy stunt or another." He eyes me with his brows crinkled, holding a forkful of fish an inch from his lips. "You did run away once. If you mean to leave me again, please wake me up to say goodbye this time."

"I won't run away again. I promise. That was a panic impulse, which isn't like me at all." I pick at the cheese biscuit on my plate and eat a tiny piece. Okay, I'm delaying. I get why he worries I'll take off again, but that will not happen. How can I convince him? By being honest and giving it time. "You can put a GPS chip on me if that'll make you feel better."

"No, lass, I willnae do that."

He goes back to eating and joking with me, and we don't mention that topic again. For the rest of the afternoon, he shows me his favorite parts of Ballachulish and Loch Fairbairn. We stop in at *Da-Shealladh*, the metaphysical shop owned by his cousin Kirsty. She's beautiful and sweet, and she escorts me around the shop to explain what the various knickknacks are. Callum hangs out at the sales counter so he can chat with Luke Turner, Kirsty's fiancé.

My hostess has just shown me the selection of candles she keeps in stock, including one that's supposed to help with summoning spirits. But now she turns to the shelf behind us where small wooden bins hold various kinds of rocks. She picks up a light green stone and sets the polished rock in my palm, folding my fingers around it. "You should have this. It's actinolite, also known as cat's eye. It has healing properties, but it also promotes balance, especially in matters of the heart."

"You think I'm out of balance?"

"Everyone knows you walked away from Callum. The news spread through the MacTaggart grapevine like wildfire." Kirsty covers my hand with both of hers. "I have *da-shealladh*, the second sight. It gives me special intuition about matters of the heart, and I sense you're conflicted. Don't let the pain of your past affect your present or your future. I'm not saying this because Callum is my cousin and I love him. I want *you* to be happy, Kate. Maybe this stone will help."

"Uh, sure. Thanks. I'll pay for the stone."

"Nonsense. It's a gift, from one woman to another."

"You're so kind, Kirsty. I feel better just having talked to you."

She leans in to whisper to me. "I'd be happy to do a tarot reading for you, or you could ask Damian Petrescu for a palm reading. He's visiting from America with his wife."

"Is he a witch too?"

"No. Damian is a gypsy and a naturist." I must look confused because she smiles and explains, "That means he's a nudist. He works at the Au Naturel Naturist Resort in Oregon. We all got to know Damian and his friends at the resort when Cat and Alex held their wedding there."

"They got married at a nudist resort?" Okay, yeah, I almost screeched that. I've never heard of anyone getting hitched at a place like that. I collect myself and ask, "Did they go nude for the wedding?"

"No," she says with a slight chuckle. "But Alex stripped naked as soon as the ceremony ended and tossed his kilt to my cousin Rory. It landed on his head."

Holy cow, I had no idea how strange this family is. Kirsty has opened my eyes.

"If ye change your mind about the tarot or palm reading," she says, "just give me a ring. Damian and his wife, Heidi, will be staying for a month."

"Sure, I'll think about it. Thank you so much for showing me your shop, Kirsty. It's a beautiful place full of beautiful things."

Kirsty smiles and pats my arm. "Listen to your heart, *gràidh*. It willnae lead you astray."

"Callum has called me *gràidh*. Is that Gaelic?"

"Aye. It means 'darling.' Callum must like you very much if he called you that. I have never heard him use that word to describe a lass he's dating. He reserves it for family."

I have no idea what to say to that. Everything I thought I knew about myself has flown out the window since I met Callum. I mean, I let a strange woman at the airport convince me to go with her to a remote medieval castle. Didn't hesitate. Emery asked me to do it, for Callum, and I went willingly. But I haven't done these things only for him. This is for me too.

When Kirsty and I return to the sales counter, her fiancé and my boyfriend are having a good laugh.

Kirsty ducks behind the counter to slip an arm around Luke's waist. "What's the joke? Must be a right good one."

"I was just telling Callum about the plan for Hugh."

His fiancée nudges him with her elbow. "You aren't meant to tell him that. It's a surprise."

"Oh, I'm not spilling the beans about the really good stuff. But I thought he'd like to know that I'll be conducting experiments on the Brit."

"Experiments?" I say. "What exactly are you planning to do to him?"

"Nothing dangerous." Luke kisses his fiancée's cheek. "Just the stuff Kirsty let me do to her when we were first reunited. I was still being an arrogant ass back then, but we had fun with those experiments."

"Are you a doctor?"

Luke chuckles. "I'm a psychophysicist."

Kirsty laughs now. "Donnae worry, Kate. That doesn't mean he's a lunatic. Luke studies physics and psychology. But I'll let him explain that to you."

"Psychophysics is a legitimate discipline," Luke says. "I study the intersection between mind and matter, as well as the concept of sensation or how we interpret what we experience. Most of my experiments involve applying electrodes to a subject to measure the skin conductance response. I've also developed some digital experiments, but I've only done those on Kirsty."

"It's a long story," Kirsty says. "But you can trust Luke. He's a good man and a good scientist."

"Are you okay with these experiments, Callum?" I ask.

"I trust Luke. And Hugh could use a wee lesson in humility. The *cacan* thinks he owns every woman on earth because he's Lord Steamy." Callum lifts his gaze heavenward. "What a bloody stupid nickname."

Hugh is hot, but in my opinion, Callum should be called Lord Steamy. That man knows how to drive me wild in bed—and on the sofa. I think we might have done the deed on the floor at one point too. Multiple orgasms fuzzed up my memory.

Callum is clearly still feeling bitter about his confrontation with Hugh the morning after I broke things off with him. I can understand that, but I want those two to work things out. Maybe Luke's experiments will help. If he studies both psychology and physics, then he might have insights that I don't. It's worth a shot.

We leave Kirsty and Luke and the cool metaphysical shop. Callum shows me a few more sites around the village, and we stop at a cafe to feast on a Scottish dessert called *cranachan*. He warns me that it contains whisky, but the confection doesn't get me drunk. It tastes delicious. After that, Callum tells me it's time to visit his parents.

"They'll want you to stay for dinner," he says. "Ma willnae let you leave until she's talked you into marrying me on the spot. Wouldnae be surprised if she has a minister waiting for us."

"Very funny. You are joking, right?"

"Partly. But Ma will cry when she meets you, then she'll gush over you and suffocate you with many hugs."

"I can handle it. Surly Scots are much harder to deal with than their excitable moms."

"Wasnae surly." He holds the cafe door open for me as we exit, then lays a hand on my back to guide me toward the Harley. "I was grumpy. There's a difference."

"Ah, yes. A very important distinction."

He climbs onto the Harley and picks up our helmets. "Haud yer wheesht and get on the bike with me, ye cheeky lass."

I get on behind him, and we roll down the street. I'm about to meet his parents.

Oh dear lord. What have I gotten myself into?

Chapter Twenty-Four

Callum

THE MINUTE WE PULL UP IN FRONT OF MY PARENTS' HOUSE, Ma rushes out the front door to greet us. I've barely set the kickstand, and we haven't even removed our helmets yet. But Ma cannae be stopped. She starts rambling in Gaelic, and Da has to hold her back so Kate and I can get off the Harley. The second Kate's feet hit the ground, Ma drags her into a bear hug.

"Oh, dearie," she coos, "we are so happy to meet ye."

She acts as if this is a surprise, but I had rung my parents before Kate and I left Dùndubhan to let them know we would stop by for dinner.

I don't bother trying to tear my mother away from Kate. "Ye haven't met her yet, Ma. All you've done is suffocate the lass."

Greer MacTaggart steps back, holding Kate at arm's length. "Let me look at ye, *gràidh*. Oh, ye are a bonnie thing. Cannae believe my boy finally found the right woman."

The right woman? I've just introduced her to Kate, and already my mother is going barmy, dreaming up a fantasy of me and Kate getting married and having twenty bairns. Jack is giving her one bairn. That means I donnae need to rush to produce more MacTaggarts. We've got plenty in the Highlands already.

Ma kisses both of Kate's cheeks. "Come inside, dearie. I need to get to know Callum's girl."

"Bloody hell, Ma," I say. "I've known Kate for two weeks. It is not time to plan the wedding."

"I haven't planned the wedding, *mo luran*." Ma smiles and winks. "You need to propose first."

Propose? She's completely off her head. But when she calls me her darling boy in Gaelic, I feel like a wee laddie again.

Kate looks at me and shrugs, which I take to mean she realizes there's no point in arguing with my mother. Ma commandeers Kate's hand as she leads her into the house. Da walks beside me and claps a hand on my shoulder.

"Just give in," Alistair MacTaggart says. "Women are crackers when it comes to all that romantic rubbish. Let your mother get it out of her system."

"You mean the way she did when Jack brought Autumn home. Ma went so far off her head that it was rolling down the street."

But aye, he's right. No one can stop a MacTaggart woman when she finds out one of her sons has a new lass in his life. Jack probably fed her a load of bollocks about how Kate is the right woman for me. Maybe she is, I donnae know. Whether she wants to be the woman for me is another question altogether.

My mother does not stop havering even when we reach the dining room. She hugs Kate again, then tells us all where to sit. Naturally, she orders me to sit right beside Kate. I would've done that anyway, but letting Ma fuss over us makes her happy. Da sits at the head of the table while Ma bustles away to the kitchen while still havering—to herself now.

"So Kate," Da says, "where are you from?"

"Toledo, Ohio. My family still lives there."

"Ye must miss them."

"I do, of course. We keep in touch with phone calls, emails, and video chats. Not the same as being there, but it's the next best thing."

I clasp her hand under the table. "Cannae imagine not seeing my family in person for more than a year."

Kate shrugs. "It was my decision to move to Scotland, and I do love it here. So I can't complain."

"Donnae need to hide the fact you're homesick."

"I'm not miserable, Callum. But thank you for being so sweet."

My father is smiling at me. "You two are the perfect couple."

"Da, ye donnae know Kate."

"A father can sense these things. Especially when your mother tells me so."

Ma emerges from the kitchen carrying a covered pot. She sets it on the table in front of Da. "Kate, I hope you like haggis."

"I've never had it," my girlfriend says. "But I'd love to try it."

She would love to try it? Most Americans either politely pick at haggis or turn their noses up at it. Kate claims to want to eat our national dish.

My mother turns toward the kitchen door. "I'll get the rest of the food."

I start to get up. "Let me help you."

"Oh, tosh," Ma says with a wave of her hand. "Sit down, Callum. I can serve the food myself. Not decrepit yet."

No point in arguing. I sit back down.

Da leans back in his chair. "Kate, I hear you're a physical therapist and a psychotherapist. Must be challenging work, especially when your client is my bloody-minded youngest son."

"Bloody-minded?" I say. "At least I didnae hold a woman hostage in my house."

My father chuckles. "Aye, Jack did behave like a wee bit of a bampot when Autumn turned up on his doorstep. She surprised him with a baby announcement, so we excuse his behavior. Don't we, Callum?"

Wee bit of a bampot? Jack wouldn't let his ex-wife leave the house, much less allow Autumn to look out the windows, answer the phone, or open the front door. My grumpy behavior doesn't compare.

"Of course we excuse him," I say. "Everybody excuses Jack."

"Donnae be cheeky."

"Why not? Every other MacTaggart is."

Ma bustles back into the room carrying a tray that holds several bowls. As she sets each bowl on the table, she tells us what the dish is. "Tatties and neeps, stovies, cock-a-leekie soup, and Scotch pies. I do hope I havenae made too much food."

"No, Ma, this looks like just the right amount for ten people to eat. Who else did ye invite?"

"Only you and Kate." She shakes her head at me while trying not to smile. "How did I raise such a cheeky lad? Your brother is so polite."

There's no point in arguing or reminding her that Jack snarled at and slammed the door in the face of everyone who stopped by his house in the week or so after Autumn arrived with her baby surprise.

Ma comes over to my chair and kisses my cheek. "Ye know I love you and Jack the same. Ye will always be my sweet wee laddie."

"I'm taller than Da."

"But you're wee to me."

Kate is grinning at us.

Ma kisses her cheek too, then hurries around to the other side of the table, taking a seat beside Da. And the meal begins.

If I hadn't been falling for Kate already, I would be now. She laughs at Da's jokes, even the ruddy awful ones, and she eats every dish on the table. Ma beams every time Kate asks what a dish is, then takes a bite, humming as if she loves it. Maybe she honestly does love all the Scottish foods my mother has cooked for us because she listens while Ma explains that stovies are an appetizer made with potatoes, sausage, roast, and spices.

"Mm, that sounds, looks, and smells yummy," Kate says. She consumes a mouthful of stovies, then half closes her eyes and moans. "Soooo good."

And my mother beams again.

When Kate tries the cock-a-leekie soup, she gets that same look on her face and moans again. I have never seen anyone enjoy soup that much. It's chicken stock, leeks, and prunes—not some decadent dessert. But that expression and the way she moans make me want to shag her right now.

Aye, she moans that way for every dish, even the haggis.

Once we've finished our meal, Ma jumps up. "I made shortbread and scones for dessert. Give me a moment to clear the dishes first."

Da jumps up too. "Let me help, *mo leannan.*"

My parents clear the table, then disappear into the kitchen. I can hear the water running, so they must be washing the dishes.

"Sorry about all this," I tell Kate. "My mother tends to go overboard with, well, everything."

"Don't apologize. Your parents are wonderful."

"Aye, they are. What are your parents like?"

"Believe it or not, they're a lot like your mom and dad. Still in love after all these years and thrilled when one of their kids meets someone new." She smiles softly as she tells me more. "They were college sweethearts who got married right after graduation. Both teachers. Mom handles third grade while Dad takes on the high schoolers. They even work at the same school."

"They sound like good folk." I suddenly realize what she said a moment ago. "You said 'their kids.' Do you have brothers or sisters?"

"One of each. An older brother and a younger sister."

"You never mentioned them before."

She winces a wee bit. "Of course I didn't tell you about my family. I insisted we were just having sex, nothing more."

"But you changed your mind. Ye came back."

"I need to spend more time with you to figure out what we are to each other. Overcoming my fears of getting hurt again might take a long time."

"Oh, I donnae think it'll take as long as you assume it will." I slide my arm over her shoulders, leaning closer. "You are a strong woman, Kate. What your husband did hasn't changed that."

"You didn't know me back then."

"But I know you now. And what I see is a braw, strong, capable woman who knows her own mind, even if she sometimes forgets that."

Tears shimmer in her eyes, but she wipes them away with the back of her hand. "You're a good man, Callum. The best, actually."

I cup her cheek in my hand and kiss her.

"Now that's what I love to see," Ma coos. "Willnae be long now until I have more grandchildren on the way."

Just stifling a growl, I roll my eyes at her. "Ma, you're on fast-forward again. Rewind and slow down, please."

Her cheeks dimple from her closed-mouth smile.

Aye, I know that look well. It means Ma is dead certain she can see my future, and it involves a dozen bairns. Maybe I would like to have children with Kate, but I can't tell her that yet. She panicked when we had sex and almost ran home to America. If my family hadn't intervened, she'd be gone.

Bloody hell. Now I have to thank the whole clan for interfering in my life.

After dessert, the four of us go out into the backyard to sit on lawn chairs and gaze at the stars. Oh, there's plenty of blethering too. Ma catches Kate up on all the clan gossip and some facts too. Tiki torches light the yard, and their flickering golden glow makes Kate look even bonnier. By the time Ma has told my girlfriend about every barmy thing my cousins did when they met the Americans they eventually married, Kate is yawning.

"Someone needs to go to bed," I say. "You're jeeked, lass."

"I'm what?"

"You're exhausted. That's what jeeked means."

"Oh." Another yawn seizes her. "I am kind of tired."

Ma glances back and forth between me and Kate. "Should I make up both spare rooms?"

She's asking if Kate and I will sleep together.

Kate responds before I can. "I'd rather share with Callum, if you're okay with that."

"Of course, dearie. We're not that old-fashioned."

My mother bustles off to get my old room ready, and Da excuses himself a moment later to go help her. That leaves me alone with Kate under the stars.

I pat my thigh. "Come over here, *mo leannan*."

She settles onto my lap, resting her head on my shoulder. "Your dad called your mom *mo leannan* too. What does it mean?"

"My sweetheart."

"I know you called me darling too. Kirsty told me that's what *gràidh* means."

"Aye. You are my darling and my sweetheart. Does that fash you?"

"Maybe it would've bothered me a few days ago, but not anymore. I like it when you call me sweet things in Gaelic."

I brush my fingers through her hair, gazing into her eyes. "Glad ye like it. It feels good to say those words to you. Feels right."

"Yeah, it does." She wags a finger at me. "But don't go thinking that means I want to make a passel of 'bairns' tonight."

"Tomorrow night, then."

She bends her head to whisper in my ear, "I hope you have condoms."

I choke on my own saliva. "Ye want to shag in my parents' house? Thought you were too jeeked to stay awake."

"Sitting on your lap woke me up. Being close to you always makes me so horny."

"Well..." I thrust a hand into her hair, pulling her face closer to mine. "In that case, aye. I've got condoms in my pocket."

She jumps off my lap. "Hurry up, then. It's bedtime."

Chapter Twenty-Five

Kate

WE RUSH INTO THE HOUSE BUT SLOW DOWN ONCE WE'RE inside. Don't want his parents to think we're so hot for each other that we can't wait one more second. Alistair and Greer are just walking out of a bedroom. Greer kisses my cheek and wishes us both goodnight, then Alistair slaps his son's arm and tells us to "sleep well." He winks when he says that, so I think his mom and dad realize we plan to have sex. They clearly don't care. I wouldn't be surprised if they have their fingers crossed that Callum and I will make a "bairn" tonight.

Oh no, it's way too soon for that. Good thing we've got condoms.

Callum shuts the door behind us.

I flop onto the bed. "Was this your room?"

"When I was a laddie, aye. Slept here until I went away to university."

Pushing up on my elbows, I regard him for a moment. "Where did you go to college?"

"University of Dundee. That's on the east coast of Scotland."

"Wow. That's far from your home." I swing my legs off the bed, letting them dangle because this bed is very tall. "I went to Michigan State University. That wasn't too far from Toledo, where I grew up. Must've been hard for you to be so far from your family, considering how tight you all are."

"It was hard. But I adjusted." He sits on the bed beside me. "These days, I'd rather be here in the Highlands, close to my large and often annoying extended family."

He smirks when he says that, so I know he doesn't actually think the other MacTaggarts are annoying. In the short time I've known these people, I can tell they're an amazing family that sticks together and supports each other. Even their spouses feel that way. Why else would Emery have driven all the way to Inverness just to convince me not to leave? Yeah, they are an amazing bunch of people.

Callum slides an arm around my waist, pulling me into his body, and feathers his lips over mine. "Donnae want to talk anymore."

"Fine by me."

I can't say anything else, not with his lips teasing mine and his hard body pressing into me. Thoughts flitter away from me, and the rest of the world seems to disappear. He wraps his other arm around me too and crushes his mouth to mine, then slips his tongue between my lips, exploring me with slow, sensual strokes. I melt for him and moan low in my throat. God, he feels good, tastes good, smells good. All I want is him inside me, right now, but I can't manage to speak, so I tell him what I need in the only way I can.

By unzipping his pants.

He lifts us both off the bed and sets me down on the floor. While keeping one arm around me, he grabs a handful of the comforter and yanks it away along with the blanket and top sheet. And he kisses me the entire time. I cracked one eye open to see him pull the covers off, otherwise I wouldn't have known what he was doing. He peels his mouth away from mine and starts kissing a trail down my throat while he uses his free hand to unbutton my top. I lose track of what he's doing, too turned on to care, and let myself revel in the sensations he evokes in me.

Suddenly, I'm naked on the bed.

Yeah, he drives me out of my mind with lust for him. No other man ever did this to me, but I love it.

Callum kneels at my feet while he ditches all his clothes and frees that glorious cock. It bounces in front of him, the crown damp and rosy. I want to lunge forward to lick up that bead of moisture, but I can't move. The vision of his nude body paralyzes and excites me at the same time, spurring my heart to beat faster and my breaths to quicken. He is more than gorgeous. He's like one of those Greek statues in museums, but he doesn't look like a young boy. No, he's a mature man with scars. But we can talk about that later.

I need him to make love to me right now.

He grabs his jeans off the floor, retrieving a condom from the pocket, then tosses them away. My body grows hotter and slicker, tingly all over, while I watch him roll the latex onto his length. Once he's done, he just kneels there at my feet, gazing at my body like he's never seen it before. We've both seen each other naked and crawled over each other's bodies for hours. But this feels like a new beginning, or maybe our real beginning. No more lies. No more sneaking around. Everyone knows we're together, and we have no reason to feel ashamed.

"Yer the most beautiful lass on earth," he rumbles as he drops onto his hands and knees to crouch over me. "Ahmno rushing this time. Want to love ye for a long time."

He means he wants to make love to me, not that he actually loves me. Would I mind if he did mean that? I don't think I would. In fact, I'm pretty sure I wish he did love me.

"Ah, lass, yer perfect." He catches one nipple between his teeth and swirls his tongue around the tip until I suck in a breath and arch my back. "*Neach-gaoil, tha thu bòidheach.*"

I have no idea what he said, but his tone of voice and the look on his face tell me everything I need to know. This isn't just sex tonight.

He doesn't need to ask me what I want. Even if he didn't already know, the way I bend my knees and spread my thighs tells him. I grip his biceps, and our gazes collide. He doesn't look away or close his eyes, not even when he pushes inside me inch by inch, taking it so slowly that I can't draw in a full breath. Seated deep, he pauses there without speaking or moving a single muscle.

Then he starts to thrust.

He keeps the pace slow and measured, and the deliberate way he takes my body makes me breathe even harder and faster while my pulse thunders in my ears. Oh God, this is even better than the wild and scorching sex we've had before. I never want him to stop, but I don't think I can stand it for much longer. The pleasure mounts little by little as he slides in and pulls out, his breaths as measured as his thrusts.

I wrap my arms around him. "Don't have to hold back. Anything you want, I want too."

"Kate, *mo chridhe*, I—" His pace accelerates, and my body shifts a little with every thrust, making my breasts jiggle. "I wanted to make love to ye slowly, but..."

"Go on. Take me however you need to. I'm yours no matter what."

He drops onto me and rolls us over, leaving me on top. "You take charge, *mo chridhe*. Fuck me."

I lay my palms on his chest and push to lift myself into a sitting position. With his cock still inside me, the fullness of him feels so damn good that I can barely breathe. "Riding you sounds way better than riding your Harley."

"Do it, *mo leannan.*"

Held up by my hands on his chest, I rock my hips, lifting with every retreat and sinking onto his length with every downward thrust. I try not to make much noise because his parents are across the hall, but keeping quiet gets harder and harder, especially when my movements grow more intense, making the bed creak.

I freeze.

Callum grasps my hips and tugs. "Donnae stop now."

"But your parents," I whisper. "They might hear."

He chuckles. "Later, I'll tell you a story about Jack and the lass he dated in school—and what they did in his bedroom."

"Yeah, later. Need to make us both come now."

"Aye, lass." He springs up into a sitting position with me still gripping his hips with my thighs. "I can help ye stay quiet."

He fastens his lips to mine, plunging his tongue deep.

While he ravishes my mouth, I ride him hard. He swallows every cry that bursts out of me, and the need for release grows stronger every second, settling into a heaviness in my belly that won't let up until I go off.

He flips us over again, pinning me to the mattress, and keeps his mouth glued to mine while he pumps into me faster, harder, the slapping of our flesh almost as loud as the creaking of the bed. The climax hits me like a lightning strike, but his mouth muffles my scream while my inner muscles milk his cock. He comes a few seconds later, his hoarse shout swallowed by our joined mouths.

When he pulls his lips away, he's almost gasping for breath and his cheeks have turned a ruddy pink.

He grins. "So much for making sweet love to you."

"You did that. But we kicked it up a few notches at the end."

"More than a few. We demolished the entire bloody post, or whatever those notches are a part of."

I can't stop myself from grinning too. "Yeah, we did."

He rolls off me and discards the condom, then draws me against his side. Enfolded in his arms, I rest my chin in the hollow of his shoulder. My eyes drift shut on their own. I feel so warm and soft and relaxed that I know I'll fall asleep any second.

Callum kisses the top of my head. "Good night, *mo chridhe.*"

As I sink into slumber, I realize I never asked him what that phrase means. Doesn't matter now. All I want is to spend the night in his arms.

Chapter Twenty-Six

Callum

I CREEP UP TO THE DOOR AND GRASP THE KNOB, ROTATING it slowly to avoid making any noise. Then I ease the door inward just enough that I can peek out into the hall. No one there. Good. I can enact my grand plan for the morning without anyone spoiling the surprise. I've never been one for grand gestures, but meeting Kate has changed me—in the best ways, I think. She seems to like me this way, but she even liked me when I was growling and snarling at her. The lass has patience and fortitude.

Those might be the sexiest qualities in a woman.

After a quick glance back at the bed to ensure Kate is still asleep, I slip out and quietly shut the door behind me. The door to my parents' room is still shut, so I assume they haven't gotten up yet. My surprise is for them too, not just Kate. My family has been as patient as Kate when it comes to my behavior lately, so I owe them all a debt of gratitude. I'm starting with Ma, Da, Kate, and Jack.

Once I get into the kitchen, well away from the bedrooms, I pull out my mobile and dial Jack's number.

"What do you want?" he grumbles, and I can hear the sleepiness in his voice. "It's six thirty in the bloody morning, Callum."

"Aye, and I called for an important reason."

"This had better be good. You woke my wife."

"Oh aye, that's the worst sin on earth, isn't it?" My brother has become a bampot for sure ever since his ex-wife came back to him and became his wife, full stop. "Tell Autumn I'm sorry I disturbed her, but I have a very important invitation for you both."

"Invitation? I worry whenever you start plotting."

"Haud her wheesht, Jack. I'm inviting you and Autumn to breakfast here at Ma and Da's house."

"Ah, I see. You're wanting to scare Kate away. Has Ma started planning the wedding yet?"

"No." But I'm dead sure that's coming—soon. "Will ye come to breakfast or not? It'll be served at eight."

"We will be there. Does my lord require us to bring a gift of fealty?"

"*Falbh a ghabhail do ghnùis airson cac.*" Yes, I told my brother to go away and take his face for a shit. He deserves it.

Jack chuckles. "We'll see you at eight."

I hang up and get to work on creating a breakfast feast for Kate and my family. Donnae think she's quite ready for a meal with the wider clan. My cousins can be... Well, let's just say they make me look sober and boring.

Kate walks into the kitchen while I'm beating eggs in a bowl. With her tousled hair and bleary eyes, she looks as if she crawled out of bed a few minutes ago. When she speaks, a yawn punctuates her words. "Morning, Callum."

"Did you just wake up, *mo leannan*?"

"Mm-hm. Wanted to take a shower, but I needed to find you first."

I rate above a shower on her list of priorities. I think I like that. "Afraid I sneaked away while you were sleeping? I wouldn't do that, *gràidh*."

"Yeah, I know." She ambles up to the counter, stopping beside me. "But I missed you."

"We slept together all night. How could you miss me?"

"Because I did. Feelings don't need justification."

"Ah, the therapist has awakened." I set down the whisk and pull her into my arms. "Time for a good morning kiss."

"Way past time."

I kiss her slowly because I've learned she loves it when I don't rush. Besides, kissing her feels too good to hurry.

When we part our mouths, she gives me a sleepy-sexy smile. "You taste like coffee."

"I made some. Want a cup?"

"Yes, please. But let me take a quick shower first."

"Have a sip before you go." I grab my mug and offer it to her. "Your morning pick-me-up."

"Mm, thank you." She takes three sips and hands the cup back to me. "Much better. Though the single best way to wake up is with you lying beside me."

"We'll do that next time."

"Can't wait to taste your cooking."

"Donnae set your expectations too high. Ahmno a gourmet chef."

"Even if you serve me gloppy eggs with half-cooked bacon, I will love it because you made the food for me."

She wanders out of the kitchen.

I love that woman.

The thought makes me freeze with the whisk in my hand. My gaze stays pinned to the doorway even after Kate disappears into the hall. I love her. That's what I just thought, and I realize I didn't mean it in an offhanded way. I shouldn't feel like this, not yet, but I cannae help it. I'm in love with Kate Wagner.

But I won't tell her that. It's too soon. Donnae want to scare her away.

I go back to making breakfast and try not to think about my revelation anymore, though it's bloody hard not to do that. I want to rush into the bathroom and jump in the shower with my clothes on to tell the lass I love her. Aye, because that wouldn't terrify her. Of course it would. *Take it slow, ye eejit, and wait until she's ready.*

Kate returns to the kitchen a wee while later with her hair still damp. She's wearing jeans and a flannel shirt that seems familiar.

"Are you wearing my shirt?" I ask.

"Yep. I didn't bring a change of clothes. Do you mind me stealing yours?"

"No. It looks better on you. Besides, I haven't worn that for ages. Left it here for the times when I stay the night after one of Ma's grand feasts."

She hunches her shoulders. "You're the first man I've slept with since my divorce. The only man I've been with besides my husband since the day I met him."

I walk over to her and pull the lass into my arms. "Forget about that *bod ceann*. You're free of him, so donnae let the *cacan* ruin any more of your life."

She snuggles into me, her chin propped on my chest. "I feel free when I'm with you. That's the best gift anyone has ever given me."

"Only because you haven't tasted my cooking yet. It's brilliant. The best meal I've ever made." I touch my lips to hers. "It's inspired by you."

"Me? Hmm, I hope it's not black pudding."

"No. I hate that rot."

"Thank goodness."

I step away and slap her erse. "Go into the dining room and wait for my masterpiece of breakfast dining. Have ye seen Ma and Da yet?"

"Yeah. They're in the dining room with Jack and his wife."

"How did they get in? I didn't hear the doorbell."

"Your parents saw them out the window and opened the door for them." Kate sashays toward the doorway, deliberately swaying her hips, and aims a teasing smile at me over her shoulder. "If your food is truly magnificent, I'll give you a gift that will make your eyes roll back in your head."

Then she disappears out the door.

Oh aye, I'm in love with that woman.

A few minutes later, I carry the first tray of food out into the dining room. Kate rubs her palms together and smiles in the most adorable way. Ma and Da seem appropriately impressed that I cooked, since I never did that when I was living at home. It's a skill I learned later when I realized it impresses the lasses if a man knows how to make at least a few dishes that aren't heated up in a microwave oven. Jack looks at me and lifts one brow, as if he's silently questioning my culinary talents. Autumn winks at me. I think that's her way of saying she believes I can create food that has no scorch marks on it and that didn't come out of a tin.

I lay down the tray and start setting the items on the table one by one, announcing them for Kate's sake. "Lorne sausage. White pudding, which I made especially for Kate, who doesn't like black pudding."

"Neither do you," Jack says. "Ye gagged the only time ye tried it."

"Donnae listen to him," I tell Kate. "Jack is a liar. He's jealous that I managed to get a girlfriend without holding her hostage."

Jack huffs. "Stealing Ma's white pudding from the refrigerator doesn't count as making it."

"Of course it does," our mother says. "He had to cook it, after all. And donnae harass your brother when he's making an effort for the sake of his lass."

"I don't care if some of the food is burned," Kate says. "But what I see so far looks yummy."

"Not done yet," I tell her as I set down another dish. "Porridge, which tastes better than the name sounds. The rowie, also called the buttery, is a kind of bread."

Kate's eyes widen. "Wow, you're really going all out. No wonder you got up so early."

I hurry back into the kitchen to get the last two items, then rush into the dining room to set each one on the table beside Kate. "Tattie scones and Scottish breakfast tea."

"Are you going to sit beside me?" she asks. "Or will you stand in the corner watching me eat?"

Rather than answering, I pull out the chair beside her and drop onto it.

"Glad you're joining me," she says. "And thank you so much for making all this food."

"I assumed you'd never experienced a full Scottish breakfast."

"You assumed right. I'd never eaten traditional Scottish food until yesterday, when your mom served us haggis and all that other yummy stuff." She takes a large bite of Lorne sausage and devours it with gusto. "Mm-mm-mm. You are one in a million, Callum. Not many men can whip up a meal like this one."

"Scotsmen can."

"Yeah, I guess I'm used to American guys who serve me hot dogs and guacamole."

"Welcome to Scotland, Kate. Here, we know how to treat a woman."

The lass goes back to eating and takes a large bite of every dish before deciding on her favorites. She eats three tattie scones, drinks two cups of tea, and enjoys an entire bowl of porridge, all while moaning with pleasure at every bite or sip she takes. I think she genuinely loves this food.

Aye, Kate Wagner is the perfect woman for me.

Now, I need to convince her of that.

After breakfast, I announce that Kate and I want to take another motorcycle day trip so she can see more of the Highlands. But Jack has a different idea. A command, actually.

"Afraid that will have to wait," he says. "We gave you time to relax yesterday, but now the radical intervention begins in earnest."

Bloody hell. I hoped everyone had forgotten about that.

Jack throws an arm around my shoulders. "You're coming back to Dùndubhan with me and Autumn. But you and Kate can travel by Harley if you prefer."

"Aye, I do prefer that. If you and I are in the car together, you'll start psychoanalyzing me and I'll strangle you. Donnae want to leave your wife to raise a child alone."

"Fair point." He slaps my arm. "You ride the Harley."

"Thank you, Jack. I needed your permission to do that, because I'm a wee laddie."

Jack lets go of me and grabs his wife, guiding her out of the house. Kate and I follow while holding hands.

Then we climb onto the bike and get on the road.

Chapter Twenty-Seven

Kate

WHEN WE GET TO DÙNDUBHAN, LOGAN AND JACK SPIRIT him away to ho knows where. Someplace inside the castle, but that's the only clue they give me. The Scots mentioned having "plans" that involve their "radical intervention" idea. I thought kidnapping Hugh and convincing me to come here was the extent of their intervention. Okay, they locked Hugh and Callum in separate rooms, but only at first. What else have they got up their sleeves today?

Autumn escorts me into the vestibule, but stops there. "Would you like to talk to Hugh? The Scots contingent wanted to toss you into Hugh's room and lock the door, but the American Wives Club talked them out of that. It's your decision, but honestly, I think he needs to hear from you."

"Is Hugh still a prisoner?"

"No. He's been free to roam the castle and the grounds, including the green. But we asked him to stay at Dùndubhan. He seemed to think he ought to go home to England."

Well, after the kidnapping thing, I can't blame him. But Autumn is right. I need to talk to Hugh and settle things between us before the MacTaggart men retake their prisoner. Autumn doesn't want to climb the stairs, but she gives me a map of the castle so I won't get lost.

"Hugh's in the tower bedroom," she says, "which is between the second and third floors. The guys wanted to lock him in until you got here, but Hugh said they didn't need to bother. I think he's a little depressed."

"I'll talk to him. Thank you, Autumn."

"Good luck."

My new friend leaves, and I trudge up the spiral staircase, bypassing the first floor on my way to the second floor. Most of this level is occupied by the long gallery, which is, predictably, a long room that extends from one side of the castle to the other. I glance out the windows as I make my way to the tower bedroom, but I can't see anything except trees and clouds. At the door to Hugh's room, I hesitate with my fist raised to knock.

What if he's mad? Well, I had told him from the get-go that I'm not attracted to him. But I do need to apologize for hiding my budding relationship with Callum.

I knock on the door.

"Come in," Hugh says, and he does sound depressed or maybe just tired.

Rolling my shoulders back, I walk into the room.

Hugh sits at the foot of the bed, feet on the floor, head bowed. He slouches, and with his elbows on his thighs, he stares down at the wood floor.

"Hi, Hugh."

The Brit's head pops up, and his gaze snaps to me, but he stays slouched there. "Good morning, Kate. How have our captors been treating you? Or am I the only prisoner?"

"You're not locked up anymore. Callum was locked up too at first, but not me."

He studies me for a moment. "Where have you and Callum been? Logan said only that you left the grounds."

"We went into the village." I shuffle over to the bed and sit down beside him. "I met his parents. We stayed the night, then Jack and Autumn joined all of us for breakfast. Callum cooked a great meal."

"Callum cooked? You must have met his doppelgänger. Cal thinks cooking means reheating Scotch pies he stole from his mother's refrigerator."

Interesting. Callum never told Hugh he can cook. I'm starting to think these two have more secrets from each other than either of them realizes. "We need to have a real conversation, Hugh. A serious one that doesn't involve flirtation."

"Yes, I figured as much."

"Are we still friends?"

"Honestly, I don't know."

"Fair enough." I start to lay a hand on his shoulder, but pull it away. He might not want me to touch him. "I'm sorry, Hugh. I should have told you I was sleeping with Callum instead of making him lie about it."

"Not your fault, pet. I should've noticed the signs. Cal isn't exactly hard to read." One side of his mouth kicks up in a sardonic smile. "Though it's clear I'm not as tuned in as I thought. My best mate had me fooled for a good while there."

"He hated keeping the truth from you. So did I. But... Oh, I shouldn't talk about that stuff."

"You can tell me anything, Kate. I'm a big boy, so I can handle it."

Well, he is taking all of this better than I expected. And I want him to understand why I kept my relationship with Callum a secret. "Okay. The thing is, I was attracted to Callum from the start. Talked myself out of believing that was true, but my subconscious couldn't deny it. Eventually, the id overcame the ego, and I lost control of my passions. Had sex with Callum in the living room of his apartment."

"That was the day I walked in and found you two behaving strangely. You ran for the bathroom, and Callum held a pillow over his lap." Hugh shuts his eyes and winces. "How did I not realize you two had been shagging just before I walked into the apartment? It was so bloody obvious."

"You trusted me, that's why you didn't see it. I vowed I did not want Callum."

"I forgive you, Kate."

"Wow, thank you. I assumed it would take longer for you to be ready to forgive and move on."

He swivels his head toward me. "I said I forgive *you*, Kate. But Callum has been my best mate for years, and he lied to me repeatedly. Swore he had no interest in you. Then I find you two had been shagging in secret, not only once, but multiple times. A man can't just let a thing like that go."

"Please don't beat the crap out of each other. Try a mature, adult approach to repairing your friendship."

"Not sure we can repair it. This was a serious betrayal."

Do I have the skills to convince him otherwise? My intuition tells me that his anger toward Callum isn't only about his best friend lying to him and sneaking around with me behind his back. Something deeper is troubling Hugh, but I've never tried to counsel someone through a crisis like this. I treat clients who have experienced injuries, not friends whose relationship has been torn asunder.

I decide my best approach is to be upfront with him. "The main reason I need to help you and Callum work things out is because I feel guilty. I'm the cause of it all, and I don't want to become the hammer that shatters your friendship."

"You are not a hammer, Kate. Callum and I did this on our own."

"Callum loves you."

Hugh smirks. "I doubt he would ever phrase it that way."

"No, but it's the truth. You guys are best friends who have a powerful bond. I think that's the main reason you're so angry with him."

"I'm angry because he's a bloody liar."

"Come on, Hugh. It's more than that." I turn toward him so I can see his profile. "Based on the things you've told me before and the way you behaved when you wanted to woo me, I think this is more about you than about me or Callum."

"How? I haven't done a ruddy thing."

"You kept struggling to win me over, even after I told you I wasn't interested. Why did you try so hard knowing your efforts would fail?"

"My efforts never fail."

Ah-hah. Finally, I have a solid clue. "Have you seriously never been turned down by a woman?"

"Only a girl or two I pursued when I was a randy teenager."

"Since then, every time you go after a woman, she falls into your arms."

He straightens and gives me a sheepish smile. "Well, yes. My dating fortunes improved vastly after I became Lord Sommerleigh. You wouldn't believe how many women want to shag a viscount."

"Uh-huh. I'm beginning to understand you at last."

"No woman has ever claimed to do that before."

"I'm a psychologist, Hugh. How many of those have you 'shagged'?"

He sighs, and his shoulders deflate. "None. I gave it my best shot, but you weren't having any of it."

"So, for the first time in all your adult life, you didn't get the girl."

"Yes." He bows his head and rubs his neck. "And the girl I lost turned out to be the only one I've ever wanted for more than a few good shags."

He means me, but he can't be saying he...loves me. I've given him no reason to feel that way, but then, emotions rarely involve logic. God, I feel horrible for him. I shouldn't have let him talk me into walks along the River Ness and picnics along its banks. But the therapist in me knows I did nothing wrong and I can't blame myself for this. It's no one's fault. As for healing the rift between Hugh and Callum, that might take a Herculean effort. I'll need more than my psychology skills to get this done. I need help from the American Wives Club, but I have a suspicion they're already working on it.

My cell phone rings. I excavate it from my pocket and answer the call.

"It's Emery, sweetie. I hope you had a good chat with Hugh because the radical intervention is about to shift into overdrive."

"Okay. Should Hugh and I go downstairs?"

"Come out to the green."

I say goodbye and stuff the phone back in my pocket. "Let's go. The American Wives Club has summoned us."

Hugh grimaces. "Do you have any idea what that lot are up to?"

"Nope. We'll find out together."

We make our way downstairs and out the vestibule door, heading straight through the walled garden and the open doorway on the other side. A crowd of people has gathered in the open, grassy area, including folks I don't recognize. I see MacTaggarts, Dixons, and Hunters who I had met on my first full day at Dùndubhan. Damian and Heidi Petrescu are here too, but they're Americans. New faces turn toward me and Hugh when we enter the green.

I notice what looks like chalk lines drawn on the grass to our left.

As we reach the small group gathered in front of the crowd, Hugh glances to our right and stops dead. His face goes blank. "Is that a shinty pitch?"

Jack MacTaggart chuckles. "Aye. Do ye know how to play shinty?"

"No. I'm British. Why in hell would I know about a Scottish sport?"

"Because you're best mates with a Scot."

"We never played shinty."

Jack approaches Hugh and thumps him on the back. "Donnae worry. We'll give you a crash course. But first, we have other events arranged for you and Callum."

"Events?"

Hugh looks genuinely nervous, and I can't blame him. If shinty is for later, what on earth do they plan on doing with Callum and Hugh right now?

Jack keeps a hand on Hugh's back as he urges the Brit to follow him into the crowd. Men and women move aside to make room for them. They move aside quite a bit. I wonder what they're about to do that needs a lot of space, but then I see what's going on. The crowd has spread out to reveal furniture set up on the grass—two tables, one long and rectangular and another small and round. Some kind of partition has been set up in the center of the long table, but the smaller one has a crimson velvet tablecloth spread over it and a crystal ball seated at its center. Two chairs flank the round table. Another chair sits at the nearest end of the long table, but two seats have been positioned at the opposite end on either side.

Kirsty MacTaggart and Damian Petrescu approach the small table, each taking a seat.

Luke Turner ambles over to the long table and sets a small suitcase on it. He unzips the bag and starts removing items from it—a laptop, electrodes, a blindfold, and some other electronic doohickeys I don't recognize.

Jack raises his arms and shouts, "Quiet, please."

All remaining murmurs from the crowd cease.

"Everything is ready," Jack announces. "The radical intervention is about to begin."

Chapter Twenty-Eight

Hugh

AM I FRIGHTENED? NO. DESPITE JACK'S ANNOUNCEMENT, I do not give a toss about whatever he and his cohorts plan to do to me. They mean to chase me away from Kate, I'm sure, but they needn't bother. I know Kate doesn't want me. Maybe she's right that my anger toward Callum isn't about her and has more to do with how I view myself.

Doesn't matter. Callum is a lying *cacan*. Yes, I've learned some Gaelic after years of friendship with a Scot. Am I jealous that he got the girl? No, of course not. I am not upset because, for the first time, I haven't gotten what I wanted—who I wanted. That's rubbish.

I glance at the two tables set up in front of us. "Electrodes and a crystal ball? What do mean to do, rearrange our brains and then tell us our fortunes?"

"The crystal ball is strictly decorative," Damian Petrescu says. "Kirsty and I have something else in mind."

"Yes, whatever. Would you lot get on with your barmy plan?"

Luke Turner waves at his long table. "Have a seat at the other end, and we'll get started."

Callum and I take the chairs at the far end. The way these lunatics have arranged things, we're forced to face each other. I have a mind to move my chair, but I suspect Logan or one of his clan will rearrange me against my will.

Luke rises to approach us and attach electrodes to our fingers. "You guys are all set."

"For what?" I demand.

He chuckles. "You'll see."

Luke returns to his end of the table and brings out his laptop computer. He taps the key and moves his fingers over the touch pad, seeming engrossed by his task. Finally, he lifts his head. "Ready to go. I'll measure your skin conductance response while you two talk through your issues."

"Talk? That's your amazing plan?"

"I'm a psychophysicist. That means I'm qualified to assess your mental state and measure the physics of your reactions."

"Wonderful."

"Time to start talking. Hugh, why don't you go first? Tell Callum why you're mad at him."

I snort. "Why? He knows the answer."

Callum folds his arms over his chest. "Aye, I know. You are an arrogant *tolla-thon* who's pouting because, for once, you lost."

"You cheated. Seducing Kate behind my back was—"

"*Falbh dàirich fhein* because nobody else will."

Yes, he just told me to go fuck myself. Lovely.

I fold my arms, mirroring his pose, though I didn't do that on purpose. "You knew I liked Kate, and you swore you had no interest in her. 'She's a harpy,' you said. 'Save me, Hugh.' I rushed to Scotland to help *you*."

"When did I beg you to save me?" He jabs a finger in my direction. "Never, that's when. Yer off yer head, ye *bod ceann*. The only reason you're angry is because Kate wants me."

The woman herself stomps over to our table, halting at the end. She plants her hands on the surface. "Does either of you care what I think? Or would you rather measure your dicks?"

"It's his fault," Callum says while glaring at me. "Hugh cannae stand that a woman chose me over him."

"Please," I say in my most sarcastic tone. "I could get her back anytime, but I didn't want to rob you of your one and only victory."

"Ye bloody erse—"

"Shut up!" Kate shouts. "Somebody grab a ruler. Let's get the measuring done with."

"Don't bother," I say. "Countless women can testify that I have an enormous—"

"Zip it, Hugh." Kate glances at my nemesis, and one corner of her mouth curls up in a slight smirk. "I know exactly what kind of equipment Callum has."

Luke Turner laughs and slaps his palms together. "Damn, this is amazing. Never seen results like this before. Both of you are displaying psychological signals like nothing I've ever measured. You guys get each other more aroused than any of my previous subjects."

"I am not aroused," I snarl.

"Relax, buddy. I'm not talking about sex. It's emotional arousal."

"Thank you for stating the obvious. An argument is emotionally stimulating. Aren't you a genius?"

Luke glances at Damian. "I think my job is done. Your turn."

"Get off your erses, laddies," Logan says. "Carry your chairs over to the other table."

I stand up. "We have to move furniture for you? I knew there was an ulterior motive."

"Do it or I will skelp ye both myself."

Callum and I exchange nasty looks as we relocate our chairs to the little round table, sitting across from each other again. Kirsty and Damian haven't moved an inch, both seated sideways to me and Callum.

"Here's how this part of the intervention will work," Damian says. "Kirsty will access her *da-shealladh* to get a bead on you while I read your palm."

I glance at Kirsty, then Damian. "She will access her what?"

"*Da-shealladh*. It's Scottish Gaelic for second sight."

"Ohhh, so we've moved on to the complete bollocks portion of the day's festivities."

Callum glowers at me. "Donnae insult my cousin. Wouldnae kill you to be more open-minded."

"You can't honestly tell me you believe in this nonsense."

"Maybe not, but I respect Kirsty's beliefs."

"This is ridiculous." I half rise from my chair. "I'm done with this carnival of Scottish lunacy."

"Sit down," Logan commands, and even from fifteen feet away, he projects menace. "Or are ye wanting us to tie you to the chair and tape your mouth shut?"

I drop back onto my chair. Not because I'm intimidated. No, I've simply decided there's no point in arguing.

Damian grabs my hand, turning it over to expose the palm. "Now just relax."

"With a crowd staring at me?"

Callum huffs. "Since when are you shy?"

"Shut your trap," Damian tells Callum. "Palmistry is a delicate art."

The self-proclaimed gypsy starts exploring my palm with his fingertips, swirling them around and tracing the line of every crease in my skin. "You've got air hands."

I grunt.

Damian glances up at me while keeping his head down. "That means you're naturally curious and excel at critical thinking."

"Well, maybe palm reading isn't bollocks after all."

"But you're also easily distracted, and if you don't get frequent stimulation, you become irritable and anxious."

Callum laughs. "Aye, that's Hugh for dead certain."

I glower at my former best mate. "This is rot."

"Oh, wow," Damian says. "Look at your Mount of Venus. It's pronounced, which means you're very sensual and passionate."

"Now that's more like it."

Damian clucks his tongue. "Your head line tells me you have a lot of lessons to learn. And this little break in that line suggests upheaval coming your way, but also a potential revelation about your life path."

"Are you done yet?"

"Yep." He releases my hand. "It's Kirsty's turn now."

The bonnie Scots lass folds her hands on the table and looks straight at me. "I've seen your future. You will lose what you believed you needed most, but a new opportunity will arise, one that will test your confidence and force you to reexamine your choices."

"Thank you for the cryptic yet annoying prediction."

Damian and Kirsty rise and start to walk away.

"Wait," I call out. "You haven't done your mystical rubbish with Callum."

Damian grins. "We gave him a private reading. You're the one causing all the spiritual mayhem, so you needed to have your reading done in front of everyone."

Logan stalks over to us. "Get up off your erses. It's time for the main event."

Callum stands up.

I stay in my chair. "Forget it. I'm done."

Logan shoves his arms under mine and hoists me out of the chair. Before I can react, Rory MacTaggart rushes over to help Logan by grasping my ankles. The pair of them carry me through the crowd and dump me on the grass near the shinty pitch they've created with chalk. Though I sit up, I stay on the ground and glare up at the two wankers who dropped me here.

Rory kneels in front of me. "Time for shinty."

"I don't know the rules."

He pats my head. "Donnae worry. We're going to give you a crash course."

Oh yes, this will be a completely fair match. I've seen how the Mac-Taggarts play shinty. Rules are a myth to them.

I am going to die.

Chapter Twenty-Nine

Callum

WATCH FROM THE SIDELINES AS MY COUSINS GIVE HUGH A quick introduction to the rules of shinty. Not that MacTaggarts give a toss about rules. We play like a clan of cavemen and always aim to win, whatever the cost. Injuring another player is one of the few things that will get a lad booted off the field, but only if he caused the injury on purpose.

Since we have so few rules, it shouldn't take more than a minute or two to explain them to Hugh. It's been longer than that. The *cacan* is probably moaning about how unfair it is to throw him into a shinty match when he's never played the sport before.

Finally, Hugh and my cousins approach the pitch.

The British contingent separates from the crowd, every man kissing his wife before heading over here.

"What's this?" Hugh asks.

Logan claps him on the shoulder. "They're here to fill out the teams."

"You get the huge monsters you call cousins, and I'm stuck with the runts who have never played shinty before."

I shake my head at Hugh. "Ye assume we'll cheat, donnae ye?"

Hugh huffs. "Why shouldn't I think that? You cheated with Kate."

"Silence, ye *baothairean*," Logan says in a soft yet threatening tone. He's calling us both idiots. "Each team will include Scots and Brits. And before ye complain again, I'll tell ye the Dixons and Hunters have learned the game. Even Bennett Montague, the former crown prince of Mithoria, is familiar with shinty."

"Oh, perfect," Hugh says. "At least Nick and Ben are massage therapists, so they can treat our torn ligaments after the match."

A woman storms out of the crowd. Kate halts near us and glances at me and Hugh in turn. "I never cheated with anyone. Hugh, it's not my fault you refused to believe me the fifty times I told you I'm not attracted to you."

I cannae help smirking. "Aye, you tell him, Kate."

"Oh, you are not blameless here. You're trying to make Hugh angry."

"Donnae need to try. He's so bloody sensitive that even a palm reading fashes him."

Hugh starts to speak, but Kate silences him by throwing a hand up. "None of this radical intervention stuff was my idea, but I think it's exactly what both of you need. Go on, beat the shit out of each other on the shinty field."

"It's called a pitch," I say. "Not a field."

"Whatever."

She spins around and marches back to the crowd, standing there with Emery on one side and Autumn on the other. The rest of the American Wives Club join them.

Logan announces who will play on each team, but he carefully chooses half Scots and half Brits on each side.

Rory strips his shirt off over his head and tosses it away.

"Taps off?" I say.

My cousin grins like the devil himself. "Not only taps off. This will be a nude shinty match."

Hugh's jaw drops. "Nude? You're completely off your rocker."

I shed my clothes. "If ye cannae handle it, princess, ye can back out."

He squints at me. "Oh, I can handle it."

"Go on, then. Show us you're not a coward."

While still squinting at me, Hugh ditches all his clothes. He spreads his arms wide. "The full monty it is."

The rest of my cousins, as well as my brother Jack and the Brits, remove their clothes too.

And the American Wives Club cheers. Emery shoves two fingers from each hand into her mouth and blows the loudest, shrillest whistle I've ever heard.

Kate's gaze veers to mine. She lifts her brows and nods toward Hugh. Then she mouths, "Be good."

I'm always good, and Kate knows it. But she really doesn't understand how MacTaggarts play shinty.

Whoever set up the pitch has placed makeshift goal posts at either end. They're actually tennis nets, but that doesn't matter. We just need a place to aim our strikes at so we can count our goals.

"There's a problem," I say as I survey the crowd. "We don't have enough men. Shinty needs twelve on each side including two goalkeepers."

"Not enough MacTaggarts?" Logan says with a chuckle. "You know better than that."

My cousin Evan jogs out of the garden door and shouts, "They're here."

Evan scans the group of Scots and Brits gathered over here, and his brows draw together. "Why are you lot naked?"

"It was Damian's idea," Logan says. "Callum and Hugh need to learn a wee bit of humility. Besides, we're more aerodynamic without our clothes."

Aye, that statement might sound like a joke to anyone outside my family. But MacTaggarts know that aerodynamics are vital in a shinty match since we do whatever it takes to win. It's not unheard of to see our players flying through the air to make a goal or tackle an opponent. That's shinty the MacTaggart way.

Our teams wind up not fifty-fifty Brits and Scots, but Hugh has the sense to haud his wheesht about that. We are in Scotland, after all, where Brits aren't easy to come by.

The lasses from the American Wives Club carry our playing sticks over to us. Each *caman* is about three and a half feet long with a curved end, sort of like a hockey stick. I explain this to Kate when she brings my *caman* to me. The lass kisses me full on the mouth while Hugh is watching us. Maybe she means to pound it into his thick British skull that she doesn't want him and never did. Or maybe she just means to wish me luck.

"Kick their asses," she says. "Especially Hugh's."

"Why especially him? I thought you liked Hugh—as a mate."

"I do. But he needs something big to knock sense into him."

Grinning, I thump my *caman* on my palm. "It's a dead certainty I'll be knocking things into and out of Hugh."

"Don't break his teeth or his nose. He has such nice bone structure."

Kate walks away.

I admire her erse until she turns around, taking up her position among the American lasses to watch the match.

Both teams walk onto the pitch and take up their positions. Gavin Douglas, my cousin Jamie's husband, is the goalkeeper for my team while Luke Turner winds up as the goalkeeper for Hugh's lot. Since we have three American blokes here, they tossed a coin to decide which two would join the match. Damian lost, but everyone agreed he should be our referee. In MacTaggart shinty, the referee doesn't intervene unless a grievous injury is imminent. Who needs all those rules? Not us.

Erica, Lachlan's wife, carries the ball out to the pitch and hands it to Damian. Then she hurries back to the crowd. Though Damian is only the referee, he opted to ditch his clothes too. That's hardly a surprise. He is a nudist, after all, and works at a naturist resort.

I think all the lasses should go nude too. Strictly to be fair.

But then Hugh would get to see all of Kate. On second thought, the lasses should stay clothed.

We all gather on the pitch with each team forming a group to discuss strategy. I donnae see why we need to do that. The strategy is to beat the other team by any means necessary.

"Aim for Hugh as often as ye can," I say to Lachlan, our team leader.

"Do we want to win?" he asks. "Or is the goal to thrash your best mate?"

"Both. Nothing will gut him more than to lose to my team."

"All right. It's no holds barred, full-on MacTaggart shinty. Are we all agreed?"

The entire team nods their approval.

I plan to thrash Hugh. My best mate. I mean to humiliate him. But is that really what I want to do? Jack and I talked earlier—as brothers, not psychologist and client—and he suggested I'm not angry with Hugh. Jack thinks I have an inferiority complex about my best mate because I believe he always gets the girl. It's a fact that he does, but Jack might have a wee bit of a point. I expect women to bypass me on their way to Hugh, and maybe I haven't tried hard enough with the lasses because of that.

Not anymore. I won Kate without any tricks. She chose me.

So, why am I about to thrash Hugh? I'll think about that later.

We take up our positions on the pitch, with Gavin as our goalkeeper. A coin toss decides whose side will make the first strike, and Damian tosses me the ball. One by one, each player wields his *caman* and prepares for the match to begin.

Damian shouts, "Ready! Set! Go!"

I whack the ball, sending it flying toward the opposing team.

And the battle commences.

The ball flies back and forth, here and there, racing across the field in a haphazard fashion as players maneuver it, focused on weaving through the crowd to make a goal. Hugh almost gets one, but Jack hits the ball in the opposite direction. Aye, Jack is on my team. My brother wouldn't aid the enemy.

"Go, Team Callum!"

I glance at the crowd and see Kate, who still has her hands cupped around her mouth as a makeshift megaphone. None of us had named our team, but Kate did it for us. Not sure my cousins and mates would appreciate the team being named after me. We're all playing hard.

My cousin Aidan, who volunteered to play for Hugh's team, ducks around Lachlan, aiming to hit a goal. But I cut him off and steal the ball away from him, heading back toward the other goal post.

Someone slams into me from the side and uses a *caman* to knock me off my feet. I glance up to find Hugh standing over me with a wicked smirk on his face.

"I played rugby at university," he says. "That's a real sport. Shinty is what Scots invented because you're all too incompetent to handle rugby."

He's insulting my home and my family. No, I cannae let that one go.

The game has kept going around us, so I spring to my feet and rush back into the fray. No one needs to ask if I want to make the first goal to get back at Hugh. They start switching the ball between them to keep the other team from getting it, and we wend our way toward the goal post. Hugh tries to trip me again, but I slam my shoulder into his to knock him off balance just long enough for Jack to pass the ball to me.

I whack it into the net.

Cheers and whoops erupt from the crowd of spectators.

"Yay, Callum!" Kate shouts. "You rock!"

I cannae resist smirking at Hugh.

He glowers at me.

The game goes on, and Hugh's team makes two goals. But then Team Callum scores two more, giving us three total. My cousins bump into each other on purpose, though they're careful not to hurt each other. Everyone on the pitch is having a bloody good time—except for me and Hugh. We have a grudge to settle between us, though I can't say for sure why. I need to beat him, to prove he doesn't always win. What does Hugh want? Kate, but he knows he's lost that battle. What else does he hope to gain?

We take a break to drink water and recover from the MacTaggart version of shinty. We're all sweating. Since we're naked, we can't wipe our faces dry with our shirts. Emery and Erica, the wives of Rory and Lachlan, rush out to hand each player a towel.

Of course the American Wives Club thought of that. Those lasses have a talent for planning—and for plotting.

The break ends, and we take the field once again.

Hugh starts the match this time, hitting the ball so hard it smacks into Iain's shin. As the oldest man on either team, he seems the most likely to get injured, but Iain never lets hardship get him down. He brushes off the strike without even flinching and hits the ball, sending it sailing through the air.

It lands a few yards from the goal post.

Evan tries to get the ball, but Rory knocks it away from him.

The ball is rolling straight toward me. If I can hit it just right, I'll make another goal. So I dodge around other players, intent on regaining control of the ball. I've just taken it away from Logan, and I'm pulling my *caman* back to swing at the ball, when a large weight slams into me from behind. I stumble and drop to the ground.

Pain stabs through my knee.

"Stop!" Kate shouts. "Stop! He's injured."

Every player on the pitch freezes—except for Hugh. He hits the ball, and it sails across the field to smack into the goal net.

"Time out," Damian declares. "Man down."

Hugh raises his stick above his head, grinning. But his triumphant expression disintegrates when he notices no one else, not even a single member of his team, is cheering for him. They all stare at him with expressions that run the gamut from confusion to disgust.

Jack offers me his hand, helping me get up. He aims a hard look at Hugh. "Donnae be celebrating when ye injured my brother."

Hugh swallows hard, the movement visible in his throat. "I thought that was how you lot played the game."

"We donnae hurt anyone. Especially a player who has a previous injury. You of all people know Callum suffered a serious accident earlier this year."

Jack is exaggerating. My accident wasn't that serious.

Kate runs onto the pitch, pushing past men who are much larger than she is, seeming desperate to reach me. She drops to her knees beside me. I've just sat up, but when I move to stand, she slaps a hand on my chest to stop me.

"I need to examine your knee," she says. Then she throws her arms around me. "I was so worried you got hurt even worse this time."

"No, I'm all right, *mo leannan.*"

Knowing she cares that much makes me feel like I could lift the whole bloody castle on my shoulders, just for her.

But Hugh needs to pay.

Chapter Thirty

Kate

I PALPATE CALLUM'S KNEE TO TEST HOW BAD HIS INJURY might be, but he barely flinches when I do that. Hugh had slammed into him so hard. I can't believe Callum's knee didn't get blown out completely, but I almost cry when I realize he can still walk. His brother and one of his cousins help him get to his feet, but he manages to move okay without their help. I ask him to keep walking back and forth so I can assess his gait.

He limps at first, but that eases up the more he moves.

The relief I feel seems incongruous with what just happened. When men play sports, they get knocked down. They get injured. It's par for the course, but I nearly screamed when I saw Callum go down. My heart is still racing, and I feel slightly nauseous, but I resist the impulse to pull him into my arms and order him to stop this match right now. Me panicking? I've never done that before. Well, except for the time years ago when a weatherman on TV announced that a tornado was heading straight for the street where I lived. My husband, now my ex, had called me an idiot for trying to make him go into the basement with me. The tornado missed us, but to this day I feel justified in freaking out back then.

Callum would never call me stupid. He would go into the basement with me and not even ask why we were doing that. God, I love him.

Holy shit. Did I just realize how I really feel about Callum? Yeah, I did. I'm in love with him. Don't care that we haven't known each other long. I refuse to overanalyze my feelings. As a therapist, I know that I need to allow myself to experience every emotion without trying to talk myself out of accepting each one before I've even taken time to process things.

Callum halts in front of me. "Well? Do I have my therapist's permission to continue the match?"

"Yes. It doesn't look like you seriously injured yourself." I can't stop myself from hugging him and kissing his cheek. "Good luck. And be careful."

He chuckles. "Ye donnae understand the MacTaggart way of playing shinty."

"Fair enough. At least try not to break any bones or snap any ligaments."

"I'll do my best."

Damian and Lachlan approach us.

"We've decided to end the match," Lachlan says. "With two caveats."

"That's right," Damian says. "It seems only fair to let Callum have the last try at a goal. Hugh's last one has been invalidated, and only the two of them will play the last round. Whichever one gets the first goal wins."

Hugh marches over to us. "Invalidated? That was a bloody fantastic goal."

Damian shakes his head. "You trampled your opponent to make that shot. The MacTaggarts might not have many rules about shinty, but Lachlan assured me that taking advantage of another player's injury is one of the rules they enforce."

"Only because you lot are all on Callum's side."

I stomp over to Hugh. "You're being a monumental jackass. Stop it before you lose every friend you've made here, not just Callum. His entire family wants to help you. That's what all this craziness has been about—saving your friendship with Callum. Don't burn that bridge, Hugh, please."

He stares at me for a moment, like he can't decide what to do. Then he rubs his eyes and exhales a long sigh. "I know you're right. I've behaved horribly ever since I got here. If I'm honest with myself, I was glad when these people kidnapped me. I don't want to ruin my relationship with my best mate, but I got caught up in...those things you and I discussed earlier."

"Yeah, I get it. End this match honorably. Please."

He nods and walks into the center of the pitch. "I'm in if Callum is."

Callum strides up to Hugh. "Just the two of us. Whoever makes the first goal wins."

They shake hands.

Everyone vacates the pitch. I stand on the sideline, hands clasped under my chin, and remind myself to keep breathing. If I pass out from lack of oxygen, I might miss the winning goal. Callum will be victorious. I know it.

Damian takes a deep breath and hollers, "Ready! Set! Go!"

Lachlan tosses the ball onto the field, and the players vie for control of it. Callum gets it first and dances around Hugh to avoid letting the Brit steal the ball away from him. Hugh finally snags it and pushes it toward the opposite end of the field. But Callum races past him, spins around, and whacks the ball away from Hugh's *caman*, sending it soaring in the other direction.

The ball crashes into the net.

"It's a goal!" Damian shouts. "Callum MacTaggart wins the match!"

Can't control myself. I leap up and down while shrieking, though I've never done anything like this before. I'm so thrilled Callum won that the joy bursts out of me. I race onto the pitch and hurl my entire body at Callum.

He catches me, lifting my feet off the ground, and we kiss. With tongue. In fact, what we're doing might qualify as public lewdness. Good thing nobody brought their kiddies to the battleground today.

The man I love sets me down but keeps one arm around me.

Hugh comes up to us and offers his hand to Callum. "The best man won. Congratulations, mate."

Callum accepts Hugh's hand. "Are we still mates? Havenae been sure lately."

"I know, and that's my fault. I'm sorry, Callum. Should never have let my pride nearly destroy our friendship."

"We can talk about that later." Callum rolls his eyes toward the crowd. "When the whole clan isn't listening in."

The two men amble off the field while Callum keeps hold of my hand. I doubt one handshake has repaired the massive rift in their relationship, but it's a start. I believe they will work it all out and be best friends again, but not overnight. Hugh has some serious issues to deal with, and I somehow need to convince him to tell Callum about that.

Sure, no problem. Because men love to share their feelings.

Damian and Luke lead us back to the two tables set up on the green.

"Ready for round two?" Luke asks. "Let's see what triggers your anger toward each other, so you guys can work out your differences as self-aware men instead of boneheaded morons."

I like Luke more every time I hear him speak—because he tells the truth. His tone is never snide or mean. He says it like it is, but with a smile and humor. Kirsty told me that Luke used to be a "flaming ersehole," but that she helped him deal with his old issues. Now, he's once again the man she fell for more than a decade ago. They're getting married soon.

Callum responds to Luke's challenge first. "I'll do it. Hugh won't, since he doesn't want to suffer another public defeat."

"This isn't a competition," Luke says. "It's a therapeutic technique."

"Public therapy? Never heard of that."

"We invented it just for you two."

Hugh rolls his eyes. "And we're so bloody grateful. Is this compulsory? If I'm going to be imprisoned again, I'll skip the public humiliation."

"You can walk away now," Luke says. "But maybe first you should think about what it might do to your friendship with Callum. How much does that matter to you?"

Callum and Hugh look at each other. The Scot lifts one brow. The Brit puckers his lips.

But then Hugh smiles and thumps Callum on the back. "If you can handle this bollocks, I can do it too. Male pride be damned."

The man I love grins. "Let's see if we can break Luke's equipment."

"I hope you mean his electronic equipment."

"Oh aye, that too."

They're both smirking, which I take as a positive sign. Men who joke together stay together, right? That's been my experience.

Luke smirks right back at the Scot and the Brit. "My equipment will survive just fine—all my equipment. Will the two jackasses take a seat now?"

The jackasses do just that. Now seated opposite each other at the far end of the table, both men clasp their hands on the tabletop.

"All right," Luke says. "My lovely assistant will place the electrodes on your fingers now."

He waves a hand, and Kirsty emerges from the crowd.

She collects the electrodes from Luke, then attaches them to the fingers of Callum and Hugh. "You're ready to go. And so you know, this isn't a con or a sham. Luke uses these techniques on subjects who need help understanding and dealing with their emotions."

"He has an office in Loch Fairbairn," Callum tells Hugh. "The bloke actually wants to spend his days experimenting on people who have emotional issues."

"Shush, Callum," I say. "Let Luke do what he does and give it a real chance. For me. Okay? That also goes for you, Hugh."

Both men nod.

Luke waves for me to approach him.

I halt beside his chair.

"Mind helping me out here?" Luke asks. "I think this might work best if you ask the questions while I monitor their responses."

"Good idea."

"You can take this chair. I'll stand."

"Actually, I think it's best if I stand at the other end of the table, right in front of those two."

Luke grins. "I like the way you think."

"Do you have a list of questions you want me to ask? Or should I wing it?"

"No list. Do your own thing, Kate."

I march down to the opposite end of the table and position myself there, facing the other end, with Callum and Hugh at either side of me. "Okay, boys. I hope you're ready for the final stage of the radical intervention. I will not be coddling your egos. It's time to get over yourselves and work through your issues."

Both men veer their attention to me. Callum's lips quirk up at the corners, but Hugh rolls his eyes.

I cross my arms over my chest. "Callum, why are you angry with Hugh?"

"We've been through this before."

"You told *me*. Now I want you to say it to Hugh."

Callum slumps in his chair and twists his mouth into a stubborn expression I saw a lot during our private therapy sessions. "Make him go first. He's the problem."

"You first. Tell Hugh why you've been angry with him. Now, Callum."

"Because he's a self-important *tolla-thon*."

"Address him, not me. Be specific."

Callum aims his gaze at Hugh. "Since Kate insists, I will tell you why you're a monumental *tolla-thon*."

"Oh, this ought to be good."

"Aye, it will be." Callum straightens and makes hand gestures to punctuate his statements. "You installed yourself in my apartment like you owned the bloody place. I didnae ask you to come here, but you did it anyway. Not to help me. To make yourself feel important."

"I installed myself?" Hugh says. "That wasn't even your apartment. It belongs to your cousin Evan. And you practically begged me to save you from the American Wives Club. I flew here because you wanted me to."

"Yer bum's oot the windae. You did what you always do—made yourself the hero and the center of attention."

The men start shouting at each other, their words overlapping so I can't sort out any of it, especially when Callum spouts Gaelic phrases.

I slam my hands down on the tabletop. "Quiet!"

Hugh and Callum freeze with their mouths open, their complaints lodged in their throats.

"That's better." I keep my palms on the table and glance at each man in turn. "Since you two seem incapable of articulating your grievances like rational adults, I'll tell you what your problem is."

Hugh lifts one brow. "You make it sound like we both share the same issues."

"Of course you do. Now shut up and listen." I straighten, eying the pair of them with what I hope seems like a determined expression. I'm starting to feel like a schoolteacher stuck with two bickering boys. "Callum, you are jealous of Hugh."

The Brit smirks.

"Don't get cocky yet, Lord Jackass," I say. "Because you are jealous of Callum too."

"What? You're off your trolley."

"Callum, tell Hugh exactly why you envy him." When Callum gives me a mulish look, I lean in to stare into his eyes from an inch away. "You know what I mean, so do it. Tell him the truth."

Chapter Thirty-One

Callum

I LOVE KATE, BUT SHE HAS LOST HER MIND TODAY. TELL Hugh what I think of him? That won't help, so there's no point in doing what she wants. Maybe I have been sort of, slightly, only a wee bit jealous of him. Hugh always gets the girl. That was what I believed for a long time, so I assumed Kate would go for him and not me, even after we had sex. But she chose me.

Why am I still fashed about Hugh? I should be over it now that I've recognized my issues—or whatever rubbish psychologists call it.

"Tell him," Kate repeats. She lowers her voice to barely a whisper and adds, "Please do this for me."

Cannae say no to Kate.

So I clear my throat and gaze at the space just to the left of Hugh. "You always get the girl, and I've been feeling, ah, sort of off my game when you're around."

"You've been feeling impotent."

"No, I am not—*Bod an Donais*. It's still my turn to tell you what a raging erse you are."

"Fine. Have at it."

"I used to like going to clubs with you to meet lasses, but lately, all you care about is getting women into your bed."

"What has that got to do with anything?"

I shake my head. "You've changed. We used to have fun together, but now I feel like I cannae tell ye anything. All you want to do is shag women and pretend you're having a brilliant time. When you went after Kate, it had nothing to do with her. You were trying to prove you're still Lord Steamy."

"Pretend? I do not need to deceive anyone. I'm so sorry that you have less luck with the ladies than I do, but that's not my problem."

Kate claps her hands twice. "Your turn, Hugh. Tell Callum what's bothering you."

"It's bloody obvious."

"So tell him."

Hugh leans back in his chair, chin lifted. "You swore you didn't even like Kate, that she was a harpy. Then you shagged her behind my back. You lied to me."

"Not on purpose. I didn't know I was attracted to Kate. It just... happened."

Kate smacks her palms on the tabletop. "Stop making this about me. If you want to go inside to discuss this in private, that's fine. But Callum, you need to be honest with Hugh about why you feel inadequate."

"Why did you announce that to the whole family?"

"You agreed to public therapy. But like I said, we can move this to a room inside the castle."

Hugh lifts one shoulder in a casual shrug. "If you can't handle public therapy..."

"I can handle it." But I need a moment to drum up the nerve to say this in front of Hugh and everyone. Only Kate knows. She's right, though, that I need to deal with the real issue. "I never felt inferior to you until after the accident."

The man who used to be my best mate just stares at me without blinking.

"I was the Super Kitten Man," I say. "A joke. The damn eejit who froze during a crisis and almost got a mate and an elderly woman killed. But it's all right. I saved the kittens. So what if I became the butt of every joke in the Highlands? I felt like a fool."

"No one thought that," Hugh says. "You're always too hard on yourself. But that doesn't explain why you hid your relationship with Kate and lied to me about it."

Kate gives me an encouraging smile.

Well, if I'm doing this, I might as well go all the way. "Before I met Kate, I hadn't had sex in almost nine months."

Everyone is staring at me now.

"After the accident," I say, "everyone treated me like I was a bairn who needed help to go to the bog. Jack kept telling me to get therapy, and you kept telling me to get laid. Didnae want to do either one. Being the Super Kitten Man was the most humiliating thing that had ever happened to me."

"I'm sorry you felt that way, Cal," Hugh says. "But you never told me any of it. And why would your accident make you envious of me?"

"Because you have everything. Money, status, women, mates. You work because you want to, not because you need to."

"Maybe I had more luck with women than you did, but you were my only real mate."

It's my turn to stare at him. "But you always had people around you. Every time we went to a club together, men and women gathered around you like flies to honey. And you've got the Dixons and Hunters as your mates."

"Yes, people gathered." Hugh rests one elbow on the table and sighs. "I didn't know those men and women. They only spoke to me at clubs and other public venues where they would be seen with me—seen with a viscount. They didn't give a stuff about me. The Dixons and Hunters are mates, but I'm not particularly close to them. Maybe that's my fault because I expect everyone to want something from me and keep my distance to protect myself."

Could all of that be true? I don't believe Hugh would lie about it. Maybe I had misunderstood what his life is like.

Kate rests her erse on the table's edge. "That was excellent, Callum. I know it couldn't have been easy to expose yourself that way."

"Actually, I feel sort of...better."

"Glad to hear it." She points a finger at Hugh. "Your turn."

"I already said my piece."

"But you haven't talked about the real issue."

He groans. "I'm getting bloody sick of hearing the word issues. But I will do my bit."

"Tell Callum the truth."

Hugh squirms and makes a face. "The truth is that I'm not actually angry with you, Callum. I'm experiencing something that has never happened to me before."

"What's that?" I ask.

"I couldn't get the girl. Kate kept telling me she wasn't attracted to me and that she didn't want a relationship. I believed her, but I also believed I could convince her otherwise." He squirms again and scratches the back of his neck. "If I want a woman, I get her. Seduction is my forte. Kate rebuffed me at every turn, but then she slept with you."

"Don't blame Kate."

"I wouldn't do that. The problem isn't that she chose you over me. It's that I failed, and you succeeded." He plants both elbows on the table and cradles his forehead in his raised palms. "I *failed*, Callum. That's never happened before, and it's knocked me off balance."

"You've both done very well," Kate says. "But there's one more obstacle. You need to confess your lies to each other."

Hugh snaps upright. "I have never lied."

"Oh please. Doesn't take a genius to figure out you two have been keeping things from each other for a long time. If you want to save your friendship, confess."

"Cal can go first."

Kate sweeps an arm toward me. "Go on."

It's my turn to squirm. "First of all, I hate being called Cal."

Hugh's eyes go wide. "What?"

"You heard me. I hate that nickname."

"Why didn't you tell me?"

I shrug one shoulder. "Didnae want to hurt your feelings."

He sinks back in his chair. "All right. Lay the rest on me."

"Well...I know how to cook."

"Kate mentioned you made a meal for her, but I assumed it was store-bought food."

"No. I made it from scratch."

Hugh gawps at me like he's never seen me before. "You have never cooked anything. All you do is nick Scotch pies from your mother's kitchen and reheat them in the microwave."

"That's partly true. I do sometimes get those pies from my mother when I don't feel like making them myself." I scratch my cheek. "But I do well enough on my own. Ask Kate. I made a right feast for breakfast."

"It's true," Kate says. "Callum is an amazing cook."

Hugh is still gawping. "But you never told me, Cal—Callum."

"Didnae mean to lie, but you were so proud of your cooking skills that I thought it was best to keep mine to myself." I wave a finger toward him. "Your turn. What lies have you told?"

"I hate your Harley. It's enormous, ugly, and outrageously loud."

"Anything else?"

Hugh bows his head for a moment, then faces me. "I wanted to hurt you on the shinty pitch today. Thought it would make me feel better, but it didn't. And I felt awful about what I'd done as soon as I'd done it."

"I know. And I forgive you."

"There's one more thing. I've been jealous of you for a long time, though I didn't realize it until Kate and I had a chat earlier."

"Jealous? Why? You're the Viscount Sommerleigh."

Hugh slouches in his chair, seeming deflated in every way. "But you have a family, the sort that I thought only existed in films or books. You all look out for each other and help each other. My family are proper English aristocrats. We don't hug. And when my father died, none of us cried. We maintained our stiff upper lips."

"You are a MacTaggart, Hugh. An honorary one, if you want that."

"I doubt your family would want it."

"Ye donnae know my family if you believe that." I rise and spread my arms. Then I shout, "Is Hugh Parrish an honorary MacTaggart?"

A chorus of ayes erupts around us. Several people whoop, and at least two whistle.

Jack walks up to slap my arm. "Any mate of yours is family to us too."

Is Hugh's lip trembling? And could those be tears in his eyes? I've never seen Hugh look so emotional before.

But he brushes it off swiftly and stands up to address the crowd. "Thank you. I'm happy to be a member of the barmiest clan on earth. May we all be crackers together."

Of course he has to be sarcastic. That's Hugh.

Every MacTaggart claps or cheers or whoops.

To know Hugh has been jealous of me eases some of my guilt. We've both assumed the other has a perfect life and perfect family, but perfection doesn't exist. We need to stop blaming ourselves for not having everything we want and instead look for ways to improve our own lives. I tell Kate and Hugh that as the three of us walk through the garden and across the driveway, on our way to the vestibule door.

Kate kisses my cheek. "You are a very smart man."

Hugh sighs with his usual sarcasm. "He's clever, but I'm a wee numpty. Is that about it?"

I drape an arm across his shoulders. "Well, ye did fail to notice the dead obvious signs that Kate and I were shagging."

"Will I never live that down?"

"Aye, ye will. In a few decades."

Once we get inside the castle, Kate suggests we go into the sitting room, where it's "cozy and comfy." The coziest, most comfortable place I know of is the bed I've been sharing with her, but I won't say that in front of Hugh. The poor sod has already lost a woman to me. Willnae rub salt on his wounds. It wouldn't be sporting.

"Stop that," Hugh says. "I can tell by the look on your face that you're extremely pleased with yourself."

"And you're jealous that I'm pleased with myself because you're a whingeing ersehole."

"We need a shinty rematch, just you and me. Then we'll see who's whingeing."

Kate grins and laughs. "Glad to see you guys are back."

Hugh gives her a confused look. "We were never gone."

"Not physically, but you did get mad at each other and almost ruin a beautiful friendship."

"Bygones, pet. If we're over it, you should be too."

"If that's true, then we should head into the great hall for the dinner party."

"We're having a dinner party?" I say. "With the whole clan?"

"Uh, no. Most of them are heading home. But Emery insisted we all need to celebrate the moment when you guys finally made up. She's been planning this party since before she found me at the airport."

"Aye, Emery always has a plan."

"Kirsty assured her you two would kiss and make up, so she acted accordingly."

"Let me guess," Hugh says. "Kirsty foresaw it with her da-shiva whatever-it-is."

"*Da-shealladh*," I say. "Learn to pronounce it. Gaelic isn't that hard to learn."

Kate turns away, walking toward the door, and glances over her shoulder at us. "Hurry it up, boys. Everyone's waiting."

Chapter Thirty-Two

Kate

DINNER WAS AMAZING. I'VE NEVER SHARED A MEAL WITH that many people, but somehow, it still felt like an intimate family gathering. We sat at one long table that was created by pushing several smaller ones together until the whole thing filled up three-fourths of the great hall. Since Emery arranged this as a buffet-style affair, we got to try all sorts of dishes, from traditionally Scottish to world cuisine. So yeah, at one point, my plate was filled with haggis, hot dogs, and empanadas.

Last night, I slept better than I had in years. Sleeping with Callum always makes me feel that way, but it's especially true now. Knowing Hugh and Callum have saved their friendship removes the last traces of my anxiety. I'm not even worried about what the future might hold. For the first time, I trust that everything will work out.

I'm currently snuggled up to Callum, both of us naked though we didn't have sex. I love just cuddling with him. Right now, he's snoring. Softly, not like a rhino with a sinus condition. That man is adorable and sexy even when he snores. After a few more minutes of lying here watching him sleep, I can't take it anymore. I have to wake him up. But I do it my way. I roll on top of him and place little kisses on his mouth, starting at one corner and traveling to the other side.

His dick starts to rouse first. Then his lids flutter open, and he gazes at me blearily. Yawning, he stretches his entire body with me still on top of him—and he palms my ass. "Good morning, *mo chridhe.*"

"Good morning, hot stuff."

"Donnae mind if ye want to call me that." His lips stretch into a lazy grin. "*Tha ball-ratha sìnte riut.*"

"Uh, what?"

"It means 'there's a lucky limb stretched against you.' And my *slat* is that limb." He shifts his hips to rub his cock into me. "Want to shag?"

"Yes, please."

He wraps his arms around me. "Kirsty and Luke's wedding is next week. Would you be my date?"

"I'd love to. But right now, all I want is to feel you inside me."

"After that, I mean to take you home—to my house."

"How many women have you taken home?"

"I've only lived in that house for nine months, so I never had a poke with anyone there." He winces. "I told you my injury made it difficult to, ah, perform."

"You've had no problems performing with me."

His lips slide into a naughty smile. "You inspire me."

I push up to sit astride his hips. "I promised if your food was truly magnificent, I'd give you a gift that would make your eyes roll back in your head."

Callum runs his palms up and down my thighs. "I remember. And you did seem to love my food."

"You are an amazing cook. I think it's time I gave you that gift."

He links his hands under his head. "Go on, *mo chridhe*. I'll give you something special when you're done."

I shimmy backward until I can lean over with my face right above his dick. It's hard and ready. So I drag my tongue over the tip to lap up the moisture there, then I moan and lick my lips.

Callum's attention stays riveted to me, to what I'm doing, and he starts breathing harder.

Braced with one elbow, I use my free hand to massage his inner thigh, edging closer and closer to his groin. My fingers brush against his sac, but I move my hand to his hip, massaging the hollow while I lower my head to lick a path up his rock-hard cock. He sucks in a sharp breath. I shift my hand down to rub his thigh again, sinking my fingers into his flesh while I close my mouth around the rosy head of his erection.

"Och, *mo leannan*," he growls. "Yer mouth is as hot and slick as yer *ròmag* must be."

I pull my mouth away. "You wouldn't believe how wet I am for you. And damn, you taste so good."

Before he can say anything else, I close my mouth around him again and give his sac a light tug. He gasps. My sex tingles, and my nipples ache, but I can wait for my climax. Right now, all I care about is making him go off like a volcano. So I close my hand around the base of his cock and pump at a leisurely pace while I lick and suck, loving the salty flavor of him and the smooth texture of his skin. My gaze remains bound to his, but the more I work his erection, the more his eyes narrow until they become the barest of slits. His cheeks have turned faintly pink, his lips have fallen open, and he's fisting his hands in the sheets.

Oh yeah, I will deliver on my promise. He's halfway to heaven already, and I love being the one to do this to him.

"*Neach-gaoil, tha thu bòidheach,*" he says, his voice rough and his breaths uneven. "*Tha mo ghion ort.*"

I have no idea what he said, though I've heard him speak some of those words before.

My hand pumps faster. I devour his cock like I can't survive without the flavor of him on my tongue, and his back bows up off the mattress. His chest heaves. Breaths explode out of him, sharp and short. I'm pretty sure he's on the edge right now, about to tumble over it.

He leaps up and flips me onto my back, then snatches a condom from the nightstand drawer and covers his length. With his body held up by his straight arms, he slams his cock into me. A cry explodes from my lips. I grip his biceps while he pummels me with thrust after punishing thrust. I can't breathe, can't move, frozen in the blissful torture of the moment before climax. He stops mid-thrust to rub my clit until the orgasm seizes me and pleasure rips through me so hard and fast that I can't even cry out. While my muscles keep milking him, he pumps into me with relentless strokes until he finally goes rigid and lets out strangled shouts, coming apart inside me.

We're sheathed in sweat and struggling to regain our breath.

Callum flops onto the bed beside me. "Kate, that was bloody brilliant."

"Yes, it was. How did you like your gift? You didn't let me finish wrapping it for you."

"Sorry. Couldnae hold back, not with your mouth sucking my *slat.*" He slings an arm around me, pulling me snugly against his side. "I need to tell ye what I said when ye had yer wee mouth on me. '*Neach-gaoil, tha thu bòidheach*' means 'my beloved, you are beautiful.' And when I said *tha mo ghion ort,* I meant I love you with all my heart."

"I love you too, Callum, love you like crazy." Can't believe we just said that, but I don't regret it. "What you said in Gaelic was the most beautiful thing I've ever heard."

Callum eyes me sideways. "You're not going to panic because I told you how I feel?"

"Nope. I'm done freaking out. Being with you has cured me of that."

"I'm the cure for getting over a bad marriage? Maybe I should be the therapist, not you."

I try to stifle my laugh, but it comes out as a splutter instead. "You want to have sex with men's wives and girlfriends to help them with their marriage issues?"

"Oh, ah, I didnae think that through before I said it."

"Relax, I'm teasing you. Maybe you are the better therapist since you helped me so much."

He kisses the top of my head. "No, *mo chridhe,* you are the best psycho-therapist slash physical therapist in the entire world. Make that the entire universe."

"I love it when you engage in hyperbole. It's hot."

Someone knocks on the door.

"Bugger off," Callum hollers. "I'm giving Kate therapy."

"It's Jack, ye erse. Breakfast will be served in fifteen minutes in the dining room."

"So it won't be the whole clan this time, eh? Cannae fit all of us in the dining room."

"Just get dressed and come downstairs."

Footsteps suggest Jack has left the vicinity.

Callum pushes a hand between my thighs. "Donnae care what Jack says. I prefer to come upstairs."

"Let's have sex in the shower before we go down for breakfast."

He smirks. "Donnae think going down is appropriate in the dining room. But I'm up for it if you are."

I adore this man with every fiber of my being.

We wind up forgoing shower sex in favor of getting dressed since we only have fifteen minutes. But Callum vows we will "have a poke" again today. After breakfast, he plans to take me on another motorcycle ride since he promised to show me his house. And I've discovered I love straddling a Harley while plastered to Callum's backside. He has the fin-est backside on earth.

Hyperbole must be contagious.

By the time we enter the dining room, which is on the ground floor, everyone else has already sat down at the table. Two empty chairs await us. Jack sits at one end of the table while Autumn sits at the opposite end, facing her husband. Emery and Rory have taken the chairs along one side of the table with a woman I don't recognize beside them. A man

I also don't recognize reclines in a chair on the other side, next to two empty seats. A third chair has been crammed in on the stranger's opposite side, but I recognize the man sitting there. It's Hugh.

A whole lot of food occupies the tabletop.

"Sit down," Jack says. "We're fair starved from waiting for you."

Callum drops onto the chair nearest to his brother, leaving me next to the stranger.

"The man sitting beside you," Jack says, "is Alex Thorne, also known as the British Bastard, the Limey Louse, and the Soulless Sassenach. His wife gave him those names before they were married, but that's a story for another day. Alex, meet Kate Wagner."

Alex Thorne offers me his hand. "Pleasure to meet you, Kate. I've heard all about the trouble these two plonkers gave you. It takes a strong woman to handle two stubborn men."

He's British like Hugh. I already figured that out thanks to Jack's introduction, but hearing Alex's accent confirms it. I shake Alex's hand, then lean forward to see the other Brit. "Good morning, Hugh."

"Have you met my wife?" Alex asks me. When I shake my head, he waves toward the brunette across the table. "This is Catriona Thorne, formerly Catriona MacTaggart. She's the sister of the Three Macs."

"The who now?"

Alex chuckles. "The Three Macs. That's what we call Lachlan, Rory, and Aidan. Their cousin Iain invented the nickname because he said they're like a wee Scottish mafia."

"I see. Well, it's nice to meet you, Catriona."

She smiles. "Aye, it's wonderful to meet you too. I'm so happy Callum found the right woman."

"Thanks to me," Jack says. "I'm the one who sent Callum to the clinic in Inverness, where he met Kate."

Callum gives his brother a fake stern look. "Are you saying it was a setup?"

"A happy coincidence. But you would never have met Kate otherwise."

"Well, I have to admit that's true."

I study the various pots and dishes arrayed on the table, but all of them have lids. "What's for breakfast? Can't tell what it is, but it smells heavenly."

"Afraid it's not Callum's amazing cooking," Jack says, with a hint of sarcasm. "But it's good, and it's hot. Autumn and I made all the food."

"That's right," his wife says. "We're the dream team in the kitchen."

Jack winks at his wife. She blows him a kiss.

Alex groans, but it's clearly sarcasm. "Must we be subjected to your saccharine displays before we've eaten? I might be too nauseous to enjoy the food."

The ribbing goes on, but I'm not paying attention to that anymore. My mind keeps replaying the moment when Callum and I said we love each other. I'd been so terrified of getting involved with anyone after my marriage ended that I gave up on dating altogether. If Callum hadn't come into my life, would I have ever started dating again? I'll never know the answer, and it doesn't matter. I do have Callum in my life. The past is gone, and the future can take care of itself.

Yes, I am happy.

Chapter Thirty-Three

Callum

After breakfast, I take Kate to my house in Loch Fairbairn. When we first met, she hated my motorcycle and ordered me not to ride it anymore. Now she loves it. I'll retrieve my car from Dùndubhan another time, but Kate doesn't seem to mind if I wait weeks or months to do that. She wants to ride my Harley. She wants to ride me too, but that has nothing to do with transportation.

"This is your house?" Kate says as we walk into the living room.

"Aye, this is where I live. Did ye think I'd bring ye to a stranger's home?"

"No, of course not. But this isn't what I expected."

"I hide my devil-worshiping gear in another room. Want to see the blood-soaked altar now?"

The lass tries not to smile, but she cannae stop herself. "I'm glad you're back to your old sarcastic self."

"How do you know this is the old me? We didn't meet until after I turned into a snarling *tolla-thon.*"

"But Jack told me what you were like before." She ambles across the room, studying everything she sees. "I guess I thought a former firefighter who's now a carpenter would go for more macho kinds of home decor."

"I can hang some rusty axes on the wall if that will make you feel better."

"No, I like this."

Kate turns in a circle to admire the whole room.

Aye, my house is not what most people think a man like me should have. But there is a reason for that, and I decide to explain it to Kate. "I cannae take credit for the interior design. My cousins Isla, Kirsty, and Elspeth decorated the house for me."

"You let the Witches of Ballachulish spiff up your home?"

"That's right. My barmy cousins insisted on doing it for free, though I tried everything short of breaking into their homes to put cash under their pillows to get them to accept payment for their work."

"MacTaggarts really are amazing. Generous, brave, smart, caring, and a thousand other things I can't articulate."

I walk up behind her, sliding my arms around her and locking my hands over her belly. "You're an honorary MacTaggart now. That means you are all those things too."

She leans backward, relaxing against me. "Could we talk about something serious?"

"No good conversation ever starts that way. But aye, we can talk about anything you want."

"How's your knee? You played shinty yesterday, so I'd be surprised if you didn't tweak your knee at all."

"It's a wee bit sore, but nothing I can't handle." I rest my chin on her shoulder. "The vibrations from my Harley make it feel better."

"Oh, so now you claim riding your motorcycle is therapeutic."

"You need to loosen up, *mo chridhe*. Not everything I do or eat or drink has to be one hundred percent healthy." I kiss a trail up her throat. "Though I think sex would be the most therapeutic, healthy thing I could do right now. For my knee."

"Guess I'd better be on top."

"Aye, ye should." I move in front of her, taking her hands in mine. "But you had something serious to say."

"Yeah, I do." She bites her lip, hunching her shoulders. But then she blows out a breath and relaxes. "Do you want to be a firefighter again?"

"Not sure. Havenae thought about it much. I've been too busy satisfying the needs of a ravenous woman."

"Very funny. But I'm serious. Do you think you would ever want to go back to being a firefighter?"

"Maybe. Not in Inverness, though. Loch Fairbairn is my home." I didn't realize until I said it that I've been considering the idea for a while, ever since I met Kate. But it was a subconscious impulse, until now. "If my knee could handle it, I might want to become a retained or volunteer firefighter."

"Not full-time?"

"I doubt it. My carpentry work started as something to do while I re-covered from my injury, but it means more than that to me now." I gesture toward the furniture in the room. "Everything you see here, I made."

"You made the sofa, the chairs, and the coffee table?"

"Aye. And I made the kitchen island too. It's butcher block." I pull her close. "But I think the creation you'll like the best is the bed I made."

"Can I see it now?"

"You can look at anything you want in this house. Look, touch, try out."

Her eyes light up, and her cheeks dimple with the sweetest smile I've ever seen. "Let's try out the bed."

Kate races down the hall.

And I run after her.

We do more than try out the bed. We test it to its limits, and I prove to Kate that my carpentry skills are top-notch. The bed survives our at-tempts to break it, but we have a bloody good time trying to do that. I used to think Kate was uptight and rigid. Now I know she's a passionate, sweet, clever, kind, and wonderful lass. Cannae believe I ever called her a she-demon.

Kate thought I was rude and insolent, so we're even.

We decide to spend the week leading up to Kirsty and Luke's wed-ding here in my house, not at Dùndubhan. We do retrieve my car, since the weather isn't always ideal for traveling by motorcycle. I show her all my favorite places around the Highlands and introduce her to more of my extended family, since not all of them attended the so-called radical intervention—which was nothing more than an excuse for revelry. Aye, to the MacTaggarts assaulting each other on the shinty pitch is a bloody good time.

Maybe my knee injury did have a psychosomatic element, but Kate has helped me deal with that. She is an amazing therapist. Since she's also a physical therapist, she offers to help me get my knee back in shape in case I want to become a firefighter again. Retained duty would mean I'd be on call. Kate seems fine with that idea, but I need to know for sure.

On the day I resolve to discuss the issue with her, we're sitting on the patio behind my house, enjoying the sunshine. Kate lies stretched out on a lawn chaise while dressed in denim shorts and a short-sleeve plaid shirt. It's not the MacTaggart clan tartan, but I forgive her for that trans-gression. She looks bonnier than ever, with her golden red hair flowing over her shoulders and those sexy legs on display.

"Uh, Kate? Could we talk about something?"

"Sure. What's up?"

"We had talked about whether I might want to go back to being a firefighter."

"I remember." She turns onto her side to face me. "What did you want to discuss about that?"

"Would you, ah..." Suddenly, I can't make the words come out of my mouth. What if Kate says she'll leave me if I go back to my dangerous former job? *Stop acting like a numpty and just ask her, ye eejit.* "Would you mind if I tried to get my old job back? Not wholetime. Retained, which means I'd be on call. Donnae even know if they'd take me, or if I'm ready for it, but I—"

"Your babbling is cute, but you don't need to be nervous. I will support you in whatever you want to do."

"I don't want to lose you."

"That won't happen. Trust me."

Of course I trust her. I've never had more faith in anyone than I do with Kate. "What about you? Don't you want to get your old job back?"

"Not in Inverness. Maybe I could find something nearby, though I don't think there's a clinic in Loch Fairbairn."

"There isn't. But maybe the village needs one."

She sits up, staring at me like I've declared she ought to become a stripper. "Are you suggesting I should start my own clinic?"

"Aye. You're very clever and dedicated to helping people. Loch Fairbairn would be lucky to have you serving the community."

"That's not a half bad idea. But I'd need to find a place that has enough room for all the equipment." Her shoulders flag, and she slumps against her chaise. "There's no way I could get the funding to start a clinic."

I chuckle. "Ye donnae understand yet, do ye? The MacTaggarts have made you part of the family. That means they will give you whatever help you need."

"But the money involved would be—"

"No problem. Trust me."

She raises her brows. "Are you secretly loaded?"

"I'm not, but my cousin Evan is a billionaire."

"Right. I forgot about that. But I can't ask your cousin to fund my new business."

"Why not?" I slide my legs off my chaise and sit facing her. "Evan owns half the village. He bought the shops and offices of all the people who had been treated badly by Rhys Kendrick. The Welsh scunner threatened to destroy their businesses just to punish my cousin Iain for sleeping with his wife."

"That sounds like a story I need to hear."

"I'll tell you sometime. Right now, I need to know if you would be open to the idea of letting my cousin fund your new clinic."

"Well... Yeah, I'd be okay with talking to him about the possibility."

"I'm sure he would invest in your clinic if that would make you feel better about the situation. I'm also dead sure he would give you the money outright." I lean forward to grasp her hands. "It's your decision, *mo chridhe*. I'll support whatever you want to do."

She lunges toward me to press her lips to mine. "I know you will. Thank you, Callum. Your support means so much to me."

This is what a relationship is supposed to be like, isn't it? I'd never had this before I met Kate. My brother and my cousins found this kind of connection, but I assumed I never would. Kate proved me wrong.

"Been wondering," she says. "What does *mo chridhe* mean? You've called me that several times."

"It means my heart."

She crawls onto my lap and loops her arms around my neck. "You are *mo chridhe* for me too. I love you more than I ever thought I could love any man. You're everything my husband never was."

"Glad I could outdo a slimy, cheating ersehole."

"There's no comparison. You are a wonderful man."

"You're a wonderful woman, Kate. You helped me get through the hardest time in my life and taught me how to accept help." I fold my arms around her and look straight into her eyes. I don't think about what I mean to say, but just say it. "Will you marry me, *mo chridhe*?"

She grins. "Yes, absolutely."

"Didnae plan this, so I donnae have a ring."

"Let's go pick one out together."

"Aye. That's a brilliant plan." I stand up, carrying her with me, and set the lass on her feet. "Let's go right now."

We jump on the Harley and drive straight to the nearest jewelry store.

Chapter Thirty-Four

Kate

I GAZE DOWN AT MY HAND FOR THE HUNDREDTH TIME TODAY, entranced by the glittering diamond ring on my finger. Callum wanted to buy me a huge, expensive boulder of an engagement ring, but I assured him that's not necessary. A bigger stone doesn't mean he loves me more. The tasteful rock on my finger is all I need.

Wow, I'm getting married again. I swore I would never do that, but Callum knew how to get under my skin and force me to reexamine my life choices. Celibacy? What a dumb-ass idea. Now I not only have my own family, but also a passel of MacTaggarts who treat me like I've always been a part of their clan.

The day after we got engaged, I call my parents to share the news. This means I'll be staying in Scotland permanently. I worry they'll be hurt by that decision, but Mom and Dad assure me they want whatever makes me happy. Callum joins in the call, and we turn it into a video chat so they can "meet" my fiancé. He informs my parents that they and my brother and sister, and their families, can fly to Scotland anytime they like—for free, thanks to the private jets owned by several of his cousins.

When we share the news with Greer and Alistair, they're thrilled too. My sister will be my maid of honor, but we ask Jack and Autumn to serve as best man and bridesmaid, and they agree without hesitation. Jack hugs his brother so hard that I think Callum probably can't breathe.

My family is happy. His family is happy. All that's left is for me to get moving on what I've been procrastinating about doing.

I meet with Evan MacTaggart.

Callum comes with me when we drive to Inverness to meet Evan at the apartment where Callum had stayed during his therapy. Evan and his wife, Keely, live in Utah most of the time. But they keep this apartment for when they come here to check on his company, Evanescent Security Technologies Limited, and for any family members who need a place to crash.

Evan is a striking man. Not only is he tall and muscular like most MacTaggart men, but he has blond hair and blue eyes so pale that they seem almost silver. He invites us to sit down on the sofa while he takes the armchair.

I open my new briefcase, which Callum bought for me as an engagement gift, and bring out a folder. I offer it to Evan. "This is my proposal, which includes a business plan."

He waves it away. "I don't need that, Kate. We're family, and I trust you. This will be a personal investment, not anything connected to my company." He hands me an envelope. "I hope this will be enough for startup capital, but I'm not an expert on clinics like yours."

I set my folder on the coffee table and take his envelope, pulling out the check hidden inside it. My jaw drops. Literally. My mouth is hanging wide open. "This is—Did you accidentally add zeroes at the end?"

"No. I'm investing five million pounds in your venture. Do whatever you feel is appropriate with the money, or if you want help, I'm always available by video chat or in person to advise you." He winks. "I have a fast jet."

"You haven't even read my business plan."

"Callum told me you're clever and determined, as well as a brilliant physical therapist slash psychotherapist. That's all the endorsement I need."

I stare down at the check and all those zeroes. Five million pounds. That must be almost seven million dollars. Maybe I'm only getting this money because of my relationship with Callum, but I kind of doubt that. A man doesn't become a billionaire by throwing away millions of dollars to make his cousin's fiancée happy. He must honestly believe I can create a profitable venture.

We talk with Evan some more about the logistics of setting up a new business. He does literally own half the village, and he offers to let me lease a vacant property that sounds like the perfect place, but I've only seen pictures of it that Evan shows me on his phone. So he gives me the keys to the building and tells me to check it out and let him know what I think.

Callum was not kidding when he told me going overboard is in the MacTaggarts' DNA. They do everything big—and with incredible generosity.

We have not forgotten about Hugh. He's still at Dùndubhan, but we've given him some time and space to adjust to the idea of me and Callum getting engaged. I feel bad for Hugh, and I suspect he's having trouble adjusting to the situation not only because of me but also because he finally realized he wants more than sex. He needs a solid relationship with a woman who appreciates him, not just his title and his body.

Though Callum and I have kept our distance lately, we decide it's time to check on Hugh. The day after we met with Evan, we drive out to Dùndubhan. Only two cars sit in the driveway, but that could be deceptive. The MacTaggarts who have kept Hugh company tend to all pile into one or two cars, kind of like a can of Scottish sardines.

Despite the cars in the driveway, we don't see another human being—not when we enter the vestibule, not when we search the downstairs, and not on the upper floors either. We return to the ground floor to discuss our next move.

"Where could they be?" I ask. "Do you think they went into the wine cellar? Or maybe the garden?"

"They're probably burying the body."

Despite his neutral expression, I know he's joking. Over the past few weeks, I've come to understand his micro-expressions. If his lips kick up the teeniest bit at the corners, and they also twitch ever so slightly, that means he's "having me on" as the Scots and Brits would say. Yes, Callum can do deadpan better than anybody I know. But I've spent a lot of time with him in the nude. There's nothing like seeing each other au naturel to give a couple super intimate knowledge of each other. No secrets when you're having sex.

"Very funny," I say. "But seriously, where do you think they've gone?"

"Cannae be the garden. I could see the whole thing when we were on the third floor." He lodges his hands in his pants pockets. "But I couldn't see the green. We should check there."

"Okay." I start to walk, then stop. "You don't think they're doing anything, um, overly macho to Hugh, do you?"

He chuckles. "Overly macho? Aye, that's the MacTaggart way. They're probably teaching Hugh how to toss cabers."

"I would've thought you already taught him that."

"No, Hugh didn't want to participate in the Highland games. He said it was 'barmy beyond belief,' and then he started calling himself Lord Sommerleigh, which always means he's harassing us."

"He invokes his title to be sarcastic."

"Aye."

We make our way outside, through the beautiful walled garden, out the door, and onto the green.

I see a much smaller crowd than last week when we had the radical intervention. Jack is here, along with his cousins Iain, Logan, and Aidan. Kirsty and her fiancé Luke have also turned up. At the far end of the green, I notice Damian Petrescu and his wife, Heidi, lying naked on a pair of lawn chaises.

Hugh stands with the MacTaggart men, and they seem to be having an intense conversation, based on their expressions. Hugh keeps nodding as if he's agreeing with whatever the others have said.

Callum and I approach the men.

Hugh smiles when he sees us. "Finally decided to check on the prisoner, eh?"

"You've stayed here voluntarily," Callum says. "I guess that means you've been initiated into the cult."

"My brain has been thoroughly washed. Nothing else explains why I've stayed here at a medieval castle with a bunch of surly Scots." He affects an exaggerated grimace as he waves toward the other end of the green. "And a pair of nudists. Yes, I have been brainwashed for sure."

"What have you boys been doing out here?" I ask. "Doesn't look like Highland games."

Logan chuckles. "No, we're teaching Hugh how to not be a *cacan* anymore."

"Donnae listen to him," Iain says. "We're instructing Hugh in the art of Zen."

"That's what *you* are doing," Logan tells Iain. "I'm getting ready to beat some sense into the laddie. There's nothing like a good skelping to straighten a man out."

Aidan raises his hands, palms out. "Donnae look at me. I'm here for the haggis Mrs. Brody is making for dinner."

Jack shakes his head, smiling at his cousins' antics. "What we're really doing here is advising our new mate on how to become the man he wants to be instead of the playboy he used to be."

If anyone can help him, it's the MacTaggarts. They are the best bunch of men and women I've ever met, besides my family. Soon, my parents and my siblings will arrive in Scotland since Kirsty and Luke have invited them to the wedding. Damian Petrescu says his parents will come too, as well as his brother and his sister-in-law. Everyone tells me Monica Petrescu is a real character, a proud gypsy who loves to play the flamboyant fortune teller.

My life will never be boring again.

The next day, everyone arrives for the pre-wedding festivities. My parents both hug Callum and treat him like they've known him forever instead of just having met my fiancé. My sister kisses his cheek and babbles silly romantic stuff about how Callum and I are "soul mates," while my brother slaps him on the back and says the usual guy stuff. Callum takes it all in stride and even teases my family the way he does with his own clan.

I think my family has fallen for him just like I did.

Even when we introduce my family to the MacTaggarts, everybody gets along and laughs together.

The wedding rehearsal dinner becomes a true extravaganza. The great hall turns into a buffet with tables lined up along one wall and more tables arrayed around the room to accommodate all the guests. The food is delicious, the company is amazing, and laughter fills the great hall.

During dessert, Jack leans over to tell his brother, "We're already planning your engagement ceilidh."

Oh yeah, MacTaggarts know how to throw a party. Our ceilidh will be a spectacle, and I can't wait for that.

I whisper to Callum, "Maybe you should make your announcement now."

"Our announcement, *mo chridhe*. But I donnae want to horn in on Kirsty and Luke's big night."

"They won't mind. Trust me."

Callum pushes his chair back and stands. "Haud yer wheesht, everyone."

His shout echoes through the great hall, and everybody stops talking. All gazes veer to Callum.

"I have an announcement," he says. "My main job will still be carpentry, but I've also been hired as a retained duty firefighter at the Kinlochleven station."

Cheers and clapping erupt around us.

Jack slaps his brother's arm. "About bloody time, ye eejit."

"I'm so proud of you," I tell Callum. Then I take hold of his face and kiss him.

Yes, I love this man.

Chapter Thirty-Five

Callum

KATE AND I ARRIVE FOR THE WEDDING EARLIER THAN MOST of the guests, but that gives us time to talk to my parents, and Jack and Autumn too. They love Kate, but that's no surprise to me. Everyone adores her, but no one more than me. We'll be getting married soon, though we haven't set the date yet. Jack insists on throwing that engagement ceilidh for us first. Hugh left yesterday, saying he didn't feel right about "crashing" the wedding when he hardly knows Luke and Kirsty. I think he just needed to get away for a while and come to terms with what he learned about himself lately.

As more guests begin to arrive, Kate and I stand behind the rows of chairs lined up on the green so I can tell her who every MacTaggart is. She's met a lot of them, but not the whole extended family, not even close to it. The lass still hasn't grasped the enormity of this clan. Kate loves learning more about the family, but one member in particular piques her curiosity.

She nods toward a man who has just walked onto the green, heading for the chairs. "Who is that? He looks like a hardcore biker."

I glance at the man in question, who wears leather trousers, a leather jacket, and a skull-and-crossbones T-shirt. His wild hair and goatee add to his devilish mystique, and so do the tattoos that peek out from under his shirt.

"That's Magnus," I say. "He doesn't like motorcycles, but he does enjoy looking like someone you wouldn't want to cross paths with on a dark street. Luke Turner calls him a demon biker, but he's just being cheeky."

"I haven't heard anything about Magnus, which seems weird considering how much your family loves to gossip."

"Magnus is a bit of a black sheep."

Two older people amble onto the green, but when they see Magnus, they veer away from him to take seats on the opposite side from where my bad-boy cousin stands.

"Who are those two?" Kate asks. "They don't seem to like your cousin Magnus."

"That's Aunt Rhona and Uncle Baltair. They're Magnus's parents."

"Guess they don't get along with their son. Your uncle is glaring daggers at him. What's their story?"

I slip an arm around Kate's shoulders. "Uncle Baltair wanted Magnus to join the police force after he left the army, but Magnus became a bounty hunter instead. Baltair still hasn't forgiven him."

"Why does he need to forgive his son for that? It's not illegal to be a bounty hunter."

"No, but Baltair thinks it's a disreputable career. Donnae know the whole story, but my uncle has made it clear he never wants to speak to Magnus again." I guide Kate toward the chairs, which all have name tags on them, and we take our assigned seats. "Most of the clan steers clear of Magnus on the rare occasions when he shows himself. They're afraid of him. But to be fair, Magnus likes having that kind of image. It makes fugitives think twice about trying to get away from him."

Magnus sits down on a chair in the last row.

Who decided to make him sit back there? Kirsty worships Magnus, which means she did not suggest they put him at the back. She would want him closer to the front.

"Back in a minute," I tell Kate as I get up from my chair. "Need to talk to Magnus."

"Sure. I'll wait here."

I trot to the last row of chairs and drop onto the seat beside my cousin. "Glad to see ye here, Magnus. But why are you hiding in the back?"

"Not hiding. This is my assigned seat."

"But Kirsty wants you in the front row."

He shrugs one shoulder. "Some people disagree."

"Cannae let small-minded eejits get to you." I tear the sign off the back of his chair. "Get off your erse, Magnus. You're coming with me."

He lifts one brow. "Since when are we mates?"

"Since the day I let you drive my Harley. You haven't met my fiancée yet, have ye? So come on." I get up and tug on his arm, which is a bit like tugging on a granite statue. "You belong closer to the front, not in the back of beyond. Donnae want to disappoint Kirsty, do ye?"

"That's a low blow, Callum. Ye know how I feel about our wee cousin."

Everyone is wee compared to Magnus, even me.

He rises from his chair and follows me to the second row, where Kate is waiting for us. I pull the name tag off the back of the chair beside her and replace it with Magnus's tag. Didnae want to sit beside Maud, anyway. My great aunt always havers on and on about her gout and her bursitis, not to mention her hemorrhoids. Aye, Magnus will be a much better neighbor. Once I've introduced Kate and Magnus to each other, I rush to the back row to put Maud's name tag on the back of the chair my cousin had occupied a moment ago.

Now everything is as it should be.

Laughter draws my attention to the other side of the green. The rest of the naturists are here. We'd all gotten to know them during Cat and Alex's wedding week insanity, so it's no surprise Kirsty invited them to her wedding. Val, Eve, Ollie, and Mara will liven up the reception with the help of Damian and Heidi. I wonder what Luke will make of the naturists. Maybe we'll have another nude shinty match, with MacTaggarts fighting over who gets Val Silva on their team. He is a former Olympic football champion, after all—and a shameless exhibitionist.

Kate and Magnus are laughing when I come back to them.

As I settle onto my chair, I give my cousin a look of fake annoyance. "Better not be flirting with my woman or I'll skelp your hide good. Donnae care how tough ye are."

"Go on and try it," Magnus says with a smirk. "I can take a wee laddie like you."

More guests begin to file onto the green, filling in the empty chairs. Jack and Autumn sit beside Kate, and my brother gives me a strange look when he notices Magnus.

"What's that look for?" I ask, whispering so no one else will hear. "Thought ye liked the demon biker."

"I do. But he's sitting directly across from his parents. Might be a bit of barnie later when Baltair and Magnus bump into each other during the reception."

"MagTaggarts love a good tussle."

We don't get to discuss Magnus anymore. Luke moves into position at the altar with only the minister beside him. He and Kirsty had decided against having groomsmen or bridesmaids, since Luke has no living relatives that he knows of, having grown up an orphan, and he hasn't quite become close enough with the MacTaggarts to ask any of us to stand up for him at the altar.

Kate cries during the whole ceremony.

Maybe I get a wee bit choked up too. It's a beautiful moment when two people who lost each other find their way again.

I look at Kate just as she looks at me, and we both smile. Aye, it's just as beautiful when two strangers find something they never expected.

After the ceremony, everyone heads for the great hall—except for me. I get waylaid by Magnus, who announces I'm urgently needed on the south side of the castle compound. Kate wants to come with us, but Magnus insists she should wait for me in the great hall. When my demon biker cousin insists on something, no one argues. While Kate wanders into the garden, I let Magnus lead me away, down the green and around the corner of the wall to the south side.

Jack and several of our cousins have gathered around a wee campfire.

"What's this?" I ask. "Doesn't seem urgent to me."

"Aye, it is," Jack says. "We decided to celebrate your new job at Kinloch-leven by giving you a fire."

"Donnae ye think committing arson to celebrate my new job as a firefighter is slightly inappropriate?"

"No," Iain says, "not at all."

I glance at Magnus. "You must think this is a barmy idea."

He shrugs. "No, I don't."

Jack hands me a bucket of water. "Here. It's time to douse your first blaze as a retained firefighter."

"Blaze? I could snuff out the wee flames with my boot." But I can tell this lot have made up their minds, and I do appreciate their barmy senti-ment. So I pick up the bucket and dump the water on the flames, dous-ing them. "Happy now?"

They all clap and cheer, and Jack hugs me.

"Can we go to the reception now?" I ask.

"Aye," Jack says. "It's time to party hearty, as my wife would say."

When I find Kate in the great hall, she's sitting at our assigned table chatting to my parents. I take my seat beside her and watch the lass, not hearing any of the words anybody speaks. But once, my attention briefly veers to Magnus. He stands in the far corner, a plate in his hand, while he nibbles at his food and scans the crowd like a true hunter.

Kirsty comes up behind me, leaning in to whisper to me, "Donnae worry about Magnus or Hugh. They'll find their way sooner than you think."

"Did your *da-shealladh* tell ye that?"

"Aye." She kisses my cheek and smiles. "And I saw your future too, but I willnae spoil the surprise."

Kirsty walks away.

Donnae need to know my future. Whatever happens next, I can handle it.

I slant toward Kate, my mouth brushing her ear. "*An toir thu dhomh pòg?*"

She turns her head slightly to see me. "I'll kiss you anytime you want, even in front of your family."

"Ah, but the kiss I have in mind involves my *acainn cungaidh*, your *brillean*, and a lot of *coinbheineadh*."

"Don't remember what all of those words mean."

I slide a hand up her thigh. "My cock, your clit, and lots of fondling."

She grins. "Sorry, guys, Callum and I need to, um, find the restroom."

We race out of the great hall hand in hand, making our way down to the ground-floor bathroom. Aye, we have a poke there. Or two. Possibly two and a half, though I've stopped counting. Once we've reassembled our clothes, Kate lays her palms on my chest.

"You're not Super Kitten Man anymore," she says. "You are a super hot firefighter slash carpenter. Don't you love having a double identity with me?"

"Aye, I'll be anything if it's with you."

Kate Wagner is *luaidh mo chèile*—the love of my life. And our journey has only just begun.

Want more of Magnus and Hugh? Experience their stories in *Relentless in a Kilt* (Hot Scots, Book Eleven) and *One Hot Scandal* (Hot Brits, Book Seven).

ANNA DURAND IS A BESTSELLING, MULTI-AWARD-WINNING author of contemporary and paranormal romance. Her books have earned bestseller status on every major retailer and wonderful reviews from readers around the world. But that's the boring spiel. Here are the really cool things you want to know about Anna!

Born on Lackland Air Force Base in Texas, Anna grew up moving here, there, and everywhere thanks to her dad's job as an instructor pilot. She's lived in Texas (twice), Mississippi, California (twice), Michigan (twice), and Alaska—and now Ohio.

As for her writing, Anna has always made up stories in her head, but she didn't write them down until her teen years. Those first awful books went into the trash can a few years later, though she learned a lot from those stories. Eventually, she would pen her first romance novel, the paranormal romance *Willpower*, and she's never looked back since.

Want even more details about Anna? Get access to her extended bio when you subscribe to her newsletter and download the free bonus ebook, *Hot Scots Confidential.* You'll also get hot deleted scenes, character interviews, fun facts, and more! Plus you'll receive the short story *Tempted by a Kiss* as well as multiple bonus chapters available in ebook and audiobook formats.

Visit AnnaDurand.com to sign up.

9 781949 406917